The Stones Of Power
Book 2
Amongst Monsters

BY AARON MCGOWAN

The Stones Of Power
Book 2
Amongst Monsters

Published 2021
Elpis Project ©2011-2021 by Aaron McGowan

McGowan, Aaron.
Elpis / Aaron McGowan

Summary: To avenge the death of his parents and the destruction of his village, Terico seeks to obtain the four fragments of the Elpis—a source of power that will allow his enemy Delkol to conquer the world.

ISBN: 000-0-0000000-0-0

1st Edition

Published by Hellfun Publishing Pty. Limited

•Part V•
A WAR OF VENGEANCE

A few hours passed before Lanek directed everyone's attention to the landscape ahead. Terico looked out the large window at the front of the bridge and found a city in the distance. It was difficult to see any individual buildings, including the royal castle where the king lived, and where an Elpis fragment presumably resided. Everyone looked out at the bright panorama, staring down in curious silence.
Terico had gotten a little used to the sensation of being this high up in the air, so he let his gaze linger a little longer at the distant scene. There was a wide river that ran between the expanse of green hills, down through the city, and on past the farmlands below. The lines of crops were dizzying to look at for long, so Terico focused more on Setar, its grand structures slowly becoming a little more clear to the eye.

"Amazing," Suran said. "The very size of these buildings..."

Terico thought it was all very impressive, but it had to be even more fascinating for someone like Suran, who was more knowledgeable in engineering. And in her case, she had only been outside of Edellerston on a few brief occasions in her life. Seeing the capital city would be a special event for her.

"It's certainly a large city," Terico said. "It looks really chaotic from up here."

"To be expected," Lanek said. "The castle and its surrounding premises are rather well organized, but there's only so much that can be done for a city at large. Especially one as old and expansive as Setar."

"It has its own kind of beauty," Suran said. "I don't think I'd ever want to live in such a big city, but it is nice to visit."

"Poor time to visit it, though," Lanek said. "If things don't work out with Terico and the Elpis, we'll probably be caught up in Delkol's invasion."

Terico would have liked to assure that everything would work out, but there was no telling what Delkol had been up to since escaping Vursa. Areo, Kitoh, and Borely continued to look out the window in silence, each of them impressed by the view the airship offered. Terico hoped Kitoh would be up for whatever lay ahead, and that Areo and Borely would be able to handle things as well.

Eventually Terico was able to make out the castle at the city's center. It was a tall structure of dark red stone, portions of which were painted yellow or purple. It was encircled by six thin red towers that stood even taller than the castle, each of which were connected together by a deep brick wall. Further out, Terico spotted a portion of the river redirected to form a moat around the central portion of the city, which included the castle grounds as well as a great deal of the city's larger buildings. Outside the protection of the moat were thousands of tiny wooden huts and patches of farmland— far too many for Terico to ever count.

"Lanek, are you there?"

It was a familiar voice, though it took Terico a moment to remember it belonged to Rilv, the head servant of the royal court.

Lanek leaned back in his chair and slipped a teal Nexi stone from his pocket. "Good afternoon, madame."

"Scouts have reported four Brotherhood airships approaching the city from the east," Rilv said. "Most of the royal fleet is away, gathering reinforcements from neighboring cities, and the remaining ships have been sabotaged by a double agent. It will take some time to get any of them in the air—I need you to hold off the airships in the meantime. Or simply take them down."

"Oh yes, how simple," Lanek said. "Four airships against one that's fortunate to even be airborne... Suddenly *The Finest Hour* takes on new meaning."
"So you can't handle it then?" Rilv said.

Lanek gripped the Nexi stone and sighed. "To be realistic..."

"You have the tools necessary to achieve victory," Rilv said. "Deal with those ships and I may accept your earlier proposition."

"Very well," Lanek said. "I guess *I'll try* then. Is there anything else?"

"No," Rilv replied. "If any airships get close to the castle, we will be able to launch Nexi stones at them. But I imagine the Brotherhood has a plan, as evident by the fact there is a traitor in our midst."
"Just leave it to me." And with that, Lanek put the Nexi stone away and stood

up to run the controls of the airship.

He turned it toward the region east of the city, leading the airship toward a few dots in the sky that Lanek identified as the Brotherhood airships. "Delkol is probably on one of those ships," Terico said.

"Sounds likely," Lanek said. "Everyone get ready—they'll start firing at us as soon as we're in range."

A part of Terico wanted to activate his Elpis stones and attack the airships himself, but he couldn't be certain Delkol was on one of them. He didn't want to exhaust himself and then be left vulnerable for when the time came to face Delkol.

Suran sat down in her chair and moved it toward some of the controls about a meter from Lanek. She placed her hands above four different levers, which Suran had told Terico were used to control each of the four Nexi cannons equipped to the airship. There were many Nexi at her disposal, so as long as Lanek piloted the ship properly, Suran would be able to both attack and defend via her mental connection with the Nexi stones.

"Two ships coming toward us," Lanek said. "The other two are continuing toward the center of Setar."

Terico could see the city far below, and realized it would probably only take a few minutes for the Brotherhood ships to reach the castle at the speed they were going. Now that they were closer to Terico, he could see these airships were massive—several times larger than the one Suran and Lanek built. Great white dirigibles each with a thick, inverted black cross painted down their sides. The dark metal machinery of the jagged ships tied beneath the blimps hung menacingly, at least a half-dozen Nexi cannons hanging from each side of them.

"One will attack while the other tries to slip past," Suran said. "If Delkol can locate where Elpis pieces are, he'll know Terico is here. They'll try to board the ship to retrieve the Elpis."

"Everyone prepare to fight then," Lanek said.

"But what about those other two ships?" Borely asked. "They're already getting away."

Lanek didn't respond, and Terico wondered if he should go after them. Rilv said the city did have defensive measures, but the Brotherhood had to know that. They had to have a strategy in mind, and it left Terico uneasy. What was Delkol's plan? Was he trying to lure Terico out of the airship? Perhaps Delkol was hoping Terico would go after those two airships.

Kitoh ran out the bridge and down the hallway, gripping a couple bright Nexi in his fist.

"Kitoh, wait!" Areo called. She turned and ran after him.

"Hold on!" Borely yelled, running after her.

Terico followed to find out what was going on. He chased Borely and Areo down the clanging hall and into the airship's entry room. Kitoh forced up a lock at the very back of the room, then began sliding open the shaking metal doorway.

"Stop!" Areo yelled.

Kitoh turned back a moment, then leaped out of the door. He fell through the sky a couple seconds, then activated his Nexi stones. The boy turned into a great dragon, just as he had at Vursa—only this time he was flying. He would have been too large to fit in the airship's entry room at this point, and was probably at least a quarter the size of the dirigible as a whole. Kitoh used his massive wings to turn himself around, then flew toward the doorway and maintained a speed similar to the airship's.

"I'll go with you!" Areo yelled over the rushing winds. "Just drop me off at one of the airships, and I'll take care of the Brotherhood!" Once Kitoh was close enough, Areo leaped out the door and landed atop the dragon's back. She nearly stumbled over the other side, but managed to hold a strong, careful grip with her claws. Once secured, she situated herself so she sat against the front of the giant fin protruding from Kitoh's back.

Kitoh was about to take off, but Borely yelled out to them. "Hold on!

I'm not letting you sneak away that easily!" Before Terico could stop him, Borely leaped out, arms and legs flailing in the air. He screamed at the top of his lungs, and for a moment it looked like he was going to miss the dragon entirely.

Kitoh swerved to the left and dived down a bit to scoop Borely up with the back of his large, thick neck. Still screaming, Borely tumbled backward, pushed by the tumultuous winds. He crashed straight into Areo, who grabbed onto Borely and slid her way in front of him. She forced Borely to wrap his arms around her stomach to keep him from flying off into the air.

"What are you thinking?" Areo screamed. "Are you insane?"

"Someone has to watch you!" Borely yelled. "You're too suspicious to be left alone at a time like this!"

Terico could only make out a groan in Areo's response, before Kitoh swooped down beneath the airship and flapped his giant batlike wings to propel himself forward. If Kitoh could drop Areo and Borely off at one of the two ships heading to the castle and then attack the other one himself, it would buy Suran and Lanek some time as they dealt with the other two ships.

Terico shut and locked the doorway, then ran back to the bridge to watch the approaching Brotherhood airships. Suran still had her hands at the controls, while Lanek guided his airship to the best spot to take on the two enemy ships. The odds were against them, but Lanek said their ship would be faster and more dexterous than the giant Brotherhood dirigibles. Terico knew though that in the end, it would come down to his skill with the Elpis stone. Delkol was seeking it, and a final battle was certain to ensue in some form.

And I have one more piece than him, Terico thought. He knew this wouldn't spell an instant victory, and knew better than to become overconfident. Delkol certainly had a plan in mind, and Terico had to make sure to not fall for it.

"One more minute," Lanek said, his rapt attention on the nearer of the two enemy airships.

"I have it," Suran said, staring wide-eyed at the same ship. She adjusted one of the levers ever so slightly, and Terico could hear the clanking of a shifting cannon at the front of the airship. From here it wasn't possible to see the tilt or direction of the cannons, but Terico assumed Suran had a good, intuitive handle for it, and her mind's connection with the ship's Nexi stones would act as a guide for her as well.

With her mind, she used a Nexi to fire one of the cannons, launching a great red Nexi stone for the nearest Brotherhood ship. Terico watched the large glowing stone tumble through the air, rushing straight for the back half of the dirigible.

A swarm of dirt rushed out of one of the enemy ship's cannons, quickly forming into a massive wall of earth that curved a good distance in front of the back half of the balloon. The red Nexi exploded into a great ball of fire, blasting apart the hardened earth floating in front of the dirigible. The detonation blew apart the shield, but had no effect of the airship itself.

"A brilliant shot," Lanek said. "But they have an equally competent Nexi user in their midst."

"I'll break through their defenses," Suran said, already working with a second lever.

The Brotherhood ship shot a series of dark blue Nexi stones, then set them off about a dozen meters from *The Finest Hour*. At the same time, Suran released a tan Nexi, which she caused to form a protective barrier in front of the airship. With a limited amount of dirt at her disposal, she had to direct portions of the the dirt to just the right spots in order to block the four blasts of water. The end result was a formation of strained, hardened earth that twisted and turned sharply in several directions. As the earth was shot, the water and dirt broke apart and plummeted toward the ground.

The second Brotherhood ship continued onward in the meantime, slipping toward *The Finest Hour* while Suran was busy defending against the first ship. The moment she had the opportunity though, she turned to a lever to control the cannon on the starboard side of the airship.

"Keep an eye on them both," Lanek said.

Suran responded by firing a tan Nexi at the second enemy ship, which continued approaching from the side. Terico thought it risky to use up a tan Nexi for an attack, considering its important role for the airship's defense— but he decided to trust Suran's judgement for now. The large tan stone transformed into a long stone spike, flying straight for the dirigible. Terico doubted it would pop like a balloon, but the damage the stalactite would cause could bring it down, he imagined.

The enemy ship fired a couple light blue Nexi toward the spike, detonating them a few meters in front of it. The spike was going to freeze and shatter into small harmless pieces, Terico realized.

Just before it crashed into the bursting ice Nexi, the giant earth spike exploded into a massive ball of dust. Apparently there was a red Nexi stone lodged in the tan Nexi cannon, and Suran detonated it just before the spike of earth was destroyed. Terico watched as a thick smoke screen enveloped the area between *The Finest Hour* and the enemy airship, as well as most of the enemy airship itself. Now her plan was a bit more clear—her goal was to create as much dust as she could, as close to the nearer of the two Brotherhood ships as possible.

"Now, Lanek!" Suran cried.

"Already going," Lanek said, pulling on a rope with one hand while adjusting a lever with the other.

The airship took a sharp, sudden dive to the right, and Terico fell to the ground hard. He managed to grab onto one of the thick legs of Suran's chair, which was grafted to the metal floor.

"Oh, and hang on," Lanek added as an afterthought.

"Thanks for the warning," Terico said.

"Always be on your toes," Lanek replied.

Terico pulled himself up and saw the first Brotherhood ship firing several red Nexi, hoping to keep *The Finest Hour* from slipping behind the thick, lingering smoke screen. Suran quickly fired a couple green Nexi from the front of the ship. As soon as they were in the air, she caused their vines to spread out in all directions and intertwine with one another. In seconds a thick, expansive wall of sprawling vines appeared. The red Nexi crashed against it, blowing it apart and burning the vines to ash. Lanek guided the airship behind the smoke screen before the first enemy ship could attack again.

The moment it stabilized, Lanek forced the airship to speed toward the second enemy ship, which was still making its way through the cloud of dust. Terico held on to the back of Suran's chair, anxiously watching for the second airship to appear. Lanek drove *The Finest Hour* onward and turned it hard to port.

The Brotherhood ship emerged from the dust, its side facing toward *The Finest Hour*. Lanek had guided his airship upward a ways, however, leaving the enemy ship vulnerable and blind about a dozen meters below.

"Fire!" Lanek yelled.

As he gave the order, Suran quickly adjusted the two forward cannons and fired a couple red Nexi at the giant blimp below. She and Terico peered out the window to watch the two fire stones crash into the dirigible. Suran caused the fire to spread quickly, sending the entire blimp bursting into flames. Lanek piloted *The Finest Hour* back a ways, trying to keep the remaining dust and the ensuing thick black smoke between his airship and the remaining Brotherhood ship.

"Nice!" Terico said. "That was brilliant, Suran."

Suran smiled but was quick to return to her seat. "There's still another one to deal with."

"Three, actually," Lanek said. "We don't know how Terico's ragtag team of misfits is holding up."

The airship jerked to the right slightly, and a terrible clanging noise erupted from the hallway.

"Terico!" an echoing voice screamed.

Terico ran to the hallway and found masked members of the Brotherhood entering the back of the airship. They had apparently used vines to reach the ship, and then forced a large opening in the floor via orange Nexi.

"Boarding party," Terico said. "Four—no, five of them."

"Go with him, Suran," Lanek said. "I'm in position to fire once the smoke clears. I can pilot and defend at the same time."

Suran got up and joined Terico, who unsheathed his sword and charged down the hall.

"Use the Nexi that Rilv gave us," Lanek called back to Suran. "And don't die! Tell Terico I'll kill him if he lets you get hurt!"

The way Lanek said it made it sound like a joke, but Terico felt pretty sure Lanek would make good on that promise in such an event. Terico wasn't going to let any of the Brotherhood near Suran if he could help it though, regardless.

He and Suran rushed into the back room of the airship and found the five Brotherhood members, each of them dressed in white clothes and silver armor. Their white masks each bore the symbol of the inverted black cross over the right eye, but only one mask had the additional smile painted from ear to ear.

"Terico!" the boy yelled. He tilted his head a bit and tossed an orange Nexi in the air a couple times. "And isn't this a pleasant surprise...

It looks like *Suran* is still alive and well."

"Terico..." Suran said in a hushed voice. "Is that... Turan?"

The boy clenched his orange Nexi tight. "Turan is no more! Turan died, but has been reborn as Lynx!"

"He was captured by the Brotherhood," Terico said. "Augurc has brainwashed him. If we can capture him without killing him, I might be able to find a way to save him."

"Your orders, Lynx," said one of the masked fighters.

"Kill Suran, the girl!" Turan replied. "I will pin Terico down and make him *watch*! And then... I'll break every little bone in his body!"

•

Areo held tight to Kitoh's back while Borely held on to Areo. The sailor wouldn't stop screaming, and it was difficult to tell if it was out of fear or enjoyment. Flying through the air on the back of a dragon was exhilarating, but Areo had to keep focus on the two airships slipping away in the distance. One of them was turning so its cannons would face toward the approaching dragon.

"Watch for Nexi fire!" Areo yelled.

Kitoh didn't respond, perhaps afraid to speak in this form. The boy flapped his long, leathery wings to bring himself higher, where it would be more difficult for the airships to fire at him.

"Hang on," Areo called back to Borely. "And quit screaming."

Borely laughed. "I had always hoped to die in a glorious way. Can't think of anything more spectacular than *this*!"

"Don't die, you idiot," Areo yelled. She squinted toward the nearest airship, the sky annoyingly bright and the winds only making things worse. The blasts of several cannons boomed through the air.

Kitoh turned to the left, avoiding a large red Nexi stone. It exploded above him, forcing him to dive downward. Two more red Nexi stone approached, detonating in front of him. Areo gripped Kitoh's back tighter, but for a second it felt like Borely was losing his grip. He managed to keep hold though, even as Kitoh flailed to the right of the bursting fire. The dragon rushed forward to avoid a fourth stone, then corkscrewed to the left to keep away from the burst of flames erupting from a fifth and sixth red Nexi.

"Hurry and drop us off at the farther airship," Areo told Kitoh.
"We'll fight them off from within, while you handle this ship." She wanted Kitoh to be able to return to the elves' airship in case the boy couldn't maintain his dragon form for much longer, so she didn't want to force him to chase the enemy ship getting further and further away. She also needed to make sure the Brotherhood didn't reach the castle, guessing they had some special means of breaking past the castle's defenses.

Kitoh rushed for the second airship, pushing his wings harder with every stroke. The first airship launched a series of dark blue Nexi at Kitoh, and once the second airship was in range, it also began firing ice Nexi. The Brotherhood's tactic was readily apparent—Kitoh was struggling to fly through the frozen air.

Areo felt her whole body grow cold as more of the dark blue Nexi burst apart mere meters away. With each detonation, the Nexi released torrents of frozen air and water in all directions. Kitoh struggled to push through, and for a moment he had trouble getting his wings to flap properly. The dragon fell several meters, scaring the breath right out of Areo and Borely.

Fortunately Kitoh managed to keep himself together and continue flying. He flapped as vigorously as he could, working his way above the pockets of frozen air released by the light blue Nexi stones. Areo couldn't stop shivering, and neither could Borely, who she worried would lose his grip around her stomach.

One ice Nexi rushed by just a few centimeters to Areo's left, and she nearly flung herself to the right in reaction. Instead she held on tight, and counted herself lucky that the stone wasn't set off when it was right next to them. Otherwise they would have all been frozen, leaving them to plummet to the earth helplessly.

Kitoh pushed above the range of the Nexi cannons, then soared toward the second Brotherhood airship. Once near enough, the dragon dived down toward it, pulling up just as he reached the bottom of the ship. Kitoh positioned himself so he was directly underneath the ship. He flew along at the same speed as the airship, and turned his head back to Areo, as if waiting to hear what to do next.

"We'll break in," Areo said. She considered having Kitoh breathe fire at the ship from here, but she wanted him to save his energy for the ship he would have to face alone.

Careful to keep hold of Kitoh's back with one hand, Areo took a green Nexi stone from her pouch and aimed it for the side of the ship. It didn't look like there were any ways in from below, so she and Borely would just have to break in from the side. If the sailor could break through the massive doorway to the Vursa council room, he could break through a door to the airship too.

She caused several thick vines of her Nexi to wrap around a railing, then reminded Borely to hang on tight again. "Be ready to fight the moment we break in."

"No problem," Borely said.

Once the vines were secure, Areo let go of Kitoh's back and leaped off. She gripped her Nexi stone tight with both hands and caused the Nexi to reabsorb its vines. With the vines clung tight to the siding of the airship, Areo was propelled through the air and pulled up toward the railing. Borely was a heavy weight to carry, but he managed to keep a firm grip on Areo. Once at the railing, Areo grabbed on to the side of the ship and pulled herself up to a set of steps leading to one of several metal doorways. She glanced back down once more to see Kitoh heading back to the other airship, flying low to make it difficult for the Brotherhood ships to shoot him down.

Once on the steps, Borely let go and walked up to the doorway. He looked flustered, but Areo didn't comment on it. She brushed off her waist and hips, a little upset Borely had to hold on to her so tight for as long as he had. "You better not hold back," Borely said, raising a fist toward the doorway. "I hate having to count on you, but you'll have to watch my back." Areo glanced away. "Watch your own back. I won't slow you down."

Borely turned back to the door and charged his fist with orange Nexi energy. He landed a solid punch, sending the entire door flying into the entry room. Areo charged in after Borely, rushing straight for the nearest Brotherhood member she caught sight of. A masked man turned around and started to yell something. Areo clawed apart his throat and ran on to the next nearest Brotherhood fighter, leaving the first to drop dead behind her.

At the same time, Borely ran for a Brotherhood fighter knocked to the ground by the metal door Borely had punched in. Areo glimpsed Borely punching the masked man just as he was getting up. Borely shattered the man's mask and knocked him out cold.

Areo saw the room was very long, running for tens of meters forward and backward. There were long rectangular windows and several small tables covered with the controls used to operate the ship's cannons. There were six Brotherhood members left to deal with, Areo quickly counted. These were competent fighters, and Areo no longer had the advantage of surprise on her side.

Borely was closer to the next nearest Brotherhood fighter. He dodged a burst of fire released by the masked man, then slammed a Nexi-powered punch into the man's chest. The man flew back, straight through one of the large windows. Borely immediately turned to the next Brotherhood fighter.

Vines grasped the sides of the broken window, and the masked man Borely had punched leaped back into the room. He had his fire Nexi raised toward Borely, who was turned away from him.

"Watch it, Borely!" Areo yelled.

She rushed for him and pushed him away from the enemy's blast of fire. The flames nearly caught on to her, but she jumped back in time to avoid the attack. In one swift motion, she spun in place and leaped for the enemy. The man ran to her and raised his red Nexi. She sliced the man's hand clean off before he could activate the Nexi stone. Still stepping toward the man, Areo finished the motion by plunging her free claws into his heart.

By the time she turned around, a long-haired Brotherhood member had released a stream of swamp material, while a short Brotherhood fighter ran toward Areo with two daggers raised. Areo ran aside of the brown Nexi substance and charged for the fighter armed with daggers. In one glimpse, Areo realized one dagger had a purple Nexi attached to its hilt, while the other had a yellow Nexi.

Areo slipped out her tan Nexi and released a burst of dirt at the fighter. Closing her eyes, Areo leaped into the cloud of dust and listened for the assailant's exact movements. With two footsteps to go by, Areo lunged for the fighter, listening for the swipe or thrust of a dagger. The Brotherhood member swung a dagger—the one with the purple Nexi, which created a spherical shockwave to clear away the dust. The blast of energy disturbed Areo's swipe toward the fighter's neck, and she ended up clawing at the assailant's mask.

The mask flung off of the fighter, revealing the face of a woman—she had short black hair and large, piercing green eyes. Areo continued her attack, slashing again for the woman's neck. The Brotherhood member activated the yellow Nexi of her other dagger, and Areo's claws slammed against the yellow glow that enveloped the woman's body. Areo stepped back to avoid the swipe of the woman's other dagger.

At the same time Areo heard an object collide with the ground just behind her. She leaped back as hard as she could, jumping over what turned out to be a brown Nexi stone—the one used by the Brotherhood member from before. The stone blew apart, releasing a deluge of swamp substance. The second Brotherhood member guided most of it toward Areo, who quickly released a burst of dirt from her tan Nexi. She coated the swamp material beneath her feet and hardened the dirt, allowing herself to run back from the thick, dark waves.

The woman with daggers ran around the rushing swamp, much faster than Areo had expected. At the same time, Areo heard footsteps coming from the side. She glanced and found a third Brotherhood fighter avoiding a blast of water fired by Borely, then sprinting on toward Areo. A tall masked bald man—an elf, Areo noted from the pointed ears. He wielded a long metal staff.

While Borely beat down the man controlling the swamp, Areo caused a large arm of earth to erupt from the dirt she left atop the swamp. She turned back to the woman with the dagger, who swung a wave of purple energy at Areo. While dodging the attack and going by the sound of the man's footsteps, Areo caused the dirt arm to grab the man's leg. The woman continued toward Areo, who readied her claws for the kill.

A blast of water slammed into Areo's back, flinging her straight for the woman with daggers. The elf apparently had a water Nexi embedded in the end of his staff, Areo realized. She crashed against the woman, who shoved a dagger toward Areo's heart. Areo slipped her claws into the the woman's hand at the last moment, forcing the assailant to drop the dagger.

The two crashed against the far wall, the enemy's head bashed hard against the thick dull metal.

Before Areo could claw at the enemy, a very large red Nexi fell to the ground about a meter away from them. An attack meant to take her down, even if it cost the Brotherhood woman's life.

The woman was dazed. Areo grabbed the dagger with the yellow Nexi from her and turned around. She leaped over the red Nexi just as it detonated into a massive ball of fire. Areo activated the yellow Nexi, creating a barrier around her body just as she was engulfed in the flames. The ear-piercing detonation flung Areo across the room for several meters, sending her crashing past where Borely and two other Brotherhood members were fighting. She tumbled across the floor, then rolled until the fire covering her body dissipated. By keeping the energy of the yellow Nexi active, Areo managed to keep from getting burnt by the all-encompassing flames.

She glanced back to where she had been, finding a massive hole in the room, now filled with dark smoke and patches of blue sky. Both the woman and the elf Areo fought were gone.

Borely batted aside vines flung by one Brotherhood fighter, then spun in place and slammed a hard punch into the stomach of the other fighter, who had charged for Borely from behind with a sword. The first fighter raised a tan Nexi, aiming it toward Borely from behind.

Areo flung her dagger into the man's back. She ran to him and clawed apart his neck before he could fight back. Meanwhile Borely continued to fend off the other Brotherhood member, who activated an orange Nexi in the hilt of his sword. Borely leaped back, smart enough to know he wouldn't be able to block the man's swings with his fists, even with his thick metal knuckles charged orange as well.

The moment he had an opening, Borely stomped forward and slammed his forehead against the enemy's forehead, activating the blue Nexi in his headpiece in the process. The jet of water sent the masked man flying back several meters, clear across the room. He crashed against the wall, just beside the door to the airship's hallway.

A large, muscular man walked into the room and stopped at the entry. A small vest left most his chest and abdomen bare, and several glowing green Nexi were grotesquely grafted to his arms. The man had a wide bandana to keep his long black hair back, and a pallid scar curving across his nose. His face was essentially a series of frowns—one from his bandana, another from his scar, and a third from his actual frown. He stared at the chaotic scene before him with cold, soulless green eyes.

Areo had never seen this man face-to-face before, but she knew of him—Augurc Shire, one of the two brother leaders of the Shire Kingdom. He was considered subordinate to his older brother Delkol, but Augurc was the one with the darker reputation. Even in Istal, Areo had heard stories of the man's sadistic experiments and monstrous creations.

The masked Brotherhood member Borely had blasted across the room crawled toward the newcomer. "They're strong..." He struggled to get to his knees, but was too injured to do so.

"No," Augurc said. "You're weak." He grabbed the man by the neck and lifted him up. Augurc held the man with his right hand, which Areo saw had an ice Nexi embedded in it.

The man's entire body froze instantly. Augurc continued to hold the man, and it took a few seconds for Areo to realize Augurc was forcing more and more icy air into the frozen corpse. For a moment the masked body glowed a bright light blue.

Augurc looked to Areo and Borely a few seconds. "You would have made interesting test subjects." His voice was monotone, lifeless.

He lobbed the frozen body toward Areo and Borely. Areo stepped back, but saw it was going to miss by a couple meters.

Upon landing, the body shattered into hundreds of small pieces of ice. Each of the pieces immediately sprouted several long icy needles, which jetted out and connected with one another. In seconds, there were thousands of these jagged protrusions, weaving a massive web of ice with needles that grew increasingly longer with each passing moment. Areo ran back and forced Borely back with her, but the freakish ice mass was growing far too quickly to escape from in time.

Areo handed Borely the tan Nexi and began clawing away at the jetting needles of ice with all the vigor she could muster. Meanwhile Borely controlled earth to push away as much ice as possible, hardening the formations of dirt to create a barrier between them and the spreading web of ice. The long, thick needles dug into the earth walls, quickly tearing it apart. Areo continued to furiously swipe apart the razor-sharp icicles, but her mad frenzy was wearing her out, and there was no end in sight to the ever-expanding web of ice.

Amidst the frozen entanglements, Areo noticed thin vines rushing through the holes and cracks of the ice formations. Augurc was guiding tens of vines toward Areo and Borely, hoping to ensnare them while they fought off the ever-growing ice needles. Borely managed to block off the vines reaching toward him, but Areo had too many icicles to fend off for her to claw apart the vines slithering toward her feet.

"Smash the ground!" Areo yelled.

Borely charged the orange Nexi for one of his fists and did as Areo directed. He quickly knelt down and punched a wide hole straight through the metal floor. The floor was thick and had multiple layers, so it took Borely a few punches to break through all the way. As Areo beat away the icicles, the web of ice grew increasingly tighter as long needles started filling in all the gaps. Once Borely tore the holes in the floor open enough for them to fit through, Areo immediately slipped out her green Nexi.

She quickly created vines to wrap around the portions of metal connecting the different layers of floor together. At the same time, Augurc's vines reached Areo's feet, then began encircling her legs.

Areo leaped down the hole and let her body dangle in the air beneath the airship. She clawed apart Augurc's vines while keeping a firm grasp on the vines from her own Nexi. Borely jumped down the hole and grabbed on to Areo's vines before he could be impaled by the expanding ice formation. He climbed down the thick green ropes until he was about a meter above Areo.

"Well, now what?" Borely asked.

Areo looked to the other Brotherhood airship. It looked like Kitoh was still battling with it, avoiding the Nexi stones the Brotherhood launched at him.

"Just hold on," Areo said.

Borely formed a thick barrier of earth over the hole above them, keeping the web of ice from reaching down to Areo's vines. Areo kept a close eye on the hardened dirt, watching for any sign of the ice needles breaking through. She didn't know what to do until Kitoh came back for them, other than hang on tight. The winds were furious beneath the airship, which had fortunately slowed down a bit following Areo and Borely's ambush. She hoped that the two of them had at least managed to make things difficult for this airship to reach the castle.

A figure lowered from the side of the airship, about a dozen meters away. It was Augurc, standing straight in the air with his arms held out to either side of him. Vines from his many Nexi stones connected his arms to the railing of the ship. He caused his vines to effortlessly reach for pieces of the airship's underbelly they could easily wrap around, and guided himself slowly toward Areo and Borely.

Incredulously, Augurc looked unfazed by the fact he was hanging from the bottom of an airship hundreds of meters up in the air. The wind pushed him far to the side at times, but still he continued to make his way forward. As he approached, he raised his right palm and caused an icicle to emerge from the Nexi stone embedded in it. The ice formed into a long, jagged spear that extended at least a meter long.

Like extra appendages, Augurc's vines pulled him toward his prey. His spear of ice at the ready, the man floated toward Areo and Borely, an entirely disinterested expression etched on his face.

"Give me my tan Nexi," Areo said. Borely tossed it down to her, and she immediately released a thin tendril of dirt toward Augurc. The man slashed away at the hardened dirt, his jagged icicle slicing through with each stroke of his arm. And all the while, his vines continued leading him toward Areo.

Borely shot off a jet of water from his metal laurel's Nexi, but Augurc easily caused his vines to slide him to the side of the blast. Augurc's control over the green Nexi in his arms seemed unconscious—as if it took more effort for the man to breathe than to control the vines from his arms.

It was difficult to think of anything more to do, dangling hundreds of meters above the ground, hanging from the vines of a single green Nexi.
Borely shot off jets of water several more times at Augurc, but to no effect. Augurc dodged every attack effortlessly, and continued to approach them.

Areo looked back and found an airship bursting into flames. She looked down and squinted into the bright blue sky, searching for any sign of Kitoh. After a few seconds of this, she glanced back to Augurc, now just a few meters away.

She turned back and found Kitoh, soaring straight for them. The dragon flapped his wings as fast as Areo could imagine him being able to, but it was going to take a few more seconds for him to reach them.

For a moment it looked like Augurc was going to fling himself down to stab Areo with the giant icicle protruding from his hand, but he caused his vines to bring himself upward at the last second. The man sliced through all of Areo's vines in one swoop, too quick for Borely to shoot with his dark blue Nexi.

Areo immediately guided the cut ends of her vines to latch on to Augurc's legs. She and Borely fell a few meters, but held on thanks to Areo's control of the vines. Augurc cut the vines wrapped around his legs, and Areo and Borely fell again.

They crashed onto Kitoh's back. Areo held on carefully with her claws while Borely grabbed Areo's leg and started screaming once more. This time though, Areo was pretty certain he was screaming in excitement.

Once she and Borely were situated safely on Kitoh's back, sitting in front of his fin, Areo looked back to the airship Augurc continued to hang from. "Now's our chance to take down that airship," Areo said. "Augurc isn't on board, and there isn't anyone running the cannons."

Kitoh turned back to the airship, flying high above it. Once near the dirigible, Kitoh swooped down and breathed a giant field of fire across the top of the great balloon. The blimp erupted in flames, and Areo directed Kitoh back down to the ground below, recognizing the boy's energy was wearing thin.

Areo looked back to where Terico and the elves were situated. It was difficult to see their airship, or the other two of the Brotherhood's airships. She had to simply hope they would pull through, and believe that Terico would manage to defeat Delkol if the time came for them to meet once more.

•

Terico and Turan clashed swords, leaving the other four Brotherhood members free to charge for Suran. Furious, Terico shoved Turan back as hard as he could. He leaped back to Suran's position and swung his sword at the nearest masked fighter. The tall, lanky man blocked with his own sword, then activated an orange Nexi in his hilt. Terico slipped back before the man could slice the blade of his sword clean in two.

Turan lifted a brown Nexi stone while Suran shot off a vibrating purple wave at the Brotherhood fighter nearest to her, knocking him off his feet—

she apparently had the Nexi stone for loose energy. A masked fighter with a large axe used a yellow Nexi to guard himself against the burst of energy, and continued rushing toward Suran.

Dodging Turan's blast of swamp material, Terico leaped in front of Suran and slammed the blade of his sword against the axe pole of the man charging for her. Terico glanced right and saw the tall swordsman pointing a dark blue Nexi at Suran.

She leaped away before the man could hit her with a jet of water. Terico pushed back against the axe of the Brotherhood member he fought, but the burly man was too strong. Suran suddenly jumped in front of Terico and slammed her purple Nexi against the axe man's stomach.

The man shook back violently, and Suran slipped to the side to allow Terico to slide his blade through the man's chest.

A series of vines immediately rushed for Terico, guided by Turan a couple meters away. Terico hacked away at them, but glanced back to Suran, noting how heavily she was breathing. She was struggling to stand, having used so much Nexi energy. Not only had she just finished shooting off a bunch of cannon Nexi, but she was utilizing a rare purple stone to fight these Brotherhood members.

She blasted away the swordsman approaching her before collapsing on her knees. Another Brotherhood member raised a red Nexi and fired at her. Terico found a brief opening from the rushing vines and ran in front of Suran. Just as the flames rushed around him, Terico slipped out his dark and light blue Nexis and created a barrier of ice to protect him and Suran from the flames.

Vines wrapped around Suran's legs, and before Terico could even turn around she was dragged away—straight toward Turan.

"No!" Terico shot off the formation of ice, slamming it against the masked fighter wielding the fire. The tall fighter with the sword leaped in front of Terico before he could chase after Suran. Terico blindly ran straight through the man, shoving his blade through the enemy's stomach before the man could swing his sword. Terico ripped his blade out the man's side and continued running after Suran.

Turan dragged Suran to him and wrapped more vines around her body to keep her from struggling. The vines stood her up straight beside him, and as Terico sprinted toward him, Turan rubbed a gray Nexi stone across the blade of his sword.

Turan stood behind Suran and placed his glowing gray blade against Suran's throat. The masked boy looked at Terico, the sadistic painted smile mocking Terico in his helplessness. Terico stopped about three meters away, but kept his sword raised.

"Stop!" Terico yelled. "Don't do it, Turan."

"My name is Lynx!" Turan replied. "But speaking of Turan, I wonder who it was that wouldn't stop for *him*. It was his supposed best friend. *Terico*. I saw it all. When he needed his best friend most, Terico *abandoned* Turan! I saw Turan... screaming Terico's name. Crying for help..." His muffled voice cracked a bit behind the mask, but then turned livid—far louder than Terico expected. "*Needing someone to save him from this agonizing fate!*"

"Turan, I'm sorry," Terico said.

"Of course!" Turan screamed. "Now you're sorry! I'll make sure you're plenty sorry! I'll—"

"It was a difficult decision!" Terico yelled. "I thought our friends at the school needed help. I thought you'd be okay... I thought things would work out..." He stared at Suran's pale face, struggling to breathe from the tightening vines. Terico considered reaching for his Elpis pieces, but knew Turan was watching his every movement. It would take a second to activate the power of the Elpis, and by then it would be too late.

"You thought things would just *work out*?" Turan yelled. He slid his blade toward Suran's neck.

"No!" Terico screamed.

A sphere of purple energy exploded from Suran, blasting apart the vines wrapped around her. The shockwave sent Turan flying back to the large hole in the floor he had made when breaking into the airship. Suran collapsed on her hands and knees, her last bit of energy spent on creating that one final blast with her purple Nexi.

The detonation pushed Terico back a couple meters, and knocked Turan's mask and green Nexi away in the process. Stumbling back, Terico grabbed the green Nexi from mid-air and immediately launched a series of vines toward Turan, already falling out of the ship.

I won't abandon you again!
"Grab on!" Terico yelled as loud as he could. He sent the vines rushing out the opening, unable to see how far down Turan had already fallen. There was no way for Turan to save himself, having just been hit that close by a full-powered blast of loose Nexi energy, and without his green Nexi stone to grab on to the airship with.

Terico continued to create more and more vines from the stone, driving them down as fast as his strength could manage. Several heartracing seconds passed before Terico felt an added weight to the vines. Terico gripped his Nexi stone tight and held on. He guided the vines back into the stone, pulling them back up into the ship. At the very end of the vines Terico found Turan hanging on, his body limp and beaten down. He still held on to his gray-glowing sword, but his grasp was tenuous. Terico dragged him onto the ship and sighed in relief. He fell to his knees and set the green Nexi down, but still kept a grip on his sword.

His mind went blank a few moments. He simply stared at Turan's barely conscious body while Suran crawled over to kneel beside Terico. He looked to her and felt his whole body start to tremble. At one moment he thought Suran was going to die, and the very next moment he thought Turan was going to die. It drove him to tears to see them both alive. Suran clasped her hand in Terico's and gave a small, exhausted smile.

Turan lifted his head and stared up at Terico. Turan's dark brown eyes were ringed with deep black marks, and his scraggly blond hair was speckled with blood. It was strange to see him without his mask again. To Terico, it almost felt like he was back in Edellerston again, and everything was back to normal. Turan coughed up blood and shook violently, still reacting from the purple energy Suran hit him with.

"I'm dying," Turan said, crimson lines trickling from his lips.

Terico stood up and walked over to Turan. Suran followed beside him, limping along wearily.

"Don't strain yourself," Terico said.

Suran closed her eyes and smiled. "I'll be fine." She took a more serious expression and added, "It's Turan we should worry about. There's a medical kit on the bridge I can get for him."

"I... I'm sorry," Turan said before coughing up some more blood. "I was wrong."

"It's okay," Terico said. "Augurc did something to your brain, perhaps heightening certain emotions you had at the time. But it will be all right.

We'll help you through this, Turan."

"I... I've hurt you, Suran," Turan said, tears trickling down his face.
"I'm so sorry."

Suran smiled as if it were nothing. "I'm just tired is all. I'm just glad you're alive."

"We still need to heal you though," Terico said, helping Turan roll over so he lay on his back. "Where do you hurt?"

The airship turned hard to the right, then shook violently. Terico fell backward and slid a couple meters before managing to grip a seam in the metal flooring. Suran grabbed on to the floor beside Turan and helped him hold on, even in her weakened condition.

What's Lanek doing? Terico thought. The airship shook again, and Terico realized the ship was descending. The Brotherhood airship was landing attacks on *The Finest Hour*.

The ship stabilized slightly, and Terico turned back to Suran and Turan.

Suran stood up and turned her head back to check on Terico. "Are you—"

Turan stood up and stabbed Suran through the chest.

"No!" Terico screamed.

He ran straight for Turan, who pulled his gray blade out of Suran's chest and shoved her to the ground. Turan stood still, staring at Terico wideeyed, as if surprised by what he had just done.

Then he grinned.

Terico swung his blade at Turan, ready to hack him to pieces. At the last moment, Turan leaped backward, letting himself fall out the hole in the airship. He had his green Nexi again, Terico realized.

Through the window, Terico saw the Brotherhood airship, flying by only a dozen or so meters away. It fired several cannons straight at *The Finest Hour*, but a barrier of earth appeared to block most of them. One connected, however, and the ship began to descend more rapidly.

Terico looked out the hole in the airship to find Turan far below, hanging on to vines connecting him to the Brotherhood ship. A part of Terico wanted to use the Elpis and go after him, but right now Suran needed him.

Suran. The moment she was stabbed, Terico's entire body had seemed to freeze over, and yet he still reacted. His heart stopped, but still he forced himself to move. He ran back to Suran's limp form, almost falling over amidst the shaking of the airship. He knelt down beside Suran and looked over her bloody wounds. The blade had pierced all the way through her chest, and on out her back. She was still managing to breathe, however—a frail hyperventilation, terrifying in the fragile balance it held.

Tears streamed down Suran's face. "T-Teri...co..."

He took out his Elpis pieces and accessed their power. His body surged with the violent energies flowing through every pore of his skin. The transformative effects quickly took hold, but the power building up in Terico felt far greater than he imagined. With two fragments of the Elpis, Terico's power was many times greater than it was with one.

I can heal her, Terico thought. He knew from experience there was healing energy in the Elpis—he had healed himself in the underground city, and was strengthened when fighting Ganto and Delkol. The pain was almost unbearable, but he survived. He could survive again.

Suran looked up at Terico, a frightened look on her face. Seeing Terico in this form must have been shocking.

"It's the Elpis," Terico said. "I'll use its power to heal you." He placed a hand over the bleeding wound in her chest, wincing at the grisly sight. Focusing all his concentration on Suran's wound, Terico shut his eyes and willed the Elpis power to shift to healing energies.

Terico's body turned boiling hot, then freezing cold, then tight and constricted, then overwhelmingly weak and nauseous. With each passing moment, the plagues of the various Nexi powers swept through his body. He struggled to seek out the healing energy, the pain of the Elpis far greater than it was the last two times he used it.

Hot tears slipped from Terico's eyes, and the blood spilling over his hand turned frigid, icy. He cried Suran's name, exerting every bit of his mental focus on healing her of this wound.

For just a moment, Terico felt as if his pains were erased, his entire body lightened and free of of the Elpis's agony. The pain of a blinding headache afflicted him immediately afterward, but Terico forced his mind to latch back on to the previous energy. He felt the healing return, and quickly willed the energy to flow from his arm to Suran's wound.

Suran fell into fits of convulsion, screaming at the top of her lungs. Terico's immediate reaction was to pull away, but he knew with a certainty this was the energy that would heal her.

"I'm sorry, Suran!" Terico yelled above her cries of agony. "Hold on just a little longer!"

Suran arched back and reached out with her arms, struggling to break away from the torment the Elpis inflicted on her. Terico held her down to keep his hand firmly over the bleeding injury.

Can't lose her now... Not now... Not when we're so close... Not when we're finally together again! Not when I've already lost everything else! Suran's screams grew louder, and her limbs contorted into painful, disjointed positions. The Elpis energy continued to flow to Suran's body, the process draining to Terico's mind and soul. He slowly felt as if his very existence was leaking away. For a moment he felt as if continuing this would cause him to disintegrate from the inside—to crumble apart and fade away forever. And yet he kept pushing himself to heal Suran, to do whatever was in his power to save her.

Perhaps a minute of this passed before blood stopped leaking from the thick opening in Suran's chest. Terico's body trembled from the rush of energy flowing out of his body, but managed to lift his hand away to look over the wound. Using his sleeve, he wiped away as much blood from the wound as he could.

The incision was gone—there wasn't even a scar left. With his clean hand Terico felt only smooth, healed skin, and noted the steady beat of Suran's heart.
He put away the Elpis stones and cut off his access to their power.

The sudden release of energy gave him the overwhelming urge to lie on his back and die, but he kept his focus on Suran and her injury. She writhed in pain for a few more seconds before settling down. Her screams faded to gasping cries, and within a couple minutes she was breathing normally again.

Terico looked her over, and as far as he could tell the wound was gone. He checked her back and saw the slit there was gone as well. The fact Suran was breathing normally again seemed to imply her lungs were healed, and Terico felt her pulse to check her heart was still beating properly. He wasn't sure if she had been stabbed in the heart, but without the Elpis Terico doubted he would have been able to heal her in time.

"How are you feeling?" Terico asked. He felt terrible himself, struggling to even sit up at this point—but he had to be certain Suran was fine before he could worry about himself.

"I'm okay," Suran said, her eyes half-open. "But Turan... stabbed me." "Does it still hurt?" Terico asked.

Suran looked up at him a few seconds. "No... I feel fine... I'm just tired... So very tired..."

"That's all right," Terico said. He knew Suran had exhausted herself already from Nexi use, and the strain of the Elpis energy would have certainly worn her out even further. "You can rest all you want now."

He looked out the window and saw the airship was still descending. The machinery of the ship had grown louder, and it was clear there wasn't much chance of it staying airborne much longer.

Terico lifted Suran off the ground and carried her with him down the hallway. It strained him to carry her, despite how light she was—but he wasn't going to leave her alone for even a second at this point. He needed to get Suran to Lanek, then find a way to save the airship. Terico wondered if he would be able to find a way to fix *The Finest Hour* with the power of the Elpis. It would likely take a lot of effort to figure out a way to do so, and by then he would have exhausted himself far too much to be able to fight Delkol.

The third piece is at the castle, Terico remembered. *I can fly there with the two pieces I have, and then the third fragment will give me even more power. I'll be able to take Delkol down easily then...*
Terico stumbled to the bridge, where Lanek was frantically working with

several different levers. He turned back for a moment, quickly noting it was Terico and Suran entering the room. He returned to his controls and pulled on a rope as hard as he could, working to stabilize the drifting airship. "What happened to Suran?" he yelled as he went back to a lever.

"She was hurt, but I healed her with the Elpis," Terico said. "She should be fine."

"You let her get hurt?" Lanek screamed. He was absolutely livid, yet continued to operate the controls as if he were having a friendly chat. "I'd kill you, but we're probably all going to die in just a minute anyways." "The ship's going to crash?" Terico asked.

"Too late to save it," Lanek said. "There were far too many jets of water to defend against while piloting the airship."

"Get on my back and I'll fly us out of here," Terico said.

Lanek turned around and looked up at Terico in callous disbelief. "You fly."

"I fly. Now come on." Terico turned and ran back down the hallway. He heard Lanek's footsteps following behind him, and continued to the gaping hole in the entry room. The airship tilted backward, making it easy for Terico to run down while carrying Suran. He gripped his Elpis fragments tight and accessed their power upon reaching the edge of the hole. The burst of torment erupting in the very center of his chest made him cry out in pain, but he managed to stop and bend to one knee so Lanek could climb on his back. Terico felt his body transform, and he filled with the pain and energy of every Nexi in the world. For a moment Terico felt he would utterly collapse beneath the weight Lanek placed on his back. Lanek was about as thin and light as his sister, but carrying both him and Suran was too much for Terico to handle in this state.

He strained himself to seek out the orange Nexi energy within the constantly shifting powers rushing through his body. For a moment it felt like his mind was going to shatter, but just as he was about to collapse he managed to grab hold of the strengthening Nexi power bursting within him. Suddenly carrying Suran and Lanek was a simple matter, and Terico was able to concentrate on levitating off the ground.

"Hang on," he said to Lanek. Terico looked down to Suran's tired face, straining to keep her bloodshot eyes open. Though he had saved Suran's life, Terico still felt uneasy about her.

She's just worn out, he thought. He forced himself to concentrate on the task at hand.

The airship shook more violently, and tilted even further backward. Terico let himself fall out of the hole, jumping forward to make sure Lanek didn't hit the edge of the jagged flooring.

The three plummeted out of the airship, falling only a little faster than the quickly descending airship. The ground was much closer than Terico expected, and he needed to start flying immediately. This ability was much more second-nature, apparently an inherent aspect of the transformation the Elpis brought him.

He flew down to the green fields below at a safe speed, then glided a good distance from where the airship would crash. As soon as Terico reached the ground, he stopped using the Elpis power, regaining his normal form once again. He knelt down so he could lay Suran down gently, and so Lanek could get off of his back.

"Are you okay?" Terico asked Suran.

She barely managed to nod in response. Too tired to speak, she shut her eyes and fell asleep on the spot. Terico and Lanek watched to make sure she was still breathing, and checked for any further signs of injury.

"She seems fine," Lanek said, "but I'll want to take her to a clinic to be certain. Wearing herself out this badly probably warrants a visit in and of itself."

Terico agreed, and sat down beside Suran so he could recover himself. His whole body was worn out, and the fact his best friend had stabbed the girl he loved was painful to think about. And in the end Turan managed to slip away, still vengeful and blind with hate. Terico wanted to believe it was all Augurc's fault, but the fact Turan wanted

Terico to suffer because Terico left him back during the attack on Edellerston... There was a sense to it. And a part of Terico felt he couldn't really fault Turan for wanting revenge.

Turan didn't want to simply kill Terico, though. He wanted to kill everyone Terico loved. He wanted Terico to hate his very existence. This was how Turan felt, Terico realized. Turan's life was a constant hell. Surely Augurc did experiment on Turan, but Turan was able to recognize what he had become. Turan still knew what he was doing—he wasn't mindless—and yet to some degree he had lost his mind to the lust of revenge. Terico thought over Jujor's and Areo's words on the subject. How different was Terico's quest for revenge?

I can't just stop, Terico thought. *Not now. Not when everyone is depending on me to bring Delkol down. He's still out there... He's probably in one of those airships, heading for the castle. I have to get there before him.* Terico turned to Lanek, who was watching his airship crash into the ground. It collapsed in a tremendous heap in the distance, loud and terrible.

"Rest in peace, *Finest Hour*," Lanek said. "What a short, unfortunate life you lived."

To Terico it was just an airship, but to Lanek and Suran it was something they had spent a great deal of time and effort on. It was also a treasure of their parents, as well as a symbol of their past, long lost to the cruelty of Delkol and his Brotherhood.

Everything goes back to him, Terico thought. *Delkol. The man who killed my parents. Destroyed my home town. Wreaked havoc in every land he stepped foot in. And through his Brotherhood, he has hurt the lives of every living person I know. Suran. Lanek. Areo. Borely. Kitoh. Turan.*
It will never end. It will never end until he's dead.
I have to find him now!
If there was a golden Nexi that could lead people to what they sought after, Terico could access that power via the Elpis. He already knew he could see great distances with the power of the Elpis—if he could combine that ability with the golden Nexi energy, he would be able to find Delkol.

Upon activating the Elpis fragments, the instantaneous surge of energy tore through his body. Terico nearly collapsed to the ground, but managed to keep to his feet.

"What are you doing?" Lanek asked.

Terico gripped his forehead and shut his eyes tight. An all-encompassing white light was surging within him, blinding his eyes—blinding his entire body. He screamed uncontrollably. One moment an icy wind blew through his bones, and the next moment he felt as if his blood were turning hard—solid and heavy. Just standing up was difficult, but Terico pushed himself to access the power he would need to find Delkol.

He opened his eyes and still felt blinded for several seconds. A Brotherhood airship came into focus for a moment, then turned blurry and fragmented. The sky split apart, and for a second Terico felt his own body was being ripped in half, tearing from his left shoulder to his right hip.

He gripped the Elpis pieces tighter and turned around, facing toward the capital city. His vision went dark, then turned into an image of the castle. It was blurry at first, but once it cleared Terico felt as if he were standing just outside the castle grounds. He noticed something flying past one of the red towers. Terico gazed at it, and his vision focused in on what turned out to be some kind of giant hawk. It was difficult to tell at first, but Terico quickly realized the demonic creature was made entirely of bones and bloody strands of muscle. How it was able to fly, Terico couldn't imagine—but it flapped its skeletal wings vigorously, propelling it from the castle and toward the area where *The Finest Hour* fought the Brotherhood airships.

Terico stared closer at the gruesome bird, bringing his vision closer to it. There was someone riding on top of the reigned beast.

Delkol.

And as Terico focused a little more, he could make out the gleam of Nexi stones in Delkol's hand. Two stones—and they continually shifted from one color to the next.

The airships were just a diversion, Terico realized. While Rilv's units were scrambling to prepare the city to defend against the approaching airships, Delkol sneaked to the castle with the help of his secret agent and obtained the Elpis piece hidden there.

I can't let him get away, Terico thought. He forced his mind to let go of the golden Nexi power and shut his eyes for a few seconds. His head was ringing violently, and a part of Terico wanted to fall to his hands and knees and retch out all the organs in his body. His insides quivered and turned soft, as if they were dissolving into liquid.

He forced himself to fly into the air. Lanek was yelling something at him, but he sounded distant. For a moment Terico wondered if Lanek was dead, then wondered why he was flying away. Something snapped in the back of his head, and he clawed at it, screaming from the pain erupting in his mind. His vision turned blurry for a few seconds, and once it cleared Terico realized he was lying on the ground, his clothes and body torn up in bloody gashes.

His body was suffering from Elpis poisoning. Even with half the Elpis, it was too difficult for him to use it too much, especially when he was completing difficult tasks. Saving Suran from death and pinpointing Delkol's location were taxing on Terico's very being, it seemed.

He cut off his mind from the Elpis energy and fell into a violent coughing fit. The agony struck at his heart and lungs the hardest, but at the same time his mind felt like it was being stabbed with a thousand tiny needles all at once.

As Terico drifted to unconsciousness, his thoughts somehow remained coherent, focusing entirely on Delkol. Terico could see the man's smug expression perfectly. His short, light brown hair flapping in the wind. His icy blue eyes, gleaming wide and eager. The macabre scar running across his right eye, from his forehead to his cheek. And that smirk. That all-knowing, pretentious smirk.

You think you've won! Terico thought. *I'll kill you. I'll kill you. I'll kill you.* He fell unconscious, all his thoughts sinking deeper and deeper into a thirst for revenge.

•

Terico woke up to find himself lying in a bed. He stared up at a ceiling painted a dark blue, about the same color as his hair. His whole body ached, even worse than it had after using the Elpis in Vursa. It strained his eyes to glance around, and he had to wince when he looked too far to one side or the other. He was apparently in a clinic, one quite nicer than the one in Edellerston. The green blankets he lay in were light and cool, and he was dressed in clean clothes—a loose, white shirt and trousers.
"Hey, he's up," Borely said, standing up from a small wooden chair in the corner. Areo and Kitoh got up from their chairs and followed after him. They walked to the side of Terico's bed and stood quietly for a few moments.

"How are you doing?" Areo asked.

"I'll live," Terico said. He glanced to the other side of the room and noted a second bed, which he found occupied by Suran. Save for the slight rise and fall of her breathing, she lay perfectly still beneath her blankets. Her eyes were closed, but she still looked exhausted.

"What happened?" Terico asked. He was struggling to piece together everything that had happened. He knew he used the Elpis, and that he was chasing after Delkol...

He tried to sit up, and Areo helped him position his back against the wall behind him.

"Lanek found you just outside the castle grounds," she said. "He brought Suran with him, and she's still unconscious. It's been about fourteen hours since the airship attack, but nothing has happened since." Borely handed Terico a couple leather pouches. "Here's your Nexi stones, and the Elpis fragments."

Terico opened the lighter of the two bags. "Two pieces of the Elpis.

And now Delkol has the other two."

"The castle was attacked," Areo said, "but we don't know any specifics yet. Rilv said she'd explain the situation once you were up again."

"Everyone's okay though?" Terico asked. "The three of you look well. And Lanek?"

"He's fine, but is... away," Areo said. She looked down to Terico, her expression grim. "And Suran... The doctor is still concerned about her condition, I'm afraid."

"She'll be fine," Terico said, his memories of yesterday's events starting to piece back together. "She was stabbed, but I healed her. I used the Elpis to save her."

"Explain more," said a man's voice. Terico turned to find a man dressed in the light green and black garb of a city hospital worker. He was a tall man in his forties, and had short, black hair and a full goatee. His ears were slightly pointed, perhaps marking him as a half-elf. "I need to understand precisely what happened to the patient."

Walking beside him was a woman only slightly shorter than the doctor. She seemed in her late twenties, and had sharp, thin eyes and silver hair that reached her shoulders. Terico inferred from the regal purple and white uniform that this was Rilv, the head servant of the royal line.

"It was just as I said," Terico explained. "The Brotherhood boarded our airship, and the two of us had to fight them all off. Suran was stabbed in the chest by one of them, but I used the healing energies of the Elpis to save her shortly afterward."

"There was no wound for me to examine," the doctor said. "And no scar left behind."

"It disappeared," Terico said. "And there shouldn't be a problem anymore. She's breathing fine, isn't she?"

"She's alive," the doctor said, "but she's extremely weak. Barely able to maintain consciousness for more than a minute at a time, and with several hours needed to recover each time. Her brother said she was worn out from Nexi use, but if that were the case she should have recovered by now... Do you remember if there was anything peculiar about the sword used?"

The questioned triggered Terico's memory of the blade glowing gray. "There was a gray Nexi stone. He rubbed it against the full length of the blade, turning it gray."

"A gray Nexi stone?" Borely said. "What does that do?"

Terico had never heard of a gray Nexi, let alone seen one used before. It must have been a very rare stone.
"A poison," Rilv said. "Incurable." "Wh... What?" Terico cried.
"She will not live long," Rilv said, as terse as she was when she spoke via the teal Nexi.

Terico turned to the doctor. "No, there has to be a way to heal her."

The man sighed and shut his eyes a few seconds. "I'm sorry, boy. The gray Nexi's energy is the power of death. It seems you slowed the effect a bit with the Elpis, but she is still dying nonetheless. Had it been a regular poison of some kind, there might have been a chance—but the gray Nexi has affected her entire bloodstream, and in turn every vital organ in her body. I'm afraid there is no possible cure... It's only a matter of time."

"No," Terico said, pushing aside his blanket. "No, that's wrong. I can use the Elpis." He struggled to turn himself so he could get out his bed, then strained himself to walk over to Suran's. He held on to the side of her bed to keep from falling to the ground, and had to take a couple slow breaths to recover.

"You can barely stand," Rilv said. "You can not use the Elpis again in this state. And with only two of its four pieces, you won't be able to last long.

You will kill yourself."

"I have to try!" Terico yelled. "I'm not going to just let her die!" "You healed one wound," Rilv said, "but can you heal every organ in her body? On top of this, her entire bloodstream has been infected by the Nexi energy. You would have to heal every drop of blood in her body."

Terico thought over how long this would take him. Hours, he realized. The agony would be unbearable, and he likely *would* die if he made such an attempt.

No. I can't just do nothing. Not again. Not now. I have half the Elpis. I can save her. It has to be possible. I'm not going to lose her now!

He took his Elpis fragments and placed one in each of his hands. Though he felt half-dead himself, he had to try. There was energy in the Elpis that could strengthen him—if he could access that energy right away, he might be able to hold out long enough to find a way to heal Suran.

"Stop," Rilv said. "You must rest."

Terico ignored her and gripped the Elpis pieces tight. His body filled with a hundred energies, each of them destroying him from the inside. He screamed, but forced himself to clasp the Elpis pieces tighter. All the wounds across his body erupted with searing heat, as if a tremendous fire was rushing out each of his cuts and pushing against each of his bruises.

Terico collapsed to the ground, sitting against the side of his bed. He fell into sudden gasps of slow breaths, his lungs heavy and dense.

Rilv walked to him, bent to one knee, and wrenched the Elpis fragments from him. Terico couldn't fight back, barely even conscious of what she was doing.
"I will return these to you after you recover," she said. "You probably need to rest at least a day before using the Elpis again. It is pertinent you regain your strength before Delkol's armies close in on the city."

Terico took long, shivering breaths. His body felt cold and tight, as if he were buried beneath a frozen avalanche. He couldn't respond to Rilv. He couldn't argue. He couldn't yell. He couldn't scream at the sheer wretchedness of his situation.

Suran is dying, and I couldn't do anything.
"I need to explain the current situation to you," Rilv said.

Suran is dying.

"I will be brief, as I have many matters to return to," Rilv continued.

Why is this happening?

"Delkol Shire has obtained the castle's Elpis fragment. He escaped with the remnants of his Brotherhood, which has joined with the Shire armies in preparation to invade Setar."

Just when we were back together... Just when things finally started to look up for us...

"Using the power of the Elpis, Delkol killed nearly every royal guard he came in contact with. Before escaping the castle, he murdered the king and each of the royal dukes. At that point, every soldier and servant he caught sight of was killed."

I have the power to save her... I have so much power, and yet I'm failing her!

"Fiefs Kingdom is now without a leader, and the Shire armies will likely be ready to invade within the next two to three days."

Why can I not do this one thing? Suran needs me more than ever... She needs me, and I can do nothing.

"The traitor within the royal guard has escaped with Delkol, who now has half of the Elpis. It is likely that it was through this agent that Delkol was able to enter the castle in secret. He is likely also responsible for Delkol learning about your father and the Elpis fragment in Edellerston, as well as the likelihood of an Elpis in Vursa."

I won't stop. I won't stop trying to save you, Suran. As soon as I can, I'll use the Elpis to heal you. I'll destroy the poison. You'll be healthy again, and live a long, wonderful life. I'll heal you, no matter what it takes.

"It is up to you, Terico, to use your half of the Elpis to defeat Delkol. If you can kill him and retrieve his two Elpis fragments, this war can be stopped before the city suffers extreme casualties."

We can still be together, Suran. I can heal you. There has to be a way to heal you.

"I am conducting every possible effort to bring in all the reinforcements I can, but time is short. Delkol has amassed a large, well-trained army, and many of our most valuable resources have been undermined.

On top of this, the death of the king has hurt the morale of our troops. The massacre of at least half the royal guard and over a hundred servants has also been a terrible blow." *I won't fail you, Suran.*

"Terico. Do you understand how vital you are to the preservation of our kingdom?"

Terico looked up at Rilv, his vision blurry. He realized his eyes were clouded with tears, and wiped them out right away.

"Do you understand, Terico?" Rilv repeated.

"You're being too harsh," Areo said. "You can't order him around like this right after being so blunt about Suran's condition."

"He must understand that there is no hope for that girl," Rilv said.

"No hope?" Terico said. "You're wrong! I still have the Elpis. There's still hope for Suran. Just give me some time, and I'll heal her."

"She is a lost cause, and you need to move on," Rilv said. "You must understand that you are the only one who can defeat Delkol with the power of the Elpis. You will be one of the most important factors in this war, and your success or failure will greatly affect the outcome of this battle."

"Why?" Terico yelled. "Why am I the one who has to do this?"
"Do you not want to kill Delkol?" Rilv asked. "He is the leader of the Brotherhood, and therefore the one responsible for this girl's state."

"I know!" Terico said. "But why? Why is it just me and Delkol who can use the Elpis?

Rilv tightened her dark, knifelike eyes a little further. She stared down at Terico a few seconds before responding. "You have royal blood. Only those descended of the royal Fiefs line are capable of accessing the power of the Elpis. You and Delkol are both descendants."

"Royal blood?" Terico asked. "My parents weren't royalty. We lived in *Edellerston.*"
"Your grandfather was King Levae Fiefs. He had an illegitimate child— your father. To keep him a secret, your father and grandmother were moved to the remote village of Edellerston. Your father adopted the last name of his mother. He grew up and had a connection to the Elpis hidden there. The royal head servant who preceded me deemed it pertinent to have someone watch over your father, just in case it ever became

necessary to gather the Elpis together. Eventually Jujor was the one assigned to Edellerston, and he deemed you to have an even greater connection with the Elpis."

Terico struggled to believe such a story, though the more he thought about it, the more everything started to make sense. And yet his whole life he never suspected a thing. His parents never acted anything like royalty. Nobody in Edellerston had even been to Setar, as far as Terico ever knew. He hardly ever knew a thing about the current events of the Fiefs government. The very notion that Terico was connected to all this was incredulous.

And he wasn't just connected to it.

"I'm... a member of Fiefs royalty," he said. The very fact these words were coming out of his mouth seemed ridiculous. He had never aspired to any such thing. The thought never crossed his mind—not even *once*.

"And the king is dead," Rilv said. "This means you are the only heir to the throne."

Terico shut his eyes and clenched his forehead. He couldn't believe this was happening. It didn't *make sense*.

"I have no intention of being king," Terico said.

"Of course. Now is hardly the time to instate you as king," Rilv said, folding her arms. "You have not been prepared for such a responsibility, and the threat of Delkol's invasion warrants greater attention. I will lead the armies for the time being. In the meantime, you must rest in preparation to fight Delkol. Focus on killing Delkol and retrieving the full Elpis. Once that is taken care of, we can deal with matters of royal succession afterward. It is best we focus on our very survival for the time being.

"Give me back the Elpis," Terico said. "I'll only use it once I'm ready." "You will die if you use it too soon," Rilv said. "It would be unwise to take that risk."

"I may not be king, but I am royalty," Terico said. "As the royal head servant, you must comply with my demands."

"My greatest priority is the safety of the kingdom," Rilv said, standing up a little taller. "I strongly suggest you allow me to hold the Elpis fragments for the time being. I will return them to you once you have recovered."

Terico stared at Rilv's placid eyes for several long seconds. This obstinate woman was going too far.

What, does she want the Elpis for herself? What is going through that head of hers?

He wondered if he could really trust her. There was no way to be certain where her loyalties lay.

"You failed to protect the Elpis piece held in this castle. I won't risk you losing these two pieces as well." Terico held out a hand. "Return them to me, head servant."

Rilv simply stared at Terico, as stone-faced as ever. Terico thought she wouldn't comply, but she at last responded with a small, curt bow. After setting the Elpis pieces back on Terico's bed, she turned and walked out the door, swift and proper.

•

Terico lay back in bed, each minute feeling like hours. Areo and Borely tried to keep Terico company for a while, but Terico simply had nothing to say. They eventually left with Kitoh when Terico stopped responding to their inquiries. He couldn't care for any of the things Rilv had revealed.

His family was Fiefs royalty all this time. He was now heir to the throne. The king and dukes were all murdered. And all the armies of the Shire Kingdom were closing in on the city.

And Terico didn't care. It all meant nothing to him. Not when Suran was dying.

The doctor said she likely had at least a day left to live. He would come back from time to time to check on her, but he never said anything more to Terico regarding her condition.

Hour after hour passed, and all Terico could do was lie still and watch Suran. With each passing minute, he wished to try to use the Elpis once more, but he knew he wasn't ready yet. His body would just crumple beneath the torment of the Nexi energies if he accessed the Elpis's power again too soon. He had to be patient.

It was the hardest thing in the world, watching his greatest love slowly die right before his eyes.

He gazed at her shut eyes, and over her face in general. She lay so quiet and still, Terico constantly worried if she were alive or not. He would get out of bed from time to time to check on her. When it looked like she wasn't moving at all, he would check her pulse. He placed an ear over her heart and listened for its faint, distant beating. The pulse of her small, weak heart was slowly fading away.

It was still too early for him to attempt using the Elpis again. He stroked her long red hair, then felt the outline of her thin, pointed elf ear. It brought back a childhood memory of when he was about five, when he first played with Suran.

She was the first elf his age he ever played with, and after they finished climbing a tree he asked if he could feel her ears. She let him, but only if he let her feel his ears. His short, rounded ears made her chuckle, and Terico couldn't get her to explain what was so funny. His ears were *normal*, he told her. It was *her* ears that were funny. Of course, she didn't think that way, and Terico had to learn for himself how much a different perspective could change things.

Terico lay back down and thought of all the people he had come in contact with since leaving Edellerston. He wondered if he had been able to see the point of view of each person he encountered. Turan, Jujor, Febraz, Areo, Borely, Kitoh, Lanek, Suran. Everyone had encountered a great deal of suffering since that fateful day Delkol attacked. They all found ways to cope. They all found ways to move on. They all struggled and fought and gave their all for what they believed in.

But Delkol. What was his perspective? To some degree, all the misery Terico's friends and associates had suffered was a result of this one man's quest for power and domination.

Why? Terico wondered. *How does this drive him to murder countless victims?* If Delkol could use the Elpis, then it meant the Shires were descendants of the Fiefs from centuries back. Terico knew the Shire Kingdom was founded when the Shires were exiled from the Fiefs Kingdom and conquered some of the surrounding territory, but he didn't know the Shires were royalty. Perhaps Delkol simply felt he was the rightful ruler of the Fiefs Kingdom.

It was all so ridiculous, and Terico didn't want to think about it any longer. There could never be a legitimate excuse for Delkol's actions. He had to be stopped—there just was no way around that.

But the time to face Delkol would come later. If what Rilv said was true about the gathering Shire armies, it wouldn't be long before Delkol would make his move. But the more pressing matter was Suran and how to save her.

Terico spent the hours either staring at the ceiling or watching Suran, always thinking of how he would use the Elpis to heal her. He knew how to transfer the healing Nexi energy to her, but he wasn't sure how to apply it to each of Suran's poisoned organs. The gray Nexi had affected each system of her body, weakening her in every way possible. Terico wondered if he'd have enough energy to heal Suran's entire body. It had taken so much out of him just to heal the wound of the sword that pierced her...

"Terico..."

It was Suran. Terico got out of his bed and stood beside her. "I'm here, Suran."

Her eyes were still closed, her entire body as still as as can be. "Terico..."

Half a minute passed, but she didn't say anything more. Terico placed a hand on her head and held his breath. He bent down a bit so he could listen as closely as he could. Suran exhaled slightly, but Terico couldn't make out any words from her breath.

"I'm here," he said again. "You're going to be okay. Just keep resting..."

She lay there, quiet and motionless, an embodiment of pure innocence. Her breaths were slow and shallow, even more so than was typical of sleeping.

She's dying, and there's nothing... nothing I can do yet. He knew he was still too weak to use the Elpis right away. Making another attempt to heal her this soon would only wear him out more, and he would need all the energy he could get in order to save her.

Suran slid a small hand out from her blanket. Terico clasped it and looked down to Suran's eyes, which were still shut. Suran's hand was so cold, it made Terico shudder when he first held it. He gripped it tight, letting her frigid energy seep into his hand.

"My... mind is far away," Suran whispered. "Tell me... a story." "About what?" Terico asked.

"Us," Suran said, her voice tired and scratchy. "Happy."

There were plenty of happy times Terico spent with Suran and their classmates. In a soft voice, Terico shared some of the happier memories he was able to quickly remember.

He started with a story of when they were seven years old. Suran

and a friend of hers had found a tiny rabbit in the forest caught in a simple snare. They wanted to free it, but were afraid the frightened animal would bite them, or that they would hurt its leg while trying to untie the rope. They found Terico and Turan and asked them to help save the rabbit. At the time Terico didn't think there was much purpose in this, since another animal would just get caught later anyways—but Suran couldn't help but sympathize with this specific rabbit. Turan pointed out that they had all eaten rabbit in the past, but still Suran wanted to free this bunny, regardless.

Once in the forest, Terico held on to the animal while Turan untied the rope. Terico managed to calm the rabbit and let Suran pet it, which filled her with emphatic glee. Terico couldn't help but smile, too. Though it might have been wrong to mess with the trap, Terico was glad to make Suran happy. Even as a child, he recognized something special in Suran's smile.

There was a faint trace of one on Suran's face as Terico told the story.
Terico moved on by recounting when they had participated in a play for the Heavenly Lights Festival. They were all twelve at the time, and their class was assigned to perform the tale of Yemadi for the village. In an attempt to put a fresh spin on the yearly performance, the class had everyone play the roles of characters of the opposite gender, with the exception of Turan, who played as a giant worm demon. Terico ended up with the part of a castle maid who happened to hear the worm's wicked plot, while Suran got the lead role of Prince Yemadi.

It was likely the most ridiculous play the village had ever seen, but most of the class managed to get through their lines without dying of embarrassment. The crowds roared with laughter whenever Turan squirmed onto the stage in his absurd worm costume, and would applaud whenever a new character appeared. Just the anticipation of seeing which girl would play as the blacksmith or which boy would play as the fortune teller was enough to hold everyone's interest. The one to get into the play most wholeheartedly though was Lanek, who volunteered for the role of Yemadi's love interest, Princess Iminia. He was probably the only one who looked just like the character he played, actually. Some of the villagers even questioned Lanek's gender for a few days, to his amusement.

The details of the story made Suran smile a tiny bit more. Her breathing was still very slow, and her hand was still nearly cold as ice.

Terico moved on to another story. About a year ago, Terico's parents had fallen gravely ill. They were sick in bed for several days, and Terico took time off of school in order to care for them. One day Terico left to buy some food, and when he came back he found Suran in the house, tidying up the mess that had grown over the past few days. She ended up helping Terico prepare a soup for his parents.

Once Terico's parents were asleep, Suran took Terico outside so they could chat. Suran was worried Terico was going to get sick himself if he didn't get enough fresh air, and wanted to let him know he could always go to her if he needed help. They walked to a field of yellow flowers, bright even under the night sky. Terico had trouble thinking of things to talk about with Suran, so they simply looked up at the sky for a while, searching for constellations and falling stars. It was probably that night when Terico realized just how much he liked Suran, though he had no idea how to go about telling her. So they simply enjoyed their time together, gazing up at the sea of stars.

"As always, you were concerned for the well-being of others," Terico said. "It made me really happy to be with you that day. And I was always glad to see you at school. I always wished we could do more together."

Suran's faint smile had faded slightly, her nearly sleeping face turning a little more thoughtful.

"And we will do more together," Terico said. "You'll be well soon enough. And once the Elpis is gathered, my work in this city will be done.

We can go wherever we wish."

She didn't say anything more, but drifted slowly back to sleep. Terico knelt down on the floor, too tired to keep standing. His hand still gripping Suran's, Terico shut his eyes and lay his head against his arm.

•

Hour after hour passed, but Terico could not fall asleep. Though the Elpis had drained him of all his energy, Terico didn't feel tired enough to sleep. Even as night drew on, he remained kneeling by Suran's bed, holding tight to her cold, tender hand. Darkness fell over the castle, and Terico kept all his thoughts on Suran and how he'd heal her.

Her tiny heartbeat pulsed from her wrist, so faint that Terico was afraid to move his hand away—as if the slightest disturbance would douse what little fire was left in Suran's heart.

The door to the room opened, but Terico didn't bother going to his bed. He listened for who approached, hearing only one person treading the thick wooden floor.

It turned out to be Lanek, who didn't bother lighting any of the wall torches. He looked down to Terico and pursed his lips.

"A part of me would still love to kill you," he whispered. "You must realize... that girl is the most important person in the world to me."

Terico looked up to Lanek. "Where have you been?"

"Working with the doctor," Lanek said. "We're searching through every text on the gray Nexi stone we can find. To call that stone *rare* would be a... vast understatement."

"I'm sorry," Terico said. "You asked me to protect Suran... but I failed."

"Yes, you did," Lanek said. "And I really do wish to yell at you for it. For hours on end. Or at least to slap you."

Terico stared at the elf, knowing better than to object. A part of Terico felt he deserved any retribution Lanek wished to deal him. If Terico hadn't saved Turan from falling out the ship, Turan wouldn't have stabbed Suran. It was thanks to Terico that Suran was in this state, dying a little more with each passing hour.

Lanek walked to Suran and placed a hand on her forehead, stroking her bangs a few times. "I need to keep searching for a cure, if there is one. You keep resting, Terico. If Suran wakes up and you're awake, you let her know she's going to make it. And when the time comes... you better heal her."

"I will," Terico said.

"I realize you and Suran have been good friends for many years now," Lanek said. "And I understand that... there's only so much I can do for her as her brother." He bent down to give his sister a kiss on the forehead, then turned away and took a long, slow breath. "When the time comes, please save her, Terico. I've already lost my parents. I can't lose my dear sister, too."

Lanek walked back to the door, his last words giving away his tears. Terico said nothing, but focused on his grip on Suran's chill palm.

•

The night passed without Suran waking up again. Kneeling on the floor for so long was painful, but Terico was too focused on Suran to let the pain in his knees affect him. Terico listened intently the entire night, but Suran didn't speak up again until morning.

"Terico..." she whispered. She was still too fatigued to open her eyes.
"Yes," Terico said in a hushed voice. "I'm still here."

"I'm..." Suran began, but she couldn't finish her sentence.

"It's okay," Terico said. "Don't push yourself. Just rest a little longer... I'm going to use the Elpis to heal you. As soon as I can, I'm going to heal you."

Suran lay still, her mouth open slightly for several seconds. "Talk..."

She needed Terico to speak to her. He thought of telling more stories of the good times they spent together, but instead felt he should finally tell her all the thoughts that had built up in his heart. For hours now, his mind had been entirely focused on Suran and all his hopes and dreams for her.

"There's so many things..." Terico began, struggling to find the right words to say. "So many things I wish to do with you, Suran. I will heal you, and then the battle will end, and everything will work out. In the end, everything will be all right.

"They might try to make me be king afterward, but I will turn them down. I don't seek power, or the strain of an entire kingdom's troubles. I would rather live somewhere quiet and peaceful. I would like it if we lived in a small town like Edellerston again. It wouldn't be the same, of course, but we belong in the countryside somewhere. We can leave all this behind. The royal courts, the wars, the Elpis, the power struggles, the constant death... We'll leave it all behind.

"We'll live together in a village, and the world will never trouble us again. We can get married... Nothing will break us apart. We'll always support each other. Every day, you can call me dear. Then I will call you dearest. And you will call me dearest forever... And... I'll call you dearest of all times, all places."

Terico couldn't say any more. His throat was so tight, it hurt to even breathe. Tears dripped onto his hand and Suran's hand, still clasped together. Terico had wanted to be strong for Suran, but he couldn't control himself. All his feelings for her were pouring out, and he couldn't stop himself.

"Once this is over, let's get married," he said.

Suran gave the slightest hint of a smile on her face. "I would... like that."

"I'll give you my... entire heart." Terico was too overcome with emotion to say anything more.

He knew what he had to do. As soon as his energy was back, he would use the Elpis to fight off the poison infecting Suran's body. He wouldn't let up until she was in perfect health once more. Even if he had to give up his entire heart.

•

The morning slowly crept toward noon, and Suran's condition continued to grow worse. Despite Terico's presence, Suran's hand only grew colder. Her pulse slowed down even more, leaving four seconds of emptiness between each heartbeat.

The doctor eventually returned to check on Suran once more. "The poison is affecting her a bit faster than I anticipated."

Terico stood up and gritted his teeth against the pain in his legs. "How long does she have? How soon do I need to use the Elpis?"

"You shouldn't use it before you're fully healed," the doctor said.

"But how much time does Suran have left?"

The doctor sighed. "It's difficult to say. I've never had a patient infected by gray Nexi energy before."

She could be hanging to her final breaths then, Terico thought. *This man doesn't know how much time Suran has left to live. I have to heal her now.* "Okay," Terico said. "I'll keep watching over her."

"Very well. Make sure you get some sleep..." The doctor looked concerned, but he also looked very weary—he may not have slept at all either.
As soon as the doctor left, Terico took out his Elpis fragments and gripped them tight, one in each fist.

I'll start by healing her mind and heart, Terico decided. He placed one hand on her forehead, the other over her heart.

"Don't worry," Terico said softly. "This might hurt, but the Elpis will destroy the gray Nexi energy inside you."

He knew he wasn't in very good condition to use the Elpis again, but there was probably no time left to wait any longer. One can only wait so long before breaking down.

I can do this, Terico repeated in his head. He activated the Elpis stones, causing them to glow brighter. The energy rushed up his arms and flooded his body with every pain imaginable. The fact he was still recovering from his use of the stones the day before only made the agony worse.

With all his might, Terico focused on directing the Nexi energies to Suran's mind and heart. He shut his eyes and exerted all his strength to separate the healing forces from the rest of the Elpis powers. Upon accessing the healing magic, Terico forced the energy to flow from his body to Suran's.

Suran's eyes shot open and she screamed at the top of her lungs. Terico wanted to cover her mouth to keep her from alerting the castle's nurses, but he couldn't move his hands away from Suran's mind and heart now. He continued to pour Elpis energy into Suran, his body trembling from the torment of the Elpis. Suran writhed beneath her blankets, tears streaming down her face.

Terico felt the healing energy collide with the gray Nexi energy in Suran's body. There was far more of the poisonous energy accumulated in her than the Elpis energy Terico was transferring to her. The gray energy negated all of Terico's efforts, then rushed up his arms and flooded his body with the effects Suran was suffering. Immediately Terico's arms went limp, too weak to even hold up.

In seconds, Terico's whole body turned weak and lifeless, and it simply became impossible to fight the Nexi energy, let alone the torment of the Elpis. He fell back and collapsed on the ground, unable to move at all for several seconds. His mind disconnected from the Elpis, and once he could move his hands he pushed the Elpis fragments away. The pain coursing through his body remained several seconds longer, and Terico almost felt certain he was going to die.

It didn't work, he thought, shutting his eyes tighter. *It didn't work at all.*

Suran's cries died away, and she lay still and quiet once more. Terico wanted to get up to check on her pulse or to see if she was breathing, but his limbs failed him. The brief burst of gray Nexi energy in his body was heightened by the energies of the Elpis, and his entire body felt numb, unresponsive.

The effects faded away after a few minutes, however, destroyed by lingering traces of the Elpis's healing powers. As soon as Terico was able to move to his hands and knees he pushed himself back to Suran's bed.

I can try again, he thought. *I have to keep trying!*
He picked up the Elpis pieces and struggled to stand on his feet again. He felt too weary to do so, and decided he had to rest a few minutes to recover.

Once he was able to stand, Terico felt for a pulse, and after several seconds felt only a single faint heartbeat. Suran held on to life with only the slightest of grips, her body threatening to give in to the poison at any moment.

"Stop!" a woman yelled. Terico glanced to the door to find Rilv entering the room.

"This is my only chance," Terico said, turning his focus back to Suran.

"You don't have the energy to save her," Rilv said. "You need to rest until you have fully recovered."

"She will die by then!" Terico yelled.

"You were supposed to rest," Rilv said. "You need all your energy for when Delkol attacks."

So this was Rilv's hope, Terico realized. She just wanted Suran to die while Terico slept, and then have Terico continue to rest and prepare for Delkol's invasion.

"Leave," Terico ordered. "I need all the concentration I can get." "You can't keep using the Elpis like this," Rilv said. "You will die." Terico ignored her and placed both hands on Suran's heart. He gripped the Elpis fragments tight and accessed their energies once more. In seconds, the power overwhelmed him. He could feel the gray Nexi in Suran's body fighting against his Elpis energy, utterly overpowering it. There was a moment of utter torment, then a moment of complete emptiness, and then a moment of pure grief.

I need more, Terico thought. *My power isn't enough. Even if I were fully rested, I wouldn't be able to fight off this poisonous energy. I need the full Elpis.*

His body turned limp and weak once more, forcing him back to the ground. He dropped the Elpis pieces to either side of him and rested his back against the side of his bed. Every centimeter of his body drummed with a stinging pain, and his headache seemed to pulse from head to toe several times a second.

"I hate this," Terico whispered, short of breath. "It's not enough. It's not nearly enough."

"You must rest," Rilv said. "If you are ill-prepared to face Delkol, he will kill you, take the Elpis fragments, and then have the powers of a god. He would be very difficult to deal with then, and thousands of people would die."

"I understand," Terico said. "I have to find Delkol... I have to find him now."
"I have scouts searching for his present location," Rilv said. "I will let you know as soon as he has been spotted. In the meantime, you must get ready to fight."
Terico sat still for a minute, going over everything Rilv had said. If Terico could get a hold of the rest of the Elpis, he would have the power to save Suran.
He just needed to find Delkol.

•

Rilv left when Terico assured her he would rest in his bed. He had to be helped into the bed because his body had gone numb, but afterward Terico lay there, thinking only of Suran.

Once Rilv was gone and Terico had recovered from his numbness, he got out of bed and used the Elpis fragments to find where Delkol was hiding. Terico had expected Delkol to use the golden Nexi stone to find Terico and fly to him right away, but it seemed Delkol was hoping to invade the city for the select purpose of obtaining the full Elpis.

Terico activated the energy and searched for Delkol the same way he had after flying out of Suran and Lanek's airship. The process was just as painful and difficult as before, but Terico forced himself to keep at it.

Seconds turned to minutes, and though Terico was able to access the golden Nexi energy, he couldn't visualize any clear image of where Delkol was. *Is he hiding himself with the Elpis somehow?* Terico wondered. He fought back the pain and continued to search. His head rang with a dozen headaches, and it soon became too much for Terico to handle. He dropped his Elpis fragments and gripped his head tight.

This can't be happening, he thought. *Why is the Elpis failing me now? Right when I need it most...*
Time passed slowly, and Terico could do little to make the pain of the Elpis go away. It lingered on, much stronger than it ever had before. He was using its power too much, and too soon. He felt as if a part of him had melted away from the inside, never to be fully healed again.

I'm dying, he thought. *If I keep using the Elpis like this...*
His own life was of little concern at the moment. He sat on his bed and stared down toward Suran, wishing above all else that he'd find a way to save her. All his efforts thus far availed him nothing, though. He hadn't even come close to saving her.

It's not right, Terico thought. *It's not right for you to die.*
Her breathing only slowed down, however. Terico tried willing himself to recover from his Elpis use, but there was nothing he could do. The pain and exhaustion only remained, and even as day turned to night, Terico still felt overwhelmed by his repeated access of the Elpis's energies.

The room turned dark, and Terico found himself kneeling by Suran's bed once more. She hadn't spoken at all since she responded to Terico's marriage proposal. He gripped her hand once more, and felt as if he was dipping his hand into icy water.

No. Not yet. Please hold out a little longer, Suran...
He stood up and felt for a pulse in her wrist, then in her neck. There was no heartbeat. He placed an ear over her heart and listened for ten seconds, but there was no response.

Wide-eyed and breathless, Terico immediately took his Elpis pieces and held them over Suran's heart. He accessed the Elpis energy and exerted every ounce of strength he had to bring healing energy to Suran's heart. It was too hard to control. In seconds the power of the Elpis brought unbearable pain to every nerve in Terico's body. He threw aside the Elpis pieces and gripped the side of Suran's bed, struggling to keep standing. Breathing heavily, Terico stared down at Suran's unmoving form through rushing tears.

"Please… wake up, Suran," Terico whispered. "Please wake up." She simply lay there, placid and soundless.

There was still no heartbeat, and her body only remained frigid and still. Suran had stopped breathing, and there was no response when Terico tried to shake her awake.

He knelt down and lay his head against Suran's, falling into a cycle of continuous weeping.

Suran was dead, and once again Terico's power availed him nothing. The night grew darker with each passing hour, and the complete exhaustion and torment of his body slowly forced him into a deep sleep. He soaked Suran's pillow with his tears, and flooded his dreams with visions of what may have been.

•

The next day came and passed, leaving Terico to rest and recover from his repeated use of the Elpis fragments. As he had expected, Rilv was displeased he had used the Elpis before he was ready, as it would make it impossible for him to fully recover in time to face Delkol at full strength. Terico could not get himself to care for Rilv's words, as she had made it clear she did not care whether Suran lived or not. In fact, Rilv was probably hoping Suran would die quickly, before Terico could try using the Elpis to save her.
Rilv went on about how Terico had jeopardized the entire kingdom, and how he had placed Suran's life before the lives of the thousands who lived in Setar. Terico felt he would have made the same choice again if put under the same circumstances. A part of him would have even sacrificed the city if it could bring Suran back, as cruel as this sounded.

He held on to one last possibility for bringing Suran back, though. The full Elpis was said to give one godlike powers. In time, Terico felt there was a chance he could bring Suran back to life.

Upon learning of her death, Rilv and the doctor prepared to take Suran away to prepare for burial. Terico demanded they leave her in bed, however. If Delkol was going to strike soon, Terico intended to obtain the Elpis from him and try healing Suran with its full power. Rilv complied with the demand, perhaps just hoping to keep Terico on her side. They both understood Terico was necessary for defeating Delkol.

Perhaps it was the one thing Terico and Rilv could see eye-to-eye on. Delkol had to die, both as retribution for what he had done, and for the safety of the Fiefs Kingdom.

In a way, it was the only thing Terico had left. His home was gone.
His parents were gone. Suran was gone. And though Turan was still alive, for all intents and purposes he was gone too. All that was left was the hope in a revenge that could ease Terico's misery. Even if it helped just a little, it would be worth it to kill Delkol.
And yet, Terico found himself questioning if even that would please him. What *would* killing Delkol do for him? It wouldn't really change anything. Everyone would still be dead.

No, the Elpis, Terico thought, staring blankly at the ceiling. *There's still the Elpis. If I have all four pieces, I can do whatever I wish. I can save Suran. I can save everyone. Nobody will be able to stop me. I can destroy the Brotherhood. I can destroy the whole Fiefs Kingdom. There won't be any more war then. Nobody else would have to suffer again.*
Rilv eventually returned in the afternoon, looking utterly exhausted herself.

Terico realized she pretty much had the safety of the kingdom on her shoulders, but he couldn't get himself to pity her.

"A messenger of the Fiefs army has brought this for you." Rilv handed Terico a thin scroll, forcing him to sit up and read it.

"The Kingdom of Fiefs will fall by tomorrow evening. I offer you, Terico, the same choice I offered your father. Give up the Elpis fragments, or I will repeat what I did in Edellerston—only on a much grander scale. You should understand well how serious I am when I say I am willing to kill every man, woman, and child in this land.
I do not seek to destroy this city. My only wish is to claim my rightful place as king of Fiefs. Unless you wish to have the blood of Setar's entire populace on your hands, I suggest delivering the two Elpis fragments you have by noon tomorrow."
Delkol's letter meant little to Terico. Obviously Terico wasn't going to give up his pieces of the Elpis. And it was a blatant lie that Delkol did not wish to destroy the city. Terico doubted there was anything the man enjoyed more than the bloodshed of innocent life.

"His armies will invade tomorrow then," Terico said.

"Yes," Rilv said. "Do you wish to respond to this message?"

Terico handed the scroll back. "There's no need. Just prepare the armies. I will try to defeat Delkol as soon as I can."

"Our armies are assembled," Rilv said. "Reinforcements may arrive tomorrow, if we are fortunate—but we can not rely on this possibility." "I will kill Delkol," Terico said.

It is all I have left to live for.
"Rest as much as you can in the meantime," Rilv said. "Do not use the Elpis until you fight Delkol." She tore apart the message Delkol sent and left the room.

Terico agreed and lay back down. His thoughts drifted from one thing to the next, and nothing in his head seemed to make sense anymore. It may have been in part due to his repeated use of the Elpis, but Terico felt he mainly just couldn't grasp the series of events his life had spiraled into the last few days. One minute Suran was alive again, and the next minute she was dead again. How was it that life could play out so cruelly? The fact that it was Terico's fault Suran died only made the pain worse, as well as the fact it was

Terico's best friend who killed her.

Every happy moment of Terico's past felt as if it had shattered. Long gone were the days Terico would sit in class with Turan and Suran, and enjoy chatting together and planning their small adventures. Though it was only a few weeks ago that he had been doing just that, it felt like an entirely different lifetime.

Some time in the afternoon, Areo, Borely, and Kitoh came to visit to see how Terico was doing. The three had been spending most their time training with some of the special forces within the Fiefs royal army, preparing for the upcoming battle with the Brotherhood and Shire armies. They each expressed condolences for Terico's loss, and recounted how they were all thankful for Suran and everything she had done for them during their brief time with her. Terico didn't want to dwell on the subject, especially with Suran's body still present in the room.

"I hope the three of you will be able to find your way once this is all over," Terico said. He knew that none of them had really wished to get so caught up in all this. "And I hope you'll all get through this battle unscathed."

"I'll be okay," Kitoh said. "I've been given this." He held up a Nexi stone that shined a very dark yellow—perhaps an orangeish yellow.

"What is it?" Terico asked.

"It was a gift from Vursa to Setar a long time ago," Kitoh said. "There are eigni who are capable of creating new kinds of Nexi stones, and this is one of the most powerful ones ever created. If the user is strong enough, a magnificent creature can be summoned."

"That's good," Terico said. "We'll need all the help we can get to hold off the Shire armies. I'm sure you'll be able to wield that Nexi stone well."

Kitoh didn't respond, but he looked less afraid than he had while on the airship. Terico hoped the boy would be able to fulfill the wishes of his parents and return to his city with the respect he'd deserve. It was probably going to be a rough life for the child, but Terico felt confident Kitoh would be able to handle the trials ahead—and likely with a reserve Terico could never be capable of.

"Don't worry, we'll watch over him," Borely said.

"You need to watch yourself," Areo said. "Remember all those times I had to save your life on that Brotherhood airship?"

Borely's face tightened and glowered, though he kept from looking back at Areo. "It's hard to forget. You've only reminded me of it a hundred times now."

"I won't be there to save you every time you get in trouble," Areo said.

"I'll be fine!" Borely yelled. "You just watch whose neck it is you sink your teeth into out there. I'll be ready to punch through your heart the moment you turn against us."

"Is this another joke of yours?" Areo asked. "There's no way you would land a punch on me in a fight, of course."

Terico looked to Kitoh and sighed. "I'm glad they're getting along so well."

"I think it *has* improved a little..." Kitoh said.

Terico didn't care to tell the two to work together any more than he already had before. They wouldn't have to be together on the battlefield, so this was probably the last time they'd be together. Unless, of course, Borely was still trying to get Areo to pay for his ship. Terico doubted things would end well for Borely if the sailor continued to push that agenda.

Eventually the three left to return to their training and preparations for battle. Terico was left alone once more, and there was nothing to do but lie in bed and ponder everything he had gone through since that fateful day. The day Edellerston was attacked had flung Terico on an adventure he never could have imagined undertaking. It was all drawing to a close now, and he knew his life would change forever over the next twenty-four hours.

His primary objective was obvious. Kill Delkol. And in the process of obtaining his revenge, Terico would also gain the remaining two Elpis fragments. With their leader dead and the full Elpis in Terico's hands, the Shire armies would have no choice but to retreat.

And then what?

I could destroy all those armies. Obliterate the Brotherhood forever.
With the full Elpis, this would be a simple matter, Terico believed. There would be no more pain from utilizing the Elpis, and Terico would be free to access any and all Nexi powers whenever he pleased.

There's only a few other things I would use it for, though, Terico thought. *Bring Suran back to life. Heal Turan, assuming he hasn't died in the battle. And bring back my parents, and all of Edellerston, if it isn't too late.*

Terico thought those killed in the attack on Edellerston may have been dead too long for Terico to bring back to life. Their spirits had left several weeks ago now, and there were likely limitations to what even the Elpis could do.

There was no telling what Terico would be able to do, however. He had to obtain the second half of the Elpis in order to find out.

As night fell, he drifted to sleep, plotting all the ways he would use his Elpis fragments in order to kill Delkol. Once Delkol was finished off for good, Terico's new life could finally begin.

•

Sleep came to Terico unwillingly. After all, how could a reasonable person sleep when the one he loved lay dead in the very same room? And yet he slept, the constant barrage of painful thoughts breaking his mind and dulling his senses.

Kill Delkol, and all will be right again, Terico thought over and over. The night passed without interruption, as Rilv had instructed the nurses to make sure Terico got all the rest he could. He received food in the morning, which helped him get his strength back. Though he still had a horrendous headache, Terico felt the pain in his body had dissipated for the most part. He was sore and numb, but he felt he'd be able to fight by the time he'd face Delkol.

He pushed himself out of bed and stood up, his weak legs nearly collapsing beneath him. Holding on to his bed and Suran's, Terico spent a few minutes just trying to get feeling back to his legs. Maintaining this position was difficult though, as Terico's arms were weak and dull as well.

Terico fell to his knees and took slow, deep breaths. Though most of the pain from the Elpis had faded away, it was more difficult to move than Terico had expected. On top of this, his vision turned blurry, and slowly darkened over the next several minutes. Terico shut his eyes, hoping his eyesight wouldn't give him any trouble when it came time to fight.

Perhaps an hour passed before Rilv arrived with a couple royal guards. Terico forced himself to stand, but wasn't able to hide his discomfort in the act of doing so.

"You still haven't recovered," Rilv said.

"I'll be fine," Terico said. "The Elpis will strengthen me."

Rilv simply tightened her gaze on Terico a bit in response.

"You worry about the Shire armies and the Brotherhood," Terico said. "I will kill Delkol as fast as I possibly can." He knew he couldn't promise a quick victory, so he didn't bother pretending. There was no doubt in Terico's mind that Delkol had a plan in mind for him, and it wasn't unlikely that Delkol had discovered new and powerful uses with the Elpis. The fight would be difficult, but Terico felt confident he would find a way to defeat Delkol. Once on the battlefield, it all boiled down to split-second decisions. Delkol may be the more experienced fighter, but Terico knew he could pull through with superior ingenuity and dexterity. He also felt he would be better-prepared to handle the pain of the Elpis, having experienced so much of it over the past twenty-four hours.

One of the guards with Rilv placed a set of clothes and several pieces of armor on Terico's bed. The other guard added some more armor, and held out a sword for Terico to use. Terico took it and looked it over. It was about the same size as the longsword he had back in Edellerston, though there was a stark difference in quality and detail. Just looking at it, Terico could tell this blade was much sharper, and the fine metals embedded in the hilt easily made this sword many times more valuable than all of Terico's previous swords put together.

"Is this the sword of the king then?" Terico asked.

"No," Rilv said. "You have not been officially instated as king yet. But I don't intend to send you out there poorly armed. This is a sword of the royal Fiefs line. Our armies will recognize you as a leader, and will be looking up to you for strength in this battle."

Terico nodded, understanding that the situation regarding the royal succession was likely a matter of great discussion amongst the ranks at the moment.
Rilv and the guards left Terico to change, asking him to join them outside the castle once he was ready.

The uniform was black with purple and gold embellishments, while the armor gleamed a brilliant white and yellow. Once he got his uniform on, Terico tied each of the metal guards to his body, covering his torso, arms, legs, and sides. The sword slid into its metal sheath with the clean, precise sound of a perfect fit.

He walked slowly toward the door, a deep, stinging pain starting to develop all throughout his body. It was difficult to push himself this soon, after using the Elpis as many times as he had.

I need the full Elpis, Terico thought. *I'll... probably die if I don't get it.* And if not by Elpis poisoning, then by Delkol's own hand.

It took some time for Terico to find the strength to walk out the door. He nearly jumped back when he opened it, finding Lanek standing directly in front of him. Lanek glared at Terico—the elf looked like a standing corpse.

"I have one question," he said, his voice low and torn apart.

Terico nodded. He wasn't sure what Lanek would do now that Suran had died. Rilv said that Lanek had mourned for Suran while Terico was asleep, and that she had kept watch to make sure Lanek didn't do anything to Terico—apparently she had learned from Lanek how Suran had been entrusted to Terico's care when the Brotherhood boarded the airship.

"Who killed my little sister?" Lanek asked, supreme loathing oozing with every word.

Terico had never seen Lanek with such a horrific expression. The elf's hair was uncharacteristically tattered and unkempt, his eyes bloodshot and ringed with fatigue.

"A member of the Brotherhood," Terico said, afraid to reveal that Lynx's true identity was Turan.

"I need details," Lanek said. "Describe him."

"He's young," Terico said. A part of him didn't want to say more, but another part felt compelled to. "About my height. Blond hair. Goes by the name *Lynx*. Wears the uniform and mask that all the Brotherhood wear."

"Short and blond," Lanek said. "Is there anything else?"

Obviously the easiest way to identify Lynx was with the large smile painted on his mask, but Terico didn't want Lanek to kill Turan. Even with Turan having killed Suran, Terico didn't want Turan to suffer if he could help it.

Lanek gripped Terico's shoulders. "There has to be something more. Tell me how I will find this boy."

"That's all," Terico said.

"Rilv does not know I'm here," Lanek said, gripping Terico a little tighter. "I need more to go off of. Think! There must be more."

Terico remembered very clearly Lanek's threat to kill him if anything were to happen to Suran.

And thinking about it, there was no reason to hold any details back

from Lanek. If Turan did die, Terico would be able to use the full Elpis to revive him.

"There's a smile painted on his mask," Terico said. "He has an insane personality." There was also a chance Turan would seek Lanek out anyways, considering Turan's goal was to kill everyone Terico knew.

"A smile," Lanek said. He let go of Terico and turned away, saying nothing more. The elf's thoughts were wholly focused on revenge.

How many more people will die today? Terico wondered. He placed a hand on the wall to keep his balance. *How many more people will seek revenge before this is over? This is hell.*

•

•Part VI•
THE FATE OF DESTROYERS AND SAVIORS

Rilv led Terico through the city, which for the most part was deserted. The general populace had relocated behind the walls of the castle, leaving only soldiers and powerful Nexi users on the streets. Everyone was grim, tired, anxious. Setar was prepared for a battle to the death, but Terico's feelings felt distant. Though the war was fresh for this city, Terico felt he had been fighting it for weeks now.

Everything had been taken from him. Was there anything left for him to fight for?

He had to keep reminding himself. Revenge against Delkol. The power of the full Elpis. A redemption of everything he had lost.

There was no certainty in any of this, though. Would killing Delkol fill any of the emptiness inside of Terico? And would the Elpis really give Terico the power of a god? Every time Terico used the Elpis, it had given him a great deal of agony. And even with the power the Elpis contained, Terico hadn't been able to save those he loved. The Elpis didn't save Jujor. The Elpis didn't save Suran.

And it certainly wasn't saving Terico.

What if even the full Elpis availed him nothing?

Perhaps that was why it was broken apart and hidden away. Perhaps there really was no way for the Elpis to be used for good. Perhaps it was a power that only granted misery to its users.

Terico stared at all the vacant stands, all the boarded-up houses. Such an empty, foreboding city. Terico just wanted to leave it all.

Once near the tall, stone city walls, Rilv and her guards led Terico through the masses of soldiers. Many of the soldiers were carrying large Nexi stones up the stairways to the catapults positioned atop the walls.

As soon as Delkol's army began its attack, there would be many defensive measures put into place to slow them down.

Some soldiers stopped to stare at Terico a few seconds. Perhaps there were rumors of him floating around already. Terico didn't care if everyone

started looking to him to be a leader or a king. The troops had their generals to guide them—Terico was just the one who could use the Elpis. There was only one person for Terico to fight, and once that was done, perhaps the battle would end as well.

Rilv led Terico past the front lines of the assembling armies and toward a stairway up the city wall.

"Our reinforcements have not arrived yet," Rilv said, "so the battle will be quite difficult at first. The longer we can delay, the better."

"I doubt Delkol will wait any longer than noon," Terico said. "I will fight him as soon as I find him."

"He will not make it easy for you to reach him," Rilv said. "He knows you have two fragments of the Elpis, same as him. If he can weaken you in any way before he faces you, he will."

And in all honesty, Terico already was in a much weaker state than he should have been. Walking this long had tired him out, and brought back the pain in all the cuts and bruises covering his body. His headache had grown a bit stronger again as well.

"I will kill him," Terico said, following Rilv up a stairway. It was all he could say. He knew that the chances of him succeeding were slim, but it was the only thing he had left to hold on to. He had to kill Delkol. What else was there left for Terico?

Once atop the city wall, Terico gazed out at the distant Shire armies, all in a grand formation that stretched out as far as Terico could see from east to west. The hills in the horizon were covered with soldiers in black armor. There were also large numbers of Brotherhood members in white—Terico imagined Delkol was amongst one of those groups of soldiers.

"They have strength in numbers," Rilv said. "They were assembled quickly, however, so they have no large machinery, save for a single airship. Our airships have been repaired enough to handle that, and to aid in the city's general defense afterward. Delkol is a significant element of the Shire army's power, however. He is a charismatic figure who has promised a great deal for his troops. The fact Delkol has killed our king gives them great confidence."

"If I kill him quickly, they'll lose the will to fight," Terico said.

"It would be best if you do so before the armies breach the walls," Rilv said. "We have suffered greatly in the Brotherhood's recent attack. The fact is we are greatly outnumbered, and it will only be a matter of time before the entries are broken down. The Brotherhood amongst the Shire army's ranks are greatly skilled with Nexi, and will likely have the means to sneak in quickly."

"I understand," Terico said. He had enough to worry about without all this pressure Rilv was piling atop of him.

The sooner I kill Delkol, the fewer lives that will be lost.
How many people will die with each passing minute it takes me to seek out Delkol and kill him?
The amount of blood that will be on my hands... Perhaps there will never be a limit to it.

•

The sun rose high above the battlefield. Terico watched the Shire army, waiting for the moment Delkol would order his soldiers forward. A small figure rose in the sky, and Terico kept his eyes on its approach. It was Delkol, flying in his transformed state. The power of the Elpis fragments had turned his armor black, his skin light gray, and his scar and eyes a sickly white. He stopped in mid-air a good thirty or so meters in front of where Terico stood.

"Hold your fire," Rilv told the nearest soldiers running the Nexi catapults.

"So he comes to me," Terico whispered, gripping his Elpis pieces. "Terico, the boy who would never be king," Delkol cried out in a booming voice. He somehow projected his voice with the Elpis. "You may have some royal blood in you, but otherwise there is no good reason for you to rule this land."

Terico didn't care about becoming king of Fiefs. All he wanted was to see this man dead.

Delkol went on without waiting for a response. "My offer still stands. Give me your half of the Elpis and allow me to take my rightful place as ruler of this kingdom. In return, nobody will have to die today. Do you wish to have the blood of an entire city on your hands, boy? I imagine you are tired of death."

"Not quite!" Terico yelled. He activated his half of the Elpis and shot himself into the air, straight for Delkol.

Already flying back the moment Terico began to transform, Delkol

blasted himself down toward his gathered armies. At the same time, a creature swooped down for Terico from above, forcing him to stop pursuing Delkol.

It was a death bird—the giant creature Delkol rode on when escaping the castle with the Elpis piece he stole from there. It reached for Terico with long, ragged talons made of bone, gleaming white and red. Terico forced himself back a couple meters to avoid the skeletal bird's attacks. The death bird swooped back up to Terico, far faster than he expected. Fighting back the pain enveloping his body, Terico created a burst of frozen air to materialize in front of him. He flew backward, letting the death bird fly into the light blue Nexi energy. Terico floated to the side, watching for the beast to plummet, its wings too frozen to fly with.

The creature rushed straight through the frozen air. Though most of its body was covered with patches of ice, it continued flapping its skeletal wings—and still headed for Terico. It was a creature of bone and bloody muscles—the fact it could fly in the first place should have been impossible. The ice simply cracked and broke apart as the death bird flapped its wings.

Terico charged toward it, unsheathing his sword and filling the blade with orange Nexi energy in the process. The death bird slowed down and pushed itself backward, just outside the range of Terico's blade. Terico swung again, but the death bird flapped its wings inward farther, slamming a giant bone against him.

Silently, the creature dove toward Terico, who careened backward, rushing toward the ground. The pain of the attack doubled under the influence of the Elpis, and Terico had trouble regaining control of his flight. He managed to keep himself from colliding with the ground, but the death bird was already upon him. At the last moment he raised his sword and released a burst of water at the swooping beast. The water blasted the death bird back a few meters, but it quickly recovered.

Terico forced himself to fly backward before the death bird could slam its giant skeletal beak into his body. Though wielding the power of the Elpis, getting torn in half would still be instantly fatal.

I'm wasting my energy on this bird! Terico thought. *Delkol's letting it weaken me while he hides amongst his armies.*

Terico considered just ignoring the bird and flying toward the Shire troops, but he knew the soldiers would attack him—and he had no intention of fighting off an entire army before getting to Delkol. Terico also considered heading back toward the city so the archers atop the wall could help him.

This would only endanger the lives of the city's first defense, however. Terico also wasn't certain if arrows would have any effect on this creature.

The death bird flapped its wings faster, gaining several extra meters on Terico with each stroke. Forcing himself to fly faster would strain his mind even more than he already had. He activated the brown Nexi energy and released it toward the death bird. The creature forced itself upward, and the majority of the sticky material missed it completely. The death bird dove for Terico, its open beak revealing dozens of thick, misshapen fangs.

An ear-splitting shriek broke through the air just above Terico. A massive red and yellow bird collided into the death bird, sinking its talons and beak into the fleshy bits of muscle holding its skeletal body together. This second bird was engulfed in flames, and as it brought the death bird plummeting toward the ground the creature's prey caught on fire as well.

It was a giant phoenix. It took a few seconds for Terico to figure out where it came from—it had to have been summoned by the special Nexi stone Kitoh was given. One of the most powerful stones the eigni had ever created, Terico remembered.

The two birds crashed into the ground. The phoenix tore into the muscle tissue of the writhing death bird, ripping apart the deadly creature's bones. The death bird pecked its beak into the phoenix and tried clawing at it, but the phoenix was quick to snap the death bird's neck. With a few wrenches of its beak, the phoenix ripped the death bird's head off entirely, though the creature still continued to fight back. The phoenix proceeded to disconnect the wings from what was left of the burning muscles of the bloody beast, keeping it from moving further.

Terico looked down to the Shire armies, which marched at a brisk pace toward the city walls. Delkol was among them somewhere, but Terico couldn't spot him. The majority of his soldiers were dressed in black, and

Delkol had surely stopped using the Elpis, considering how his transformed state would make him easier to notice. He was also conserving energy, while Terico would waste away if he didn't find Delkol quickly. The Shire armies reached the phoenix, which flew away from the burning remains of the death bird. A number of archers tried shooting down the phoenix, but the giant bird managed to avoid them. The legions of soldiers continued toward the city walls, where catapults began to fire giant Nexi stones toward the approaching masses. The city defenses began with large green Nexi, which blew apart into dozens of thick vines upon landing. Some soldiers were taken down by the stones themselves, but many more were tied up by the swarming vines. A number of soldiers fought off the vines with their swords, while others used fire Nexi to burn them down.

The Fiefs armies continued by launching brown and red Nexi into the crowds of charging Shire troops. Many Shire soldiers became stuck in the swamps that burst out from the brown Nexi while tens of others were blown apart by the fiery red stones.

Terico continued to search for Delkol, careful to keep out of range of the archers' arrows. Though it was agonizing, Terico forced himself to access the golden Nexi energy in order to locate Delkol's position. Terico screamed from the pain, his body trembling in mid-air high above the hundreds of enemy soldiers passing below him. There were so many people all in one location, it was difficult to search through them, even with the Elpis guiding his vision.

Shutting his eyes, Terico caught sight of several groups of Shire soldiers—some armed with lances, some with swords, and others with longbows. They were closing in on the castle walls now. Members of the Brotherhood led the way to three of the city entryways, blasting away at the massive doors with red, orange, and tan Nexi stones. Fiefs soldiers fought them back with Nexi stones thrown down from above, but for every Shire soldier that was killed, several more rushed in to take his place. The Brotherhood members also managed to avoid most of the attacks, using their skills with the Nexi to create effective defenses.

His head pounded twice as fast as his heartbeat, but Terico forced himself to keep using the Elpis to locate Delkol. The sooner he found Delkol, the better chance he had of attacking Delkol before the Elpis wore him out.

The golden Nexi energy guided Terico's vision to an area far from the city walls, where many Brotherhood fighters were congregated amidst the Shire armies. Terico's sight focused in on a caped figure standing amongst some of the masked fighters in white. It was Delkol, unsheathing his sword.

Delkol activated his Elpis fragments, transforming back into his demonic form and rising a couple meters off the ground. Terico's vision pulled back a ways, revealing the phoenix swooping down toward Delkol. A number of archers tried shooting the bird down, but the phoenix was too fast for their arrows. Delkol held his sword back and charged it with orange, white, and purple Nexi energy. His blade shifted between the three colors, vibrating violently and releasing sparks of blinding light.

With an extra burst of speed, the phoenix rushed down for Delkol. Just before the creature could tear Delkol in half with its fiery talons, Delkol shot off a bolt of lightning through the nearest wing, causing the phoenix to turn slightly. The next moment, Delkol was suddenly flying straight into the phoenix's body, slamming his blade through the bird's chest. The screeching beast blew apart into bloody, fiery chunks all around Delkol, who continued to push his vibrating blade through the phoenix's body.

Once through the other side, Delkol turned around and enveloped himself with water to douse the flames of the phoenix that caught on to his body. The phoenix turned its long neck and attempted to jab its sharp beak into Delkol's torso. Delkol flew to the side of the bird's attack and proceeded to lob its head off in one swoop. The giant bird collapsed in a smoldering heap, the passing Shire troops raising their swords and cheering for their victorious leader. Delkol floated above the corpse of the beast and stared directly at Terico, who had to be at least a hundred meters away.

Delkol closed his eyes and smiled. His control of the Elpis was extraordinary, to say the least. In half a minute he took down the summon of one of the world's most powerful Nexi stones, and he didn't look the slightest bit troubled by it.

There was no doubt about it—with the full Elpis this man would easily vanquish everything that stood in his way, just as he easily killed everyone in the Edellerston cathedral.

Terico opened his eyes and cut off access to the golden Nexi energy. He had Delkol's location. It was now only a matter of killing him.

The Elpis energies surged within Terico's body, and with the proper focus Terico forced the power to send him flying toward Delkol. The masses of Shire soldiers turned into a blur beneath him, while Terico's mind broke into pieces, the building torment of the Elpis reaching a horrific climax.

He unsheathed his sword and dove for Delkol, prepared to kill him by any means possible.

•

A flood of Shire soldiers stormed into the city. Borely readied himself for the moment he could jump into the fray.

Hold them off until Terico gets the full Elpis, Borely thought. *And then...* He still wasn't quite sure what he would do next. Trying to persuade the hundred-year-old vampire woman to pay him back for his boat had turned fruitless. She kept saying she had payed him back by saving his life on the Brotherhood airship, but Borely argued that he wouldn't have been on the airship in the first place if he hadn't lost his boat.

No use expecting her to cooperate, Borely decided. *She is a vampire, after all...* He forced himself to forget about Areo. Now was the time to focus on the approaching Shire soldiers. Borely wondered how many he could defeat by the time the battle ended. Beating down some enemies would help him blow off some steam, Borely decided.

The front lines of the Shire troops were taken down by the repeated volleys of Fiefs archers. A number of Brotherhood members leaped over the corpses and activated tan Nexi stones, forming a barrier from the next series of arrows fired. Fiefs swordsmen rushed in to hack away at the barrier, followed by lancers who took down the Shire soldiers slipping in from the sides. Several red Nexi were thrown over the wall of dirt, sending tens of Fiefs soldiers bursting into flame.

The Shire and Fiefs armies converged upon one another, and the area around Borely turned into a battleground littered with the dead and dying. The air filled with the clanging of metal, the whooshing of arrows, and the sounds of glowing Nexi stones. One Fiefs soldier ahead of Borely was knocked back by a jet of water, while a Fiefs soldier to Borely's right ran a lance through the side of a Shire soldier wielding an axe.

Borely found an opening and powered the orange Nexi stones embedded in his fists' metal knuckles. He knocked a Shire swordsman in the side, sending him flying into the back of another. Hearing the growth of Nexi vines, Borely turned and shot away the approaching plant appendages with the blue Nexi in his metal headband. A Fiefs archer shot the enemy, allowing Borely to turn and block the attack of a large Shire swordsman. Borely nudged the blade to the side and landed a Nexipowered punch on the man's face, knocking him out cold.

With a few seconds open to breathe, Borely looked to where Kitoh was positioned atop the city wall. The eigni boy didn't have his special Nexi raised in the air anymore, implying he had stopped controlling the phoenix he summoned. Borely wondered if Kitoh lost control of it, or if the phoenix had somehow been killed. Neither situation sounded likely, but there was no way for Borely to find out from here. He resumed fighting the nearby Shire soldiers, careful to watch for their weapons and Nexi elements.

An especially tall Shire lancer shot off a stream of swamp substance from a brown Nexi embedded in his spear, but Borely managed to deflect it with the water of his dark blue Nexi. With an extra push of energy, Borely directed the water into the man's stomach, flinging him back a few meters.

All at once, a dozen or so Brotherhood members charged into the area, assisting their fellow Shire soldiers against the Fiefs troops. A particularly fast Brotherhood fighter with long, thick blades attached to his arms sprinted through, slashing apart every Fiefs soldier he passed. Borely positioned himself and timed his punch for this masked man.

"Eat this!" Borely powered his punch with an extra boost of energy, but instead of connecting with the man's head, Borely got him in the shoulder. There was an earsplitting snap of broken bones, but the Brotherhood fighter didn't react in the slightest. Instead he swung a blade for Borely's head, completely taking Borely by surprise. Borely turned his head and activated his dark blue Nexi at the last moment, pushing the man's bladed arm back.

The man stumbled back a bit, and a nearby Fiefs swordsman blasted him with a fire Nexi. The Brotherhood fighter charged for the swordsman, completely disregarding the flames enveloping his body. The Fiefs soldier was stabbed with both blades, and in seconds the masked man was leaping back toward Borely.

"This is just wrong!" Borely yelled. This man was *on fire*, but was *still* fighting with the tenacity of a ravenous wolf.

Borely shot a jet of water at the man, who dodged and slashed a blade toward Borely's chest. At the same time, a nearby Shire lancer jabbed his weapon at Borely from the side, but Borely dodged him while stepping back from the Brotherhood fighter. In one quick movement Borely grabbed the lance from the Shire soldier and slammed the end of it into the Brotherhood man's neck.

The Shire soldier immediately lifted a tan Nexi stone and flung a large rock at Borely—one bigger than his head. Borely turned and landed a punch on the stone, shattering it with the force of his orange Nexi. Before the soldier could attack again, Borely ran at him and knocked him out with a punch in the face.

"Lynx!" a boy screamed, probably about ten meters east of Borely. The voice sounded familiar, and Borely caught a glimpse of an elf with long turquoise hair rushing toward the area where Borely was fighting. It was Lanek, one of the elves who ran the airship that took him to this city.

A figure stood up directly in front of Borely. It was the Brotherhood fighter he had stabbed through the neck with a lance. The man ripped the weapon out of his throat and jabbed it toward Borely.

"You've got to be kidding me!" Borely yelled. He bashed aside the lance, knocking it out of the masked man's grasp. Not only was this masked man still on fire, but he was fighting with a shattered shoulder *and* a hole through his neck. And not even crying out in pain!

Borely repeatedly blocked the man's swinging bladed arms, waiting for a good opening to beat him down. The man was fast though, and didn't seem to grow tired at all from his rampage.

The Brotherhood fighter swung both his blades inward, straight for Borely's neck. Borely grabbed both blades with his metal gloves. Before the enemy could push away, Borely fired his dark blue Nexi, shooting the man directly in the face. The man's head tore off entirely, the neck already cut up from the lance earlier.

Borely turned and found Lanek releasing a blast of purple Nexi energy, knocking away a couple Shire swordsmen in his path. The elf rushed toward a Brotherhood member—one wearing a mask with a smile painted across the bottom of it.

The Brotherhood member released a stream of brown Nexi substance. Still charging, Lanek used his purple Nexi to push away the swamp material. Borely had to dodge a large glob of it, while the Brotherhood fighter used an earth Nexi to block the majority of the swamp substance.

"Die!" Lanek screamed, quite louder than Borely imagined him capable of. As he blasted aside a Shire soldier with Nexi energy, Lanek unsheathed a long, thin rapier. He connected his purple Nexi stone atop the small circular handle, charging the blade with loose energy.

Just as Lanek was upon him, the masked fighter called Lynx brought up his sword to block the attack. Lynx's sword shattered into several pieces, one of them flinging back into his right arm. Like the man Borely fought, Lynx didn't cry out in pain or even seem to notice the injury.

Some of the Brotherhood fighters are experimented on, Borely remembered. Perhaps some were capable of fighting at full strength, even when suffering life-threatening wounds.

Before Lanek could jab his rapier into Lynx's chest, Lynx slipped back and fired another jet of swamp material. Lanek avoided the attack, but the opening gave time for Lynx to grab a sword from a fallen Shire soldier. Lynx charged it with orange Nexi energy and rushed toward Lanek.

Borely turned at the sound of screaming coming behind him. A Fiefs soldier was yelling for everyone to fall back, and it took a few seconds for Borely to find the source of the screaming. He stepped back upon sighting several Fiefs soldiers in the distance flying several meters into the air. At least a dozen vines were zipping through lines of soldiers, picking out those from Fiefs and tossing them in random directions.

It was Augurc, assisted by a number of Brotherhood members and the endless masses of Shire soldiers continuing to push their way through the gates. While Fiefs soldiers fought against the Shire armies, Augurc would control all the vines running out his arms, picking up several Fiefs soldiers at any given moment. Borely watched from a distance as Augurc picked up swords and lances from the ground and began impaling the Fiefs soldiers he held entangled in his vines. Once they were impaled, Augurc swung them around the battlefield. The blades sticking out of the soldiers' bodies slammed into the heads of other Fiefs soldiers, preoccupied with the Shire soldiers they were already fighting.

Several Shire soldiers gathered together and simultaneously activated fire Nexi toward Augurc, hoping to catch his vines on fire and guide the flames to his body. Augurc raised his right hand and instantly formed a cloud of frozen air around him, and even managed to harden it into solid ice. The massive wave of fire melted away at the ice, but there was just enough of it to defend himself. As soon as the fires dissipated, Augurc sent all his vines for these Shire soldiers. With the assistance of a couple Brotherhood members, they were all killed in seconds.

Fiefs numbers were dwindling fast, and though Borely was managing to hold his own against the Shire soldiers that came against him, he knew he wouldn't last long against more of the Brotherhood fighters. And having seen Augurc's power on the Brotherhood airship, Borely was reluctant to go against him.

I didn't come here to fight a war, Borely thought. *I just need to survive. Just get out of here...*

As soon as he thought it, he felt a twinge of guilt. People were dying at the hands of the two Shire brothers. Borely couldn't just abandon this city and let the Shire armies destroy everything.

And besides, wasn't this the sort of adventure he lived for? He took a deep breath and ran forward, grinning.

•

A lance flew just to the left of Areo's head—she had heard the weapon thrown at her and knew to not move her head at the last moment. As soon as the lance passed her, Areo tore her claws out of the Shire swordsman she had slain and leaped at the lancer a couple meters away. Upon slitting the man's throat, Areo turned and found a Brotherhood member shooting a large rock at her. Areo quickly took her tan Nexi and fired a similarly-sized rock at it. Once the two stones collided and deflected out of her path, Areo sprinted for the masked fighter.

She sunk her claws into the man's chest, but he responded by lifting his tan Nexi and activating it again. Areo shoved him aside, causing his torrent of hardened earth to pass just to Areo's right. She slipped behind the fighter and stabbed him in the back. He immediately slammed his elbow hard against Areo's face, not even crying out in pain from his injuries. Areo ignored the bruise forming around her black eye and tore her claws out either side of the man. Though she knew she had cut apart his lungs and heart, Areo took a couple steps back just in case the man would get back up again. To her relief, the Brotherhood fighter stayed dead this time.

Seeing she had a couple moments to spare, Areo sunk her teeth into the man's neck. Once she had taken a few gulps of his blood, Areo let the corpse drop back to the ground. Filled with a renewed vigor, Areo hurried toward one of the stairways leading up to the wall, taking down a couple Shire soldiers along the way.

Kitoh was still where Areo had left him, guarded by the archers who continued to fire upon the Shire armies below. Areo had asked Kitoh to wait a bit before turning into a dragon, worrying that Delkol would seek out Kitoh just as he had the phoenix Kitoh summoned. There were now tens of Shire soldiers fighting their way up the thin staircases. Most were taken down by the Fiefs troops stationed on the wall, but the continual pressure of the ever-growing number of Shire soldiers was wearing them out.

Areo rushed up the stairway, clawing away at any Shire soldiers she came across. Once atop the wall, she found Kitoh helping man a catapult with ice Nexi. She turned at the sound of vines. Tens of vines worked their way up the wall, grasping onto nooks. Areo looked down to find several Shire soldiers sliding upward, forcing the taut vines into their green Nexi stones. Before they could bring themselves up to the top of the wall, Areo tore apart each of the vines with her claws. Most of the soldiers managed to reactivate their Nexi's vines to grab onto footholds, keeping them from falling all the way to the ground.

A few dozen meters away, Areo saw at least twenty other soldiers in black working their way up the wall. There was nobody there to stop them from climbing onto the wall—the Fiefs soldiers there were killed in arrow fire. Areo looked the other way and found even more Shire soldiers using vine Nexi to ascend the wall. A number of Fiefs guards used red Nexi to burn down the vines, but several more vines would appear every time they managed to burn one down the entire way.

It was only a matter of time before the walls were overrun with Shire soldiers. Areo needed to get Kitoh out before they were overwhelmed. She ran to the boy and informed him of the situation.

"I can join the battle," Kitoh said. "Terico is fighting Delkol, and I'm needed now."

Areo looked down at the swarms of Shire soldiers pouring through the broken gates. With her heightened vision as a vampire, she was able to spot a number of individuals very quickly. Lanek was fighting a member of the Brotherhood, and Borely was rushing toward a number of Shire soldiers. Just past them was Augurc Shire, the man Areo and Borely had to escape from back on the Brotherhood airship. Augurc was flinging soldiers around with the vines coming from his arms, taking out dozens more with each passing minute.

"We need to get down there," Areo said, pointing toward Augurc. Kitoh nodded and took out his transformative Nexi stone. It was all he needed at this point, he had explained.

Areo held a hand atop of Kitoh's fist. She looked sternly into the eigni boy's eyes. "Are you sure you wish to do this?"

"My people expect me to," Kitoh said. "This is what my parents want me to do."

"Are you sure *you* wish to do this?"

Kitoh looked up into Areo's eyes a few moments before nodding again.

"Let's go, then."

After scoping out the area a bit, Kitoh leaped off the wall, jumping toward the battlefield within the city. Areo jumped after him, and as Kitoh fell he transformed into a large blue dragon. Areo landed atop his back just as Kitoh spread out his wings, causing himself to lift from the ground just in time. He glided straight down the cobble-stoned street, letting his long, batlike wings bash against Shire soldiers. Kitoh had enough control of his dragon form to keep from hurting any of the Fiefs soldiers in his path, to Areo's relief.

"Take me to Augurc," Areo said. She kept her eyes on Borely, who was fighting off a couple soldiers at once. He was being way too reckless, far too rash.
Not that this came as a surprise to Areo, of course. But did she have to keep saving his life like this? She considered just leaving him to fend for himself—after all, they weren't in this together anymore. But then she remembered that evening spent on his ship. His boorish attempt to win her over through a fish dinner and sentimental conversation.

He's an idiot, Areo thought, *but he doesn't deserve to die.* She leaped off of Kitoh and slammed her claws through the neck of a Brotherhood fighter about to fire a red Nexi at Borely.

"Thanks for dropping by," Borely said before turning to punch a swordsman away.

"I just happened to be in the area," Areo muttered. She tore her claws out either side of the Brotherhood man's neck, nearly beheading him. Areo glanced past Augurc, watching Kitoh land atop a couple Shire archers. The dragon was quick to bash away the remaining archers with his long, bony arms, keeping them from firing their arrows at him.

There were still a couple more Shire soldiers accompanying Augurc, who stared toward Areo and Borely with the same emotionless face he maintained back on the airship. He dropped the dead, impaled Fiefs soldiers his vines carried, then turned away to face Kitoh. Augurc's vines each ripped out a sword or lance from one of his dropped corpses, effectively arming himself with at least a dozen weapons. Kitoh meanwhile charged through a group of Shire soldiers, batting them away with his wings and stomping on those that fell over.

One soldier ran to Borely while the other charged for Areo. Borely was quick to blast away his enemy's sword with a brief jet of water. As the man fumbled for a Nexi stone, Borely slammed a hard punch in his face. Areo faced her opponent, who wielded a couple hand axes. He charged both of them with orange Nexi energy and leaped toward Areo. Blocking with her claws would be futile, and so would forming a barrier of earth. Knowing that her enemy would know this, Areo used her tan Nexi to create a wall of earth in front of her. As the soldier hacked straight through the hardened earth, Areo dashed around the back of the wall and slid her elongated claws into the man's neck. He fell to the ground, gagging.

Areo considered getting more blood, but Kitoh was already turning to face Augurc, who walked toward the massive dragon with an air of indifference. Kitoh breathed a torrent of fire directly at Augurc. The man placed his right hand over his face just before the giant waves of flames engulfed his entire body, as well as the bloody corpses of soldiers piled about the vicinity.

The fire flowed all around Augurc, covering him entirely. Areo hoped this was the end of him, but waited to see his melted or charred remains lying on the ground.

After a few long seconds of this, the fire passed and the smoke cleared away. Augurc stood right where he had been, covered in water and bits of ice sliding down his body. He had continually frozen himself as the dragon's flames enveloped him.

Borely charged after Augurc from behind. Augurc heard Borely's stomping and turned around, utterly disinterested. Augurc raised his hand and charged his light blue Nexi stone. Areo ran to Borely and pulled him back before he could be engulfed in the massive burst of frozen air Augurc released.

"Watch it!" Borely yelled.

"Don't just charge in there," Areo said, pushing Borely back. "He'll freeze you to death if you get too close. Unless you think you can punch away freezing air." She took a few steps to the side to separate herself from Borely.

Augurc was surrounded on three sides by Areo, Borely, and Kitoh. He pointed some of his vine-controlled weapons toward Borely, some toward Areo, and the rest toward Kitoh.

"You two again," Augurc said. "And the dragon."

Areo wondered if he would say anything more, but Augurc's tightlipped face only tightened further. Was he... *upset*?

To Areo's surprise, Augurc turned to Kitoh and sprinted toward the dragon. It took a moment for everyone to react to this decision, including Kitoh. The dragon lurched forward and snapped his jaws at Augurc, faster than Areo expected. Yet despite Kitoh's speed, Augurc managed to step aside of the dragon's fangs. At the same time, Augurc caused a vine to shove a lance into Kitoh's left eye. The dragon roared, but Augurc remained unfazed. He leaped forward and slammed his right hand against Kitoh's long neck, releasing a burst of frozen air against the dragon. Kitoh roared louder and stumbled to his side, half his neck frozen.

Meanwhile Areo and Borely both ran toward Augurc from behind, but somehow the man was able to fight them both off with the many weapons held by his vines. Even while fighting a dragon, Augurc was able to take on both Areo and Borely without needing to see them. Areo dodged one sword and batted away a second one, then sliced apart the vine holding a lance. The vine instantly grew a bit longer to grab the lance before it hit the ground. Augurc continued to attack Areo with multiple weapons, keeping her from reaching him.

Areo leaped back from the vines and various weaponry, then activated her tan Nexi stone. She caused a large stalagmite to burst out of the ground beside Augurc. He leaped aside just before he could get impaled. Borely meanwhile avoided Augurc's attacks and fired a jet of water. Incredulously, Augurc also managed to avoid this as well.

Augurc turned toward Areo and caused several more vines to jab their weapons at her. The man's control over the vines was uncanny—they were not only fast, but incredibly precise. Areo dodged a sword shot for her leg, then a lance jabbing toward her head. Immediately she had to step aside of a sword swinging for her side, then step over a second sword and duck beneath a third one. She relied more on her hearing and sense of the vines' motion rather than on her sight, and managed to keep up with Augurc's repeated attacks.

Areo heard Borely fall, and she realized he was about to get impaled with a lance. She turned and clawed past a couple vines holding swords. Borely managed to jet away the lance aimed for him at the last moment, still having enough energy to activate his dark blue Nexi. Several vines zipped behind Areo all at once.

Simultaneously they shot for her, and Areo realized there was no way to avoid them all. She positioned herself to take the attacks as best she could. One sword cut through the side of her left arm while a lance pushed through the right side of her hip. The other two swords barely missed her head and chest. Screaming, she immediately turned and clawed away the vines holding the sword and lance that hit her.

Without even a moment's pause, the two cut vines flew against her, shoving her backward.

Straight into the path of another sword. The vine shoved the blade through Areo's back and out her stomach. Before she could even react, a knifewielding vine lurched down for her head. Areo tried to leap back, but was held in place by the sword in her waist.

In one swift motion, the knife slit across Areo's throat.

•

Terico and Delkol exchanged blows, managing to block one another's attacks with their swords. They each charged their blades with orange energy, then white energy, then finally purple energy, knocking each other back with every attack.

After one such impact, Terico flew back a ways and forced more sparking white Nexi energy into his blade. His vision turned a blinding white for a few seconds, but he could still see where Delkol was and what he was doing—Delkol's very presence was abundantly clear in Terico's mind, just from the sheer amount of Elpis energy emanating from him. Terico shot off a bolt of lightning at Delkol, who created a barrier of earth out of thin air in front of him. The floating wall of dirt exploded into bits, which Delkol then launched at Terico, each of them sharpening into small spikes. Terico released a shockwave of purple energy around him, blowing away each of the sharp stones before they could reach him. Delkol was immediately upon

Terico, swinging his blade with the added force of orange Nexi energy. Terico's insides still shook from the purple Nexi energy he had accessed, but he managed to activate a burst of red Nexi at Delkol. The detonation of fire pushed Terico back, but he wasn't able to maintain a strong connection with the fire, which Delkol easily swatted away with a release of light blue Nexi.

Before Terico could attack, Delkol released a series of vines from his sword. Glowing silver feathers ran up the vines, causing them to fly for Terico more quickly. Terico caused a layer of brown Nexi substance to surround him. The silver Nexi-powered vines shot straight through the floating swamp material, but the vines were slowed down, making it possible for Terico to keep track of all of them. The instant the vines poked through the other side of the swamp substance, Terico set the vines on fire with red Nexi energy. He fought through his burning headache and caused the flames to rush down the vines, straight back to Delkol.

Terico blasted apart the swamp substance with purple Nexi energy, then shot himself toward his enemy. Delkol caused his vines to fall off his sword before Terico's flames could reach him. Terico shot off a blast of light blue Nexi from his sword, but Delkol managed to cover himself with protective yellow energy in time. Delkol shot up to Terico and swung his blade for Terico's head. With orange Nexi powering his sword, Terico blocked Delkol's attack.

Delkol's blade also glowed orange, but Terico realized there was gray energy flowing through it as well. He felt his heart skip a beat. His eyes widened at the sight. The reminder of all he had lost.

"One of my brother's subjects informed me of your most recent loss," Delkol said, unable to hide his glee. "Poisonous Nexi energy... There is no Nexi greater than this. Save for the full Elpis, there is no force on the entire planet that can stop the cold grip of death!"

Terico shoved Delkol's blade back, but Delkol immediately caused a blast of purple energy to knock Terico to the side. Silver feathers sprouted from the end of Delkol's blade, growing several meters in four razor sharp arcs. Terico avoided the feathers, but flew straight into a second blast of Delkol's loose purple energy. Terico rebounded toward Delkol, barely avoiding the gray and silver blade.

Vines suddenly emerged from the sword and encircled Terico's body. Orange energy filled the vines, causing them to tighten before Terico could slice away at them. Terico tried accessing the purple Nexi energy to free himself, but the agony of the Elpis was overwhelming him.

Delkol swung Terico down straight for the ground, flinging him into the hard earth from at least twenty meters in the air. Terico slowed his fall with the loose purple energy he finally managed to access, but the impact still nearly knocked him unconscious. Accessing the Elpis's energy filled Terico's entire body with unthinkable agony. His muscles felt like they were tearing into little bits when he tried to move. Even screaming from the pain became too difficult to do, his voice fading away and his throat filling with icy, stinging blood.

Delkol floated a couple meters above, an ecstatic grin spread across his transformed face.

"Did you think you were my equal, simply because you have two pieces of the Elpis, just as I do? You never stood a chance against me, Terico. You are young and naïve, while I am an experienced swordsman and master of Nexi. I have killed at least a hundred times as many people as you have.

"Did you think your determination would be enough for you to defeat me? My determination far exceeds yours! You may have the burning of revenge in your heart—at least a couple weeks' worth. But I have hundreds of years' worth of the Shire line's lust for revenge built up in my heart. I am ready to explode! I am ready to overpower everyone that opposes me with the pain and misery of over half a millennium!"

•

"Areo!" Borely screamed. He punched away a vine-guided lance and avoided the swing of a sword.

With Areo stabbed through the stomach, she was unable to avoid the attacks Augurc followed up with. A vine brought down a long knife and slashed it at Areo's throat.

"No!" Borely yelled. He punched aside two more swords and sprinted to Areo before Augurc could stab her even further.

With all the concentration Borely could muster, he activated his dark blue Nexi and shot off a thin jet of water. Slight motions with his head directed the water to slice through the vines near Areo, including the one attached to the sword lodged through her back. Before Areo could fall to the ground, Borely grabbed her and continued to run away. He glanced back and found Augurc sending several weapon-wielding vines toward him. Borely considered shooting another jet of water at them, but didn't feel he'd have the energy to fire one and still be able to keep fighting much longer.

Several massive water jets fired through the vines and weapons approaching Borely. He stumbled forward from the sudden bursts of water, but managed to keep hold of Areo. Once he regained his footing, he turned and found a group of Fiefs soldiers charging into the area—accompanied by a troop of eigni in red and teal uniforms. Borely guessed they had come to assist the city at Rilv's request. The eigni repeatedly fired large bursts of water toward Augurc, who was forced to call for reinforcements. A troop of Shire soldiers fighting atop the city walls headed down a number of staircases, rushing toward Augurc's location.

Borely carried Areo to a spot past a group of Fiefs soldiers who worked together to hold back a couple Brotherhood fighters. This was the safest area Borely could find, but he knew it probably wouldn't stay that way much longer. He looked down at Areo and found her wounds just as terrible as he expected. There was no way Borely was going to be able to heal her, even if he did have the means to perform the first aid or operations her body required.

"Blood," Areo whispered.

She needed blood. Of course—vampires could regenerate if they drank enough blood, Borely remembered. He looked around for any nearby corpses, but found he had brought Areo past the region of greatest bloodshed. Borely would have to work his way past the nearby skirmishes in order to take Areo to a corpse for some blood. There wasn't enough time.

Can't believe I'm doing this, Borely thought. He lowered his head down to Areo's mouth, then brought her head up a bit so she could bite into his neck.

"Borely..." Areo breathed out.

"Hurry up," Borely said. "You need blood to live. I have some. Just don't turn me into a vampire. I'll kill you if you go too far."

Areo immediately sunk her fangs into Borely's neck. As Areo sucked blood from Borely's body, he felt his skin turn a little cold. His insides felt numb, but there was a scratching feeling in his bones. Perhaps it was the altered flow of blood in his body. For at least a minute, Areo continued to devour Borely's blood.

"A...Areo..." Borely struggled to say. His eyes rolled back for a moment, but he forced himself to keep conscious. "Stop..."

Areo took a few more gulps of Borely's blood before lifting her fangs from his neck. She stepped aside of Borely, who lay on the ground, all the strength in his body drained away. Gritting her teeth, Areo wrenched the sword out of her stomach. She screamed and fell to the ground, blood pouring down her waist.

Fangs clamped down into Borely's neck once again. He pushed back instinctively, memories of his brother flooding through his semiconscious mind. Areo held Borely down and sucked more blood from his neck. Apparently the first round of blood sucking was just to heal her neck, and this time she needed to heal her stomach now that the sword was pulled out.

Borely felt all the energy in his body fade away, and any effort he made to resist Areo was hopeless. Long, weary seconds passed, and Borely slowly found himself unable to even move. His limbs hung lifeless, and he felt his heartbeat slow down, growing quieter and quieter.

She's killing me to save herself, Borely thought. *I wish... I wish...*
"I wish... I could have lived... a little longer," Borely whispered. He felt Areo's teeth release from Borely's neck. "Quit being so dramatic. You'll be fine."

Borely opened his eyes and sat up. He blinked a couple times, regaining his vision. His breathing returned to normal, and though he was greatly weakened, he didn't feel he was in any danger of dying. He looked over at Areo and saw that her neck and waist were free of the wounds Augurc had inflicted on her.

"Thank you," she said. "I'm afraid you won't be able to fight anymore right now, but I'll make sure you get through this alive—no matter what." "Just hurry and kill Augurc," Borely said.

And hope Terico kills Delkol, he added in his head.

Areo nodded and turned back to the battlefield. Borely watched her join with some of the eigni assisting the Fiefs soldiers against Augurc, and realized a couple of the reinforcements were Kitoh's parents. This group of eigni must have come from Vursa. Augurc used a number of free vines from his arms to push himself away from the jets of water the eigni shot at him, and still had the power to control other vines to kill off every soldier that drew near to him.

Borely realized he still had some energy held up in his metal gloves. If he could find the strength to land a good punch, he could use his orange Nexi stones at least a couple more times. He pushed himself to his feet and followed a couple Fiefs soldiers who finished off a Brotherhood member. Borely quickly found himself back in the fray, where soldiers on both sides of the war utilized weapons and Nexi abilities of every kind. In the center of it all was Augurc, taking down several Fiefs soldiers with every swing of his blade-wielding vines.

"Master!" Areo exclaimed. "Brother!"

Borely looked to where Areo was looking, and found five vampires leaping down from the roof of a nearby building. Each of them wore hooded black robes, though Borely imagined they all had pink Nexi stones to enable them to be in the sunlight at all. Apparently Areo knew two of these vampires.

"How are you all here?" Areo asked.

"Little Sister!" one vampire exclaimed. "Setar called for aid, so we borrowed some Rite Nexi and hurried over."

"Now's not the time—Augurc takes priority," one of the vampires said. He was a man who looked worn-out with centuries of age, despite having the appearance of someone in his late twenties. "Jenba, Areo— come with me." Areo and one of the other vampires followed, this one a man with thin eyes, and perhaps in his thirties. The three rushed toward Augurc, their claws all extended.

The remaining vampires assisted the eigni and Fiefs soldiers, who were beginning to get overwhelmed by the ever-increasing masses of Shire soldiers.

Borely fought off a Shire swordsman that leaped in front of his path. It was difficult to keep up with him, as Borely relied solely on what little strength his body held. His head turned dizzy from all the effort of blocking the man's attacks, and it was difficult to find a good opening to counter with. He didn't want to use what little power he had left for his Nexi stones—it was vital to save them for Augurc.

The swordsman swung for Borely again, and this time Borely simply blocked the blade with the metal palm of his left hand, then delivered a punch to the face with his right fist. Once the man was knocked out, Borely continued toward Augurc.

Areo and the two other vampires slashed away at Augurc's vines, which failed to retrieve their fallen weapons as the three continued to cut through the growing vines. Augurc continued to grow more and more vines, now just hoping to grab at least one of the three vampires. They were all fast, but Areo was especially quick, energized by the blood Borely offered her.

As he held them back with his vines, Augurc bent down to the corpse of a Fiefs soldier and lifted him off the ground. Augurc pushed his right hand into a deep wound in the man's body.

"Get back!" Borely screamed, recognizing what Augurc was about to do. Areo was too busy with the vines to notice, and the other two vampires wouldn't know the full extent of Augurc's abilities.

A web of interconnecting ice shards exploded from the corpse's body, expanding even faster than it had back on the Brotherhood airship. Areo rushed out of the way, just barely fast enough to avoid the long, thin icicles growing toward her. One of the other vampires was quickly stabbed in the leg by an icicle, and about to get impaled a half-dozen more times. The vampire who led the two rushed back to him and pulled him away before they could get caught in the web of ice.

From a safe distance, Borely circled the ever-growing ice formation. He was careful to avoid all the fighting Shire and Fiefs soldiers, and rushed toward Augurc from the side. From atop a nearby building, Borely caught sight of a Brotherhood member—a masked woman with long purple hair. She raised a bow and arrow and aimed it toward the vampire carrying his injured comrade. With the vampire nearly surrounded by the growing mass of ice, there wouldn't be any way to dodge the arrow.

Borely fired a jet of water at the woman, forcing her to leap aside. She released her arrow in the process, but it flew into the web of ice harmlessly. Borely nearly fell to the ground, his energy almost depleted. The Brotherhood member raised her bow again, quickly arming it with another arrow. Borely realized she was aiming for Areo this time. Areo was still escaping from the growing web of ice, which had expanded to where many Fiefs and Shire soldiers were fighting. Most turned and fled from the attack, while others were impaled, ally and foe alike. It was an ability too powerful for even Augurc to manage perfectly.

Before the Brotherhood member could fire at Areo, Kitoh appeared from behind the building, his neck apparently healed from Augurc's ice Nexi attack. The woman turned, but Kitoh bashed her off the building with his wing before she could fire at him. Kitoh flew from the building toward Augurc, who launched all his vines toward the dragon. Before his wings could get entangled in the vines, Kitoh diverted himself toward the many Shire soldiers continuing to force their way into the city. He released a giant blast of fire at the soldiers, breaking up their ranks and giving an opening for more Fiefs soldiers to attack.

Borely turned back to Augurc, who still appeared unfazed despite the great deal of Nexi energy he had surely expended. The web of ice was expanding more slowly, and the icicles were not growing as far as they had before. Areo turned toward Augurc from the side, slicing her way through the web of ice shards. At the same time, Borely continued toward Augurc from the other side. To reach Augurc, he would have to break through some of the tangled ice shards. He activated the orange Nexi in his left fist and plowed his way through, keeping it powered only the slightest bit. There was just enough energy for him to punch through the ice with one long, continuous punch.

Augurc was still bringing his vines back from his attempt to entangle Kitoh. He looked from Borely to Areo, then back to Borely—perhaps trying to decide who to attack. In an instant, a large, thick icicle emerged from Augurc's right palm. Borely was just a few steps away.

Without warning, Augurc turned back to Areo and thrust his spear of ice at her. Areo was faster than Augurc anticipated. She was already past his attack, and clawed up and down Augurc's chest with two swift swipes. Augurc stumbled back—straight to Borely's other fist. Borely used the energy of his right fist's orange Nexi to power the attack, landing a solid punch into the side of Augurc's head. Augurc took the hit and stumbled to his left, turning toward Borely in the process.

It didn't knock Augurc out, incredulously. The large man just took a punch powered by an orange Nexi straight to the head. To Borely's astonishment, Augurc held his ground and looked back at Borely, his eyes utterly void of emotion. Before Borely could even react, Augurc thrust his ice spear into Borely's chest.

What... was all that came to Borely's mind. He was too weak to move, too exhausted to scream. The frozen weapon remained in his body, the pain unbearable—and yet Borely could do nothing.

"Borely!" Areo screamed. She jabbed her claws toward Augurc's face. Augurc turned in time to release his hand from the icicle that grew from his palm. He stepped back and ran, clutching the deep, bleeding wounds across his torso.

Borely fell to his knees, but Areo knelt down to keep him from collapsing. She quickly pulled the icicle out of Borely's chest, and this time he screamed from the pain. It simply took his senses a few seconds to realize just what had happened.

He was dying.

The icicle had punctured a lung, and perhaps cut into his heart as well. It was difficult to tell—all Borely could feel was the unbearable pain of the deep wound, burning all the way through to his bleeding back. Areo looked over Borely's wound, frowning deeply.

"It's a fatal wound... but I can still save you," Areo said, her voice trembling. It wasn't like her to get nervous.

It took a few seconds for Borely to realize what Areo meant. "No. Don't do it."

"This will be extremely painful," Areo said. "And it will take a lot of effort to adjust..."

"No! Don't do it!"

Areo bit into Borely's neck once more. She sunk her fangs in and injected her blood into Borely's body.

Unbearable pain flooded through Borely's entire body, as if all his blood had turned into acid. For perhaps an entire minute, Areo continued to transfer more of her blood to Borely's body.

He was changing. His very being was transforming from the inside. Borely screamed, visions of his past flooding his mind.

In his mind, he was a child again. A child who lost everything all at once. His parents. His home. His way of life. His very innocence. He was a child who had to kill his own brother.

An insane, bloodthirsty vampire.

Borely's vision slowly grew darker. He could see Areo lifting her head from Borely's neck, but he could feel nothing but the agony of his transforming body.

Areo looked down at Borely, blood dripping down the side of her mouth. For a moment Borely thought she was crying, but the moment passed quickly. Vines wrapped tight around Areo's body all at once. She was lifted into the air, then pulled away violently, unable to move any of her limbs.

Borely's vision went out entirely, and his limp body fell flat against the bloody stone street. He could still hear the rage of the battlefield around him.

"Save for my brother, you are the one person who has ever scarred my body," Augurc said. "You will make a valuable test subject, vampire." Borely wanted to curse Augurc. He wanted to curse Areo. He wanted to curse himself.

But before he lost consciousness, a singular thought formed in the center of his mind.

Living will be worse than dying.

•

Terico stared up at Delkol, unable to move as Delkol's demonic figure transformed further. Thick black horns emerged from Delkol's whitened hair—a large one curved upward from the left side of his head, while a smaller one curved downward from the right side. What looked like giant teeth emerged from his shoulder guards, while his arm guards unraveled, his light gray skin forming long, jagged spikes. His armor emanated a darkness that clashed with the swirling white patterns glowing within, and a tattered silver shroud emerged from his back. In a way the strands were shaped like feathers, but the wind circling around Delkol showed they flowed more like hair.

Delkol gazed down at Terico, his eyes entirely white. "My control of the Elpis is greater than yours. Victory against me was impossible from the very start." He pointed his sword toward Terico's face and filled his blade with sparking white Nexi energy. The light blinded Terico, forcing him to shut his eyes. It was too difficult to move on his own—he needed to use the Elpis to get him to move.

His whirling mind accessed the tan Nexi energy within the Elpis. Delkol released a bolt of lightning just as Terico caused the earth beneath him to erupt. Terico flew in the air, and the lightning passed into the mass of earth he lay on. His sword lifted forward, Terico crashed into Delkol, who barely managed to avoid Terico's blade.

They both fell to the ground, Terico's hand grasping Delkol's face.
Terico remembered one of the Nexi stones his mother used when fighting Delkol. The clear Nexi, used for transferring abilities from one person to the other. If it was impossible for Terico to reach Delkol's level of Elpis control on his own, Terico could simply *take* some of that power. He accessed the clear Nexi energy within him and forced as much of Delkol's power to flow into him as he could. For several seconds Terico found his mind clearing, gaining a better understanding of the Elpis. His vision improved, his limbs strengthened, and the many forms of agony flowing through his body lightened a little bit.

I can still fight, Terico thought. *And I can still kill you, Delkol. I know how you fight, and I know what you want. I will kill you!*
Screaming from the pain of the transfer, Delkol swung his sword at Terico's side. Terico caused a thin wall of silver feathers to materialize between him and Delkol's blade, blocking the attack. Delkol gritted his teeth, his face contorted with rage. His body glowed the gray light of the poison Nexi, and Terico immediately let go of Delkol's face. Terico flew back a few meters, a reinvigorated force building up within his very soul. He felt his body transforming in a way similar to Delkol. His hair lengthened, extending nearly a half-meter backward. Two thin horns curved upward atop his head, and swirling black flames breathed in and out of existence amidst his hair. His armor glowed black, and filled with white spirals that pulsated with a shaky, metallic echo. Terico's arm guards turned to ice, forming sharp, jagged protrusions down their entire length.

Delkol pushed himself off the ground and floated to the same height as

Terico. At first Terico thought he was going to say something, but Delkol simply stared at Terico with empty, ominous white eyes.

A massive section of earth blew out of the ground, at least fifty meters long. Delkol slammed his sword down into it, then released a shockwave of purple Nexi energy to break the earth into giant chunks. Terico flew back from the exploding earth, avoiding the hardened dirt and stones that collided and broke apart around him. Delkol pointed his sword at Terico, exerting the tan Nexi power to send hundreds of rocks toward Terico.

Terico enveloped himself in yellow Nexi energy, protecting himself from the stones that flew into him. The chunks of earth battered him back and forth, and once he spotted an opening he sent himself flying toward Delkol, sword raised for the kill.

A sphere of fire encircled Delkol, then blew out in all directions. Terico caused water to surround him, then launched a series of vines from his sword once he passed the wall of flames. Delkol caused the air between him and Terico to freeze, forcing Terico's vines to turn to ice. Terico immediately accessed the light blue Nexi energy, and used the frozen vines to cause icicles to extend toward Delkol. Before the ice could reach him, Delkol charged his sword with orange energy and beat apart everything Terico sent at him.

Delkol's blade swirled with dark blue and gray energy. Terico cut through his vines and flew down toward Delkol, waiting for his attack. Delkol fired a giant stream of pallid gray water, which Terico barely managed to avoid. From the water emerged vines covered in thin silver feathers, reaching out for Terico. At the same time, Delkol caused another massive portion of the earth to burst up from the ground, and even used red Nexi energy to melt the rock—effectively creating a stream of molten lava under his command.

Terico covered himself with yellow Nexi energy and created a series of barriers made of earth, swamp, and silver feathers. He deflected the majority of the vines, hacking away at those that slipped past his defenses. Delkol redirected his jet of poisonous water, which Terico was simply unable to avoid, as the stream of lava reached for him from every other direction. Terico flew through the water, using the silver feathers to deflect the majority of the poisonous energy. The water quickly wore down the glowing yellow barrier protecting him, so Terico forced his mind to access the purple Nexi energy. He created a shockwave around him to blast away the water, then flew as fast as he could, escaping Delkol's barrage of poison before it could weaken Terico.

But before Terico could fly to Delkol's location, several more bursts of lava erupted from the ground, all flying toward Terico far faster than he could keep up with. He encircled himself with several layers of ice. As soon as the lava impacted the barriers, Terico rocketed out of the sphere of steam that ensued, avoiding the chunks of molten rock that followed.

If he kept having to defend against constant attacks from all sides, Terico knew he'd wear himself out quickly, even with the power of the two Elpis fragments. The pain within his body was steadily growing more and more torturous, but he kept from screaming. He had grown so used to the pain, that it seemed to simply be a part of who he was—it was almost as normal a function as breathing.

Accept the pain, Terico thought. *It was pain that brought me to this point. This is my driving force... This is what I have become. I am agony.*
He flew toward Delkol, charging his sword with red and green energy. At the same time, Delkol launched himself toward Terico, filling his sword with light and dark blue energy. Their blades clashed, unleashing the elements against one another. They each covered themselves with protective energy, then turned the yellow glow into a blinding white light. With every swing of their blades, they whittled down each other's strength and power, little by little.

Delkol screamed, causing his cloak to expand and create hundreds of silver feathers. Terico floated back a few meters, watching as the feathers began vibrating, their hue turning to a violent gold. Terico immediately accessed the power he felt most heavily amongst the Elpis energies flowing within him.

Black flames enveloped his entire body.

Delkol's golden feathers launched for Terico, too fast to even see. The blurs of golden light exploded around Terico, the feathers melting the instant they came into contact with Terico's black flames.

Accessing this power drained Terico considerably, and it suddenly became difficult just to keep himself flying in the air, and keeping his sword lifted up and steady. As soon as Delkol's golden feathers were expended, Terico cut off access to the black flames, which resumed to flickering sporadically in his hair.

Sweat dripped down Delkol's face, and Terico could tell he was breathing heavily. There was no way Delkol was going to relent, however.

Delkol swung his sword repeatedly, flinging a series of icicles, rocks, and jets of water at Terico. They were blind attacks driven by rage, but it was difficult to keep avoiding the projectiles. Terico was hesitant to use the yellow Nexi energy any more than he already had, knowing that every move he made from this point on would be vital for his success. It wouldn't be much longer before the pain of the Elpis overpowered Terico's determination to kill Delkol—there was only so much the body could withstand, and Terico had accessed the fragmented Elpis far too much over the past few days.

While flying back and forth between Delkol's attacks, Terico focused his mind on the Elpis energies within him, searching for the teal Nexi energy. As soon as he felt access to it, Terico stared down at Delkol and focused as hard as he could on the words he wished to communicate to him.

You are a disgrace to the Shire family line.
From the very beginning, you were a failure, Delkol.
We are ashamed you had ever been born.
With descendants as hopeless as this, there is no chance for regaining our rightful place as rulers of the Fiefs Kingdom.
Terico projected these words into Delkol's thoughts, filling Delkol's mind with the vague, shadowy voices of his beloved family line.

"No!" Delkol screamed. He stopped firing projectiles at Terico and gripped his head with his free hand. "I'm the one who learned of the Elpis! I've given my entire life to reclaiming the throne! I won't stop! I won't stop now!" As he shrieked, a whirlwind of silver feathers circled around him, keeping Terico from attacking.

The fact Delkol was able to maintain such power even while screaming at the voices in his head was unsettling. It meant Delkol's control over the Elpis was still much greater than Terico's. Strength and determination wasn't going to be enough for Terico—not when he was in this much pain, and with so little energy left to spare.

"I'm not a failure!" Delkol yelled amidst the flurry of silver feathers. "Every day of my life, I've worked toward this point! You will accept me! You will all accept me! You will be overwhelmed with pride when you see me, Father!"

As Delkol screamed, Terico shot himself down to Delkol and exerted all his strength to covering his body with yellow Nexi energy. Upon reaching the spinning barrier of feathers, Terico released a burst of purple energy, pushing away enough feathers to create a brief opening. Terico flew in, but the speed at which the feathers flew still caused some of them to fly into him. Most deflected off his yellow barrier, but a few sliced through his armor and scraped his skin. The beating of the Elpis energy within him filled the gashes with stinging pain, but Terico instead focused on his sword, filling it with orange and white Nexi energy—just as his father had when fighting Delkol.

Delkol heard Terico breach through the barrier of silver feathers, and turned just as Terico swung his sword at him. Delkol shot backward, his remaining swarms of feathers following to either side of him. Still swinging, Terico released the white energy from his blade, and sent it flying with the added strength of the orange energy. The orange-glowing bolt of lightning shot straight through Delkol's torso, leaving a gaping, bleeding hole the size of a fist.

"No!" Delkol screamed, falling toward the ground. Terico flew after him, intent to keep attacking him.

Delkol released several vines from his sword, forcing Terico to slow down to hack away at them. At the same time, Delkol's wound began to heal—he was flooding his body with the healing energy of the Elpis.

He's weakening, Terico thought. *I have him!*
Terico forced a giant arm of dirt to emerge from the ground beneath Delkol. Before the hand could smash him, Delkol flew to the side and sent himself upward once more. His wound was almost entirely healed, and even his armor was beginning to piece back together somehow.

Delkol flew higher, and Terico pursued, following Delkol toward the city. Still flying backward, and his sword pointed toward Terico, Delkol bellowed an order at the top of his lungs.

"By the royal blood flowing within me, I command you all to rise and destroy my enemy!"

All at once, hundreds of white glowing lights appeared from the ground below. Terico looked down to find figures of people—ghostly apparitions— flying straight toward him.

The spirits of the Shire soldiers slain in the battle below.

Terico found Delkol glowing with indigo light—the energy of the soul catcher Nexi. Delkol was able to control the souls of those under his command.

Hundreds upon hundreds of souls flew up to Terico, their ethereal weapons raised and gleaming. They chanted Delkol's name, their voices distorted and distant, despite how quickly they drew near. Fighting Delkol's fallen army would be suicide, Terico knew—he would quickly run out of energy to fend them off. The only option was to kill Delkol.

Immediately.

Terico blasted himself to Delkol, who raised his sword with an expression of pure satisfaction. The soldier spirits were quickly gaining on Terico, encircling him from all sides. Terico ignored them and forced himself to fly faster.

At the same time, Terico and Delkol both filled their blades with orange Nexi energy. Terico slammed his blade against Delkol's, and they both flew downward. Delkol held strong, but Terico forced himself to continue pushing down on Delkol, flying toward the earth as fast as he could.

Delkol grinned. His shroud spread to either side of him, the sharp, hairlike feathers separating and turning golden. Even while guiding hundreds of spirits toward Terico, he still had the strength to activate his shroud of razor-sharp blades. Delkol launched the feathers at Terico, a dozen of them zipping clean through Terico's armor and body in an instant.

Screaming, Terico pushed himself back, away from Delkol, and straight to the swarms of spirits behind him.

With orange Nexi energy built up in his arms, Terico threw his two Elpis stones away. Terico launched one stone dozens of meters to his right, the other he sent flying far to his left. Terico's transformed state held, his mind still connected with the two Elpis fragments.

"The Elpis!" Delkol screamed.

At the same time, Terico collided straight into the spirit masses, all of which thrust their weapons at him. In an instant, Terico's entire body was punctured with ethereal swords, lances, arrows, axes, and knives. The weapons afflicted his spirit with deadly wounds, so it was his soul that was tearing apart and dying. The pain was still there, however. The allencompassing agony was akin to an explosion from every pore of his body, but Terico accepted it.

He was about to have his revenge.

Delkol blasted toward the Elpis stone tumbling away to his right, his eyes wide and his outstretched hand trembling. As the spirits continued to stab at Terico's soul, Terico kept his eyes fixed on Delkol, able to see him through the vaguely transparent spirits with his heightened vision.

Just as Delkol's hand and face neared the glowing fragment, Terico activated the red Nexi energy inherent to the Elpis. The fragment released a massive detonation—a fiery blast that exploded directly into Delkol's arm and face. The flames melted Delkol's arm away and disfigured his bleeding face and torn-open neck. At the same time, the massive shockwave sent Delkol flying backward—straight toward the other Elpis fragment.

Terico activated the green Nexi energy within the stone, causing vines to wrap around Delkol's body and bind him tight. With what was left of his energy, Terico shot out of the multitude of spirits, directing his flight toward Delkol. Though skewered with at least twenty glowing, transparent weapons, Terico pushed himself toward Delkol, filling the blade of his sword with all the silver and gray energy he could muster.

Gray feathers flew within Terico's blade, and Terico suddenly felt an overwhelming sense of exhaustion—as if he had never slept in his entire life. His spirit was dying, and as he stared down at Delkol—the man's bound form steadily drawing closer—Terico wondered if it had all been worth it. Terico slammed his blade into Delkol's chest, and immediately silver feathers began tearing Delkol apart from the inside. Delkol screamed, blood flying from his mouth and neck. The poisonous energy within Terico's sword flooded into Delkol's body, and Terico continued to fly downward. As Terico and Delkol neared the ground, Terico found his energy entirely wasted. He let go of the sword and let his connection with the Elpis fragments slowly dissolve. Terico fell back, separating from Delkol, who continued to plunge toward the earth.

For a moment, Terico felt like he was floating in the air. The wind rushed all around him, and the sky was a vast, infinite blue. Delkol's army of spirits had faded away, leaving nothing but an empty sky. An endless expanse. The very embodiment of limitless possibilities.

He reached up toward the sky, wishing for something to hold on to.
Anything to keep him from falling.

There was nothing.

Terico crashed against the hard earth, landing flat on his back. His body filled with a jolt of pain, but by this point Terico had grown entirely numb to it all.
The weapons that had impaled him faded away, leaving behind a shattered, dying spirit.

He lay still, perfectly still. His transformed state was slowly dissipating, his connection with the Elpis tenuous, fleeting.

He was too tired to feel anything.

It's over, he thought, and he closed his eyes.

•

With the only hand he had left, Delkol gripped the sword sticking out of his chest. The blade dug into his palm, and thick blood slowly dripped down his forearm. He couldn't feel anything. Just the overwhelming beat of his heart, pounding pain into every fiber of his being. It might not have even been his heart, actually. When he concentrated on it enough, he realized his heart was beating very slowly, weakly.

Delkol stared up at the sky, barely able to see anything. He wanted to scream, but it hurt to even breathe. It was too difficult to look to either side of him, and everything was a bright, painful blur anyways. He doubted he would see anything but bloody corpses, but if there was a chance the other two Elpis pieces were nearby...

He slipped his weary hand into his pocket, pulling out his two Elpis fragments. There was just enough strength inside Delkol to maintain a connection with them. He gripped them tight and tried to heal himself— any part of himself.

It was a useless effort. Over the course of his fight with Terico, he had drained himself of energy. Perhaps if he hadn't summoned the army of spirits, he would have enough strength to pull this sword out, at the very least.

But he had wanted to be sure. He wanted to ensure Terico's death, no matter the cost. He couldn't hold back—not even the slightest bit. He had to give his all.

Perhaps he went too far. Perhaps he had become *too* determined.

No, Delkol thought. *No. No. No! I never wavered! I gave my all, each and every day!*

He felt the last of his energy fade away, his connection with the Elpis finally severed. His body reverted back to its normal state, a painful transformation that did nothing to heal Delkol's wounds. The poison of the gray Nexi sunk into every organ of his body, the agony accentuated by his use of the fragmented Elpis.

If I had all the pieces... I'd live.
They were so close. In mere walking distance!

He struggled to sit up, but he couldn't even move. The poison weakened him, and the wounds Terico inflicted on him were killing him on their own.

No! Delkol tried to scream.

This world was robbing him of the one thing he ever aspired toward.

I'm so close... So close!
He could see his father looking down at him, deep concern etched in his eyes.

One day you will regain the land of our forebears, Father said. *This continent needs a strong ruler again. One who can bring peace and stability to the world. One who has not only the royal blood of the great ones, but the will and might to instill both fear in his enemies and reverence in his subjects.*
The Fiefs line has become corrupted over the centuries, Delkol. The Shires are a part of that royal line, but in our separation we have maintained our integrity. One day you will claim the throne of the Fiefs Kingdom, and the land will become one again.
A strong kingdom... with an inspiring king.
Delkol's eyes burned in the light of the sun. He set down his Elpis fragments, and with a weak, shaking hand, he forced what was left of his eyelids shut. He let his hand linger, feeling the cross-shaped scar across his right eye.

Brother... Delkol thought. *You have the strength to finish what I've started. It was you who gave me this scar. With that strength... scar this entire land. Then once this kingdom has been humbled, take what is rightfully ours.*

•

Slowly Terico felt life fading away from him. The pain lingered on—in fact, it seemed to intensify—but he could tell he was passing away. He still had a faint connection to his two lost Elpis fragments, deep in the recesses of his icy, pounding mind. His body was still in its transformed, demonic state... There was still time.

It was difficult, but Terico fought through the pain of the Elpis, struggling to access the healing energy once more. The remaining Elpis pieces were close... There was still hope for him, and for everyone he had lost. It was impossible to scream, and barely even possible to move, but Terico could still feel the Elpis's power. He shut his eyes as hard as he could, concentrating on its healing energy. His body seared with pain, but inside— deep inside—he could feel something. It wasn't cold, wasn't hot. Just the sense of things melding back together. As if the healing energy was filling in the punctured holes in his soul, keeping it alive.

Terico's body and armor transformed back to normal, and he lay on the earth. Motionless. Barely breathing. Knowing his time was short. He had exhausted every ounce of his energy, and now his connection with the Elpis was thoroughly dissolved. His spirit was intact, but it was too late to save his body. He had used the fragmented Elpis far too much, and now he paid the price of its poisoning effect.

Perhaps if he had gained the full Elpis, everything would have been different. Any attempt to move was hopeless at this point, and it took all of Terico's effort just to think of anything besides the pain.

Delkol is dead, Terico thought, and for that he could smile—if only in his mind. Delkol would never again kill an innocent victim. The world was a better place without him, and the blood spilled in Edellerston was at last atoned for. Delkol received his just punishment, and Terico was glad to be the one to deliver it.

He knew though that deep down, nothing had really changed. It was good that Delkol died, but that didn't bring back Terico's parents. It didn't bring back his friends. It didn't bring back Suran.

Could the full Elpis have done that? Terico already had his doubts, but now it felt even more certain that some things simply couldn't be changed. And what if his loved ones were happier where they were now? Even if bringing them back to life was actually possible, would it have been the right thing to do?

Suddenly all of Terico's wishes felt strange, complicated. What had he been working for all this time? What did he ever hope to accomplish in his life? It was all over, and Terico wasn't even certain if the path he walked was the right one. What would become of him now?

Was his revenge worth it? Was killing Delkol worth dying for?

Terico felt the life fade away from his body, and through his closed eyelids he could make out a white silhouette. Slowly, ever slowly, the pain inside of him dissolved, and the pounding in his head dissipated. The agony he had become faded away, bit by bit.

And as the pain disappeared, Terico found his vision improving. The white silhouette turned blurry and gained its color.

Through tear-filled eyes, Terico looked up at Suran. She smiled at him, the same smile she always gave. Back when they were in Edellerston.

Suran bent down and took Terico by the hand. Terico sat up and let Suran lift him up. She helped him to his feet, and it took a few seconds for Terico to grasp where he was.

An entirely different world. A field free of corpses, free of blood, free of agony.

His heart had stopped beating entirely, and Terico realized he wasn't even breathing anymore. He was a spirit, and this was Suran's spirit holding his hand.
Suran pointed ahead, and Terico found other spirits appearing a couple meters away. Jujor and Febraz were there, and so were all the people Terico knew in Edellerston. Suran's parents, as well as Terico's classmates, his associates, and his neighbors.

And at the very front stood Terico's father and mother.

Terico turned back to Suran and squeezed her hand. Her smile turned into a silent giggle, and Terico found himself smiling as well. In a way, he had gotten precisely what he hoped for.

•

Lanek dodged the burst of swamp material Lynx fired at him, then jabbed his rapier toward the masked boy's arm. Lynx took a few steps back, taking a couple heavy breaths. Lanek also felt weary, but was determined to kill this boy—even if it was the last thing he did.

"Fall back, Lynx!" a deep voice ordered. "Gather all the Brotherhood you can."

Lanek looked past Lynx to find a large man with a bandana and vest, and a series of green Nexi embedded in his arms. This was Augurc Shire, Lanek realized. There were a number of vines sticking out of his arms, and wrapped amongst them was a young, unconscious woman. The vampire who came with Terico... Areo, Lanek recalled.

Lynx muttered something unintelligible beneath his mask and the chaos of the battlefield. Lanek rushed for Lynx, not willing to let him get away. In one swift movement, Lynx turned around and sprinted off, quite a bit faster than Lanek could hope to keep up with. At the same moment, Lynx tossed back a red Nexi stone, letting it arc right back to Lanek.

Immediately Lanek swung his rapier against the stone, hitting it in mid-air. The stone flew off to the side and exploded a couple meters away. The blast knocked Lanek to the ground, but he had hit it far enough to keep the flames from reaching him.

Lanek pushed himself back to his feet and ran in the direction Lynx dashed off to. All around him, Shire and Fiefs soldiers fought to the death. Amongst them he saw eigni, vampires, a dragon, and even Brotherhood members, but the boy in the smiling mask was gone.

A couple Shire soldiers got in his way, and Lanek dealt with them as fast as possible. But once he was running again, Lanek could find no sign of where Lynx disappeared to.

Members of the Brotherhood started to retreat, slipping back outside the city walls. Many of the Shire soldiers followed, and in turn the Fiefs soldiers pursued, not about to let their enemies escape so easily. A number of eigni used their dark blue Nexi stones to create a giant sea serpent made of water, which they caused to fly amongst the fleeing Fiefs troops alongside Kitoh, still in his dragon state. The tide was turning on the battle, but Lanek hadn't found the revenge he was looking for.

I'm sorry, Suran, he thought. *Perhaps it was pointless in the first place, but I needed something... I needed some way to rectify this...*
Perhaps there was no way to make things right. Suran was lost, and the world would never be right again.

Lanek ran with some Fiefs soldiers, following them outside the city gates.

He soon found himself standing amidst a sea of corpses. Many still had arrows sticking out their backs or torsos, while others rested as burnt, smoking remains—the victims of fire Nexi. Others still lay strangled in vines, while others rested with the deep, bloody wounds of the sword.

Walking to a small open area, Lanek couldn't help but wonder how it all came to this. The power struggles this world had to endure... How much blood was spent this day, Lanek could never imagine.

Amidst the fields of decay Lanek found a boy with dark blue hair, lying lifelessly, about a dozen gashes spread across his armor and deep into his body.

It was Terico, Lanek realized. Lanek bent down and checked his pulse, but there was nothing. There was no heartbeat and no sign of breathing. Lanek searched the area and found Delkol's fallen body as well, lying perhaps ten, fifteen meters away. He was clearly dead.

So Terico was successful, Lanek thought, *but died in the process.* A number of emotions passed through Lanek's heart, but he felt too numb and hollow to let them linger for long.

He checked both Delkol and Terico's bodies for the Elpis fragments, but didn't find them in their hands or in any of their pockets. Lanek searched the area and eventually came across two of the pieces, hidden amidst the field of corpses far away from one another.

Lanek continued searching until his eyes grew sore, but there simply was no sign of the other two fragments. They were gone.

•

The days passed, and once the battlefield was cleansed everyday life in Setar resumed just as it always had. Lanek mused that most of the populace was entirely unaffected by this brief war, but he decided that was for the better.

It was a bright, hot day, and Lanek busied himself with fixing his airship. Its crash left it a complete disaster, but he didn't want to just give up on it. This wasn't just his airship—but his parents' airship, and Suran's airship.

Though he didn't particularly enjoy it, this was a time for him to get his hands dirty.

Once evening fell, Lanek stopped his work to take a rest and look up at the stars for a while. It was something he would do with Suran from time to time. She told him that it was something she would do with Terico, as well.

Perhaps they could have been happy together, Lanek thought. He had always been reluctant to let anyone grow close to his beloved sister, but over the past few days he found himself realizing that Terico probably would have taken good care of her. Perhaps if Delkol had never set his sights on Edellerston, things would have worked out nicely for Suran and Terico. Just imagining how life could have been for them... it filled Lanek's heart with misery.

The sound of approaching footsteps broke Lanek's train of thought. He stood up and found himself face to face with Rilv, the head royal servant who dragged him and Suran into this unfortunate venture in the first place.

"Good evening," she said. "I have answers for your questions."

"I'm surprised you came to me personally," Lanek said, folding his arms.

"It is the least I could do, after you retrieved half the Elpis," Rilv said. She glanced to the right a moment. "I could also use the fresh air."

Lanek had asked to be informed of anything Rilv learned concerning the missing two pieces of the Elpis, as well as anything regarding the location of Terico's associates.

"The two pieces of the Elpis you found are still hidden in the castle, where only I can access them," Rilv said. "They are being kept under constant watch, as you can imagine."

"But the other two pieces?" Lanek said.

"It is likely that Augurc has them," Rilv said. "Once it became clear that Delkol was killed, Augurc hurried to the location his brother had fallen to and retreated with the two Elpis fragments. He was in a hurry to leave— otherwise he probably would have searched for the other two pieces."

"They weren't by Terico," Lanek said, "and I believe Augurc had little energy left at that point. Terico's associates all fought him, and he probably wouldn't have been able to fight any longer."

"He is probably experimenting on the Elpis as we speak," Rilv said.

"We will have to retrieve the fragments from him as soon as we ascertain his current location."

"Does he want the same things his brother wanted?" Lanek asked.

"Possibly," Rilv said. "Augurc's greatest concern has been with his experiments, with creating the perfect army. Now that his brother is out of the picture, there is no telling how Augurc will choose to use that army." Lanek sighed. "And what of Terico's associates? Kitoh, Areo, and Borely?"

"Kitoh has returned to Vursa with his parents," Rilv said. "He lost an eye and suffered a few other bad wounds, but he will live. There is still no word on Areo—she is likely still being held captive by the Brotherhood. What Augurc intends to do with her, I can not imagine. As for Borely, it seems he has left with the vampires who came from Istal. What business he has with them, I do not know."

Lanek let all this information sift through his mind a bit before he nodded. "Sounds like everyone is worse off."

"Misfortune always accompanies a battle," Rilv said. "In the end, Delkol was defeated, and the city suffered no civilian casualties. War has been averted, potentially saving thousands of lives. This is about the best one could hope for."

"I suppose," Lanek said.

Perhaps in the end, in the great scheme of things, things had worked out quite favorably. But how could he go on with his life like this? Every day felt hollow... empty.

It was going to be a struggle to get up each day. To keep working on this airship. To go to sleep every night.

It was always going to be a struggle, Lanek realized.

•

Lanek stared up at the full moon, unable to sleep. After gazing at it for some time, he tinkered some more with a few airship parts. He didn't get much of anything done. It was just to fill the time. He couldn't sleep, and there was nothing that could satisfy him anymore. Minutes passed. Hours passed. It was all the same to Lanek now.

He sat down on the ground and focused on the cool, soft breeze. He stared out at the fields, which not so long ago had been covered in blood, craters, weapons, and corpses. Beneath the soft glow of the moon, everything looked pristine once more.

There were footsteps. Light, gentle footsteps, barely discernible beneath the soothing wind.

Lanek squinted toward a faint glow in the distance, and his eyes slowly adjusted to the small, white lights. Two figures. A boy and a girl.

Terico and Suran.

They walked through the field, hand in hand. Lanek smiled, and his heart suddenly felt a little lighter. And yet at the same time... a little less empty.

Lanek blinked, and they were gone. How long the spirits of Terico and Suran lingered, Lanek couldn't be certain. But he continued to gaze out across the field all through the night, thankful that these treasured souls had at last found peace.

•Part VII•
FIVE YEARS LATER

Lanek fought the urge to keep a hand at the hilt of his rapier. It had been some time since Rilv had last summoned him—five years now?—but he still remembered quite clearly the dangers this castle represented. Though he had a guard leading him down the posh hallway, he didn't feel any safer. Perhaps he couldn't get himself to fully trust the royal guard. Or perhaps he just couldn't trust anyone anymore.

I'm just tense, Lanek thought. *It's being here in this palace. This is where... she died.*

His sister, Suran. He didn't want to dwell on her senseless death—the way she slowly suffered through a malicious poison, how he had been so utterly helpless to save her, the fact he had failed to avenge her in the tumultuous battle that followed. In the end, nothing Lanek did made things better for his beloved sister. And though he felt Suran and her friend Terico were in a better place now, the fact that Suran's murderer still lived unnerved Lanek.

That boy in the smiling mask, Lynx. One of the Brotherhood's most treacherous followers. Though Lanek had spent most his days the last five years focusing on his airships, he always noted any rumors involving the Brotherhood. He still looked forward to the day when he would see Lynx again. The day Lanek would have his revenge, and Suran's soul could fully find peace.

Lanek took a deep breath. *I need to relax. I need my wits about me for this meeting.*

It was difficult to calm his nerves, when such terrible memories were so deeply engrained in this place. The pristine white walls, the polished cherrywood floors, the immaculate works of art, the smell of lavender, the crisp echo of footsteps, the colored light flowing through stained glass windows... The whole castle was steeped in eclectic elegance, meaningless magnificence.

All the power in the world was gathered at this city, and what did it avail anyone? The prestige of the royalty, the intelligence of the elite, and the energy of all four Elpis pieces—none of these things were enough to save Suran. Everything deemed great and marvelous about this world... What did it bring this world? A city stained in blood. A field littered with corpses. A thousand dreams and hopes, utterly shattered forever.

And yet, life moved on. Lanek kept the legacy of his family alive through his production of airships. Rather than work directly for the royal air fleet as Rilv suggested, Lanek continued to work alone, and with the assistance of a few mechanic-savvy elves in a small village called Oedin. He would assist Fiefs engineers from time to time, but for the most part the government had left him alone for five trying years. Work was difficult, money was hard to come by, and there just wasn't much to live for anymore.

But at least he hadn't been caught up in the tumult of world affairs. Until now.

When a group of royal guards delivered Rilv's request to attend a council meeting in Setar, Lanek had no choice but to fly his airship the eleven-hour trip it took to get there. It left him weary and nervous, and even now he felt ill-prepared for whatever news this meeting would bring him.

He wondered if he was dressed appropriately for the occasion. His dark turquoise uniform, black pants, gloves, and boots were better than his work clothes, at the very least. He kept his long, light turquoise hair tied back in a ponytail—a more efficient look than what he went with when he was younger.

The guard led Lanek to the polished doors of the council room. What this meeting entailed and who precisely would be in attendance, Lanek wasn't certain. All he knew was that it was about to begin.

Inside, Lanek found Rilv wrapping up a conversation with a couple guards. She turned to Lanek and nodded. There was no emotion in her face—apparently she still didn't have an opinion of Lanek even after five years.

"You made it on time," Rilv said. "You pass."

Not exactly the welcome Lanek was expecting.

"Wonderful to see you, too."

"Your airship is undeniably the fastest in the Fiefs Kingdom." Rilv ignored Lanek's greeting entirely. She was just as to-the-point as Lanek remembered her. She had the same sort of purple and white uniform she wore before, so he took it Rilv was still the royal head servant of the Fiefs House. Though she was now in her early thirties, she had the same sharp, thin eyes and silver hair reaching down to her shoulders. Lanek noted a deep weariness in her eyes, however. Rebuilding the government of a country surely couldn't have been easy for her, considering how the king and every royal duke in Setar was murdered during Delkol Shire's rampage.

"So my coming here was just a test," Lanek said.

"Don't worry," Rilv said. "You're welcome to remain for the meeting, and share your opinion on a couple matters that may interest you." She motioned to a long, white marble table—it was shaped like a thin triangle, and had about ten chairs running down its two longer sides. At the small third side was a slightly taller, more delicately carved wooden chair with white cushions embedded within it—clearly meant for the one who would preside in the meeting.

"Take a seat," Rilv said. "Just behave yourself, and be sure to stand when the king enters."

Lanek's eyes widened. "The king?"

Rilv turned to speak with another guard, but Lanek could tell she was smirking. She had completely taken Lanek by surprise—and she knew how Lanek worked hard to never appear flustered or worried.

He motioned a hand in front of his face and took on a cool, reposed expression. "Of course. The king. What an honor."

Lanek looked over the people already sitting at the table. They were all men, so it was difficult to decide who to sit next to.

A bunch of aristocrats, Lanek thought. It didn't take long for wealthy elites the whole kingdom over to come to Setar to fill the void in the capital's rulership. Of course, a new king was needed, and in the end a young man named Enlia Tehns was deemed to have the most royal blood. With the death of the previous king and Terico, there were no full-blooded Fiefs left in the kingdom. There was the Shire Kingdom's family of the same name— their ruler Augurc had enough royal blood to wield the Elpis, but there was no chance the Shires would ever be allowed to rule in the Fiefs Kingdom. Especially after the war their previous ruler insinuated, and the continued existence of Delkol's murderous organization, the Brotherhood.

These aristocrats at the table were surely involved in many of the Fiefs

Kingdom's dealings both internally and with foreign nations. Though it was the monarch who had the final word, King Enlia Tehns Fiefs was only in his early twenties—Lanek's age—and relied on the experience and knowledge provided by royal councils.

It felt odd for Lanek to be here, but he kept calm as he sat patiently, letting the others at the table continue their conversations with one another.

"Good evening, Lanek."

Not recognizing the voice, Lanek turned and looked up at an eigni boy in his mid-teens. He wore a white jacket and pants, and had a black vest with the golden insignia of some kind of Nexi research team, it looked like. There was something familiar about this boy...

"Ah, you must be Kitoh," Lanek said.

Smiling at the recognition, the eigni sat down in the open chair to Lanek's right. "Glad you remember me."

"You're taller than I remember you."

"It's been five years, hasn't it?" Kitoh said. "You haven't changed much, though you don't look quite as smug as I remember you."

Lanek closed his eyes, frowned, and flicked a hand to the side. "The nerve of some people. You've sharpened your tongue over the years, I see. You're not cute at all anymore."

"Five years of intense research can really drain you," Kitoh said.

Lanek opened his eyes and smirked. "Studying Nexi stones?"

"Better. The Elpis stone."

"Really? What have you found out?"

Kitoh held up a knowing finger. "You'll see. I'll be sharing my team's findings in this very meeting."

A few more seats filled up, and Lanek glanced at the door from time to time to watch for the king. Lanek had never seen him in person, though he had seen a few drawings of him in bulletins posted at the village assembly hall.

Lanek looked over each person sitting at the table, analyzing whatever he could from their appearance, how they dressed, their subtle hand gestures, their manner of speech, the things they talked about, and the directions their eyes glanced toward. He decided that there were seven aristocrats and four others at the table—Lanek himself, Kitoh, an elf woman who specialized in ancient languages, and a human man who probably worked as a special operative. Neither of the latter two had outright said these things in their conversations, but Lanek knew how to piece things together and deduce their hidden meaning.

He heard the doorway open and turned to find two men walking in. First entered a man in the uniform of a guard, but with a small bucket-like hat on his head—it marked him as a head colonel of the castle guard.

Beside the colonel was a young man in white clothes and silver armor. He wore a white mask with an inverted black cross over the right eye.

The Brotherhood.

Lanek stood up.

He realized there was more to the mask. A long, thin black smile was painted across it.

Lynx.

Lanek drew his sword.

While everyone reacted in surprise at the exposed rapier blade, Lanek rushed toward the one who murdered his sister.

The colonel turned and raised a green Nexi stone toward Lanek. Lynx leaped to the side and slid out a small, thin knife from the inside of his mask. Lanek rushed through the vines sprouting from the colonel's Nexi, and continued his swing straight toward Lynx.

The Brotherhood fighter dodged Lanek's attack, then leaped toward Lanek, his blade outstretched.

The knife fell out of Lynx's hand.

At the same time, Lanek's rapier slipped from his grasp.

The two weapons floated into the air, and in their moment of confusion

Lanek and Lynx collided into each other. Vines immediately wrapped around them both and pulled them away from each other.

Lanek struggled to break free, but the colonel's control of the green Nexi was too strong to resist. The vines wrapped so tight it became difficult to breathe. Lanek glanced toward his sword, shocked to find it still floating in the air.

A second later the rapier fell to the floor, a couple meters away from him. The knife fell as well, clinking a safe distance away from Lynx.

Rilv walked toward them, holding a strange Nexi stone in her hands. It glowed a bright purple, but had a series of thin, dark blue swirls circling beneath its glassy surface.

"At least four of us have made a grave error," she said, as serious as always.

She looked to the guard first. "I expect better work from you, Colonel. This is a delicate situation. We can't risk anything like this happening in the presence of his majesty."

The colonel didn't lower his face or glance away. "Understood."

Rilv turned to Lanek. "I told you to behave yourself. You didn't."

"He's from the *Brotherhood*," Lanek said through clenched teeth. "He *killed* Suran!"

"If you don't calm down now, I will force you to leave," Rilv said.

"I didn't ask to come here *in the first place*," Lanek said.

"I assumed you would have an interest in bringing down the Brotherhood once and for all," Rilv said. "If I am mistaken, then you would not be of any help in our mission anyways. In which case, you should leave."

"Of course I wish to put an end to the Brotherhood," Lanek said. "What does it look like I'm doing?"

"Lynx has been assisting us for some time now, working as a double agent," Rilv said. "He has supplied valuable information regarding Augurc Shire's experiments and ambitions."

"I wouldn't believe him," Lanek said. "He could be—"

"Enough," Rilv said, widening her eyes. She held her piercing gaze on Lanek for a few seconds, forcing him to stop in mid-sentence.

She slowly lowered her eyelids until she wore her default expression once again. She looked over to Lynx and frowned. "I have placed a great deal of trust in you, Lynx. And yet you have betrayed a bit of that trust. Did you not agree to give up all of your weapons upon entering the castle?"

There was a long silence.

"I asked a question, Lynx."

"I agreed," a muffled voice behind the mask responded.

"The fact you had a knife hidden behind your mask supports my opinion you should give up the mask."

"The mask stays," Lynx said. "You won't get any more information about the Brotherhood's movements if my identity is given away."

"Understood, but I must require your cooperation in return," Rilv said.

She folded her arms and glanced back to the colonel. "Unbind them."

The man looked uncertain.

"Lynx will sit between us, in three seats furthest from the king," Rilv said. "I trust you and your subordinates will keep any harm from befalling anyone during this meeting."

"Yes, we will keep a vigilant eye on the premises." The colonel took the rapier and knife off the ground, and proceeded to loosen the vines so Lanek and Lynx could stand. Once they were up, the colonel caused the vines to return into his green Nexi stone.

"I demand the most orderly of conduct from you both," Rilv said, glancing from Lanek to Lynx.

Lanek couldn't stand to even look at Lynx. The very idea that Rilv and the royal court was working with the one who killed Suran... It was the most outrageous proposition he could have ever imagined. Every fiber of Lanek's being wanted to strangle Lynx to death right here and now—but he knew that would just get him detained. Lynx wasn't an easy person to kill, and there was no telling how Rilv would lash out against Lanek.

How had my weapon slipped from my grasp? he wondered. *I was going to kill him... After all these years, this is the time and place he appears? I could have avenged Suran's death...*

For now Lanek acknowledged the wisest course of action was to cooperate with Rilv. He needed to find out what lies Lynx was feeding the royal court, and what Rilv's plans entailed regarding the Brotherhood's destruction.

But there was a fourth person Rilv said was to blame for the present circumstances, Lanek recalled. The head servant looked to a far wall, not looking at anyone in particular.

"Perhaps all of this could have been avoided though, had I taken the proper measures to ensure a clash would not break out between you two," she said. "I was not certain Lynx was going to attend, and I failed to recall the animosity Lanek held toward him. As such, I am to blame for this disturbance."

She turned to the council seated at the table and bowed her head. "The sincerest of apologies. This will not happen again."

Lanek wondered if anyone intended to respond, but the room remained entirely silent for several seconds.

Rilv looked to Lynx and pointed to a chair. "Take a seat. I will sit to your left. The colonel will sit to your right."

The three sat where Rilv intended, and Lanek returned to his spot on the other side, between Kitoh and an elderly aristocrat with a gray goatee and slicked-back gray and black hair.

"I was worried this would turn into a dull meeting," the man said. "That was a splendid performance, Sir Elf."

"It's Lanek, and I'm not a duke."

"Ah, I didn't recognize you, so I wasn't certain what it is you do."

"I build air ships," Lanek said. "And I don't forget who my enemies are."

"Yes, I was surprised to see a Brotherhood member here too," the man said, scratching his chin. "I suspect Head Servant Rilv will explain everything soon enough."

All but three seats were filled now—the one at the end, and a seat to each side of it. The conversations around the table died down once the doors opened once more.

The king and two captains of the castle guard entered the room. Everyone stood up immediately.

There was a look of extreme disinterest on the king's face. He was certainly dressed like a king, with purple and white robes, a black cape, and a thin crown of golden vines and ruby flowers clasped across his forehead—but the way he walked across the room and to the seat at the end of the table... The young man didn't strike Lanek as very kingly. He had black curly hair, light green eyes, and a rather small frame for one his age.

Once the king sat down, the two captains of the guard sat in the seats to either side of him, followed by everyone else at the table.

"Good, everyone's here," the king said. He had a slight country accent, though this didn't surprise Lanek. Sir Enlia Tehns had grown up in a small hamlet in the east most his life—it likely made him stick out amongst the nobility in Setar, most of whom were either from cities or country estates in the west.

"Let's deal with the most pressing business first," the king went on. He looked down to Lynx. "Where will the Brotherhood strike next?"

"Leading members of the Brotherhood have been collaborating with a group of elite vampires," Lynx said. "Plans are being made to incite an insurrection in Istal. One of Augurc's top experiments will likely assist in the operation."

"When will this transpire?" Rilv asked.

"In a matter of days, I imagine," Lynx said. "I was not able to attend the actual meeting where this operation was discussed—my information comes from second-hand sources."

"You're certain Istal is the Brotherhood's next target though?" the king asked.

Lynx nodded. "Augurc has been anxious to gain allies amongst vampires for some time now. This will likely be the Brotherhood's largest operation since Delkol's attack on Setar."

"Why would Augurc be so willing to engage in such a large-scale project for a group of vampire elites?" Rilv asked. "How does it benefit the Brotherhood?"

"Brotherhood losses will be minimal," Lynx said. "Most of the combatants will be vampires, and the brunt of the work will be performed by one of Augurc's most powerful experiments."

From what Lanek understood, there were a number of people experimented on, essentially turning them into one-man armies—or so the rumors went. Several villages and small towns had been decimated over the last couple years, each occurrence deemed the work of the Brotherhood. In some instances, it was said to be the work of a single super-soldier.

The king clasped his hands together and frowned. "And then Augurc will gain the trust and assistance of a league of powerful vampires."

A man with dark brown hair and a green suit leaned forward, placing the fingertips of his white gloves together. Lanek felt this man was an operative who worked for Rilv.

"Four days ago, a caravan approaching the Refe Forest north of Istal was entirely massacred," the man said. "Distant witnesses only noted a handful of people who walked away from the scene. I believe this experiment spoken of was among them."

"Surely the caravan had guards," the king said. "Were they that helpless against Augurc's experiment?"

"Most Brotherhood operations of late have involved very few members," the agent said. "Ever since Delkol's war, the Brotherhood has dwindled in numbers, as support from the Shire ruling family continues to lessen with each passing month."

"Support which was never supposed to exist at all," the king said. "Not that we can expect the Shire Kingdom to keep its word."

"The Shire government is in shambles," an aristocrat spoke up. "They're barely managing to maintain power over their own people. With Augurc essentially king in name only, it's only a matter of time before the Shire family cuts off all ties from him. They're in no position to risk war with our kingdom."

"It seems increasingly apparent," the agent said, "that Augurc Shire has little interest in continuing his late brother's goals. The Brotherhood conducts acts of terrorism, but none of these procedures have gained the Shire Kingdom anything."

The old aristocrat beside Lanek spoke up. "Fear tactics. Or perhaps Augurc simply wishes to test the power of his experiments. Regardless, the Shire Kingdom will need to pay for the lives lost in our lands, and in surrounding territories."

"The Shire family's ruling council will always deny support of the Brotherhood," the king said. "Threats can be made, but troops are spread thin as it is, trying to keep this entire kingdom guarded. Launching an attack on the Shire Kingdom would be costly, and do little to stop the problem. In fact, war would likely increase the Brotherhood's numbers."

"Operatives have been tracking several groups within the Brotherhood," Rilv said. "And with the information Lynx has supplied, I feel we can begin a number of counter-operations to finally bring an end to the Brotherhood."

The king raised a hand. "First, is there any more information you can provide us, Lynx? Are there any other operations you know of within the Brotherhood's ranks?"

"There are always more being planned, but I don't know of any others that will be staged in the near future."

"Regarding Istal," Rilv said, "I have the means to warn a reliable ally of the situation. With any luck, a proper defense can be established before the Brotherhood attacks."

"But even with assistance from rebelling vampires," an aristocrat with a thin mustache said, "how could the Brotherhood hope to bring down Istal—the strongest vampire city in the world?"

"All I know is a powerful experiment will be deployed," Lynx said.

"And Augurc's experiments should not be taken lightly," Rilv said. "He has the ability to wield the Elpis, and with half of it at his disposal, there is no telling just how much power he is able to place in his test subjects."

"It's been five years since operatives have gone on the hunt for Augurc and his pieces of the Elpis," the king said. "What progress can we expect to see on this front?"

"The Elpis Research Team has made great progress over the past month," Rilv said. "Based on their findings, I have formulated a plan that will return the full Elpis to the Fiefs Kingdom and bring an end to the Brotherhood's destructive acts." She looked to Kitoh and pointed a hand toward him. "Kitoh will share with us all his team has concluded."

Kitoh unrolled a scroll and placed small metal cubes on each of the corners to hold the paper down for everyone to see. Everyone at the table leaned in a bit for a better look. From what Lanek could tell, this was a sketch of some kind of device involving the two pieces of the Elpis held in the castle. The glowing stones rested on a small triangular pedestal, in front of which lay a map of the world. There were long needles sticking out of various points on the map, which was surrounded with silver rectangles placed in seemingly random locations.

"We can not utilize the power of the Elpis," Kitoh said, "but we have created a device that analyzes the Nexi energy naturally emanating from the stones. These metal blocks contain pieces of Nexi stones placed in such a way that pins can be guided to specific spots on a map. These points on the map show us where unnaturally high levels of Nexi energy can be found."

Kitoh pointed to two spots on the map—one in Fiefs Kingdom, the other in Shire Kingdom. "The strongest Nexi energies are found here in Setar, and in this remote locale in the Shire Kingdom. We can expect these to be where we could find the two halves of the Elpis."

Once this information had sunk in, Kitoh pointed to several spots on the map. "We have been able to determine five other locations with a particularly strong level of Nexi magic. Not as strong as the Elpis fragments, but much more powerful than even the rarest of Nexi stones."

"What are they?" an aristocrat asked.

The elf woman Lanek identified as the linguist spoke up. "Based on my research of ancient texts, it's likely these are what were called *Haders*. They were created centuries ago, designed to be used by specialists in order to fight against wicked rulers who used the Elpis."

"Anti-Elpis weaponry," the operative mused.

Kitoh nodded. "When many of them are gathered together, it is believed their power would rival that of the full Elpis."

"I've never heard of them," an aristocrat said.

"Information about the Haders is difficult to come by," the linguist said. "Most texts that mention them are either in an ancient elvish or eigni language. It would appear the minds behind the Haders' inception didn't want the world at large to know of these weapons. Most are likely lost, but there may be people out there who have one. I imagine they wouldn't want people to find out the source of their power."

Rilv placed a Nexi stone on the table—it was the purple and blue one Lanek saw her with when he fought against Lynx. "Our goal over the coming weeks will be to collect as many Haders as we can. Once I managed to obtain this one, Kitoh's device was able to pinpoint more precise locations of all the rest. I will create a team to gather them for the sake of combating Augurc's Elpis-powered experiments and ultimately retrieving the full Elpis."

"How will the Elpis help now?" the aristocrat beside Lanek asked. "There is nobody left in our nation who can use it."

"I intend to destroy it," Rilv said. "There may come a time when relations of the Fiefs royal line will be able to use the Elpis, but King Enlia Tehns Fiefs has asked that we find a way to destroy the Elpis for good."

"The Haders may provide the means to do so," Kitoh said. "Once we have obtained more of them, we will be able to conduct better tests on both them and the Elpis."

The operative pointed to Rilv's stone. "So this is a Hader, then. What does it do?"

"Telekinesis," Rilv said. "This particular Hader allows me to move objects through mental willpower."

Lanek assumed this was how his rapier flew from his hand, then. Rilv had used her Hader to force it from his grasp—and had also managed to pull the knife from Lynx's grasp at the same time.

"There is likely a cost associated with it," Rilv said, "so I will only use it when absolutely necessary. The Elpis fragments gave their users Nexi poisoning, and though the Haders are not broken, they hold a volatile power."

"So you wish to obtain all the Haders," Lanek said. "How do you plan to go about doing that?"

"I will lead a small team to each location Kitoh's device points us to," Rilv said. "We will act in such a way that the Brotherhood will not not learn of the operation."

"Is the Brotherhood searching for the Haders as well?" Lanek asked.

"Haders have never been brought up amongst the Brotherhood's ranks," Lynx said. "Augurc will rely on the Elpis and his experiments. I doubt he'll want to search for the Haders and thin his troops out even further."

"There is a town in the Shire Kingdom," Rilv said, "where there are two Haders stones. Though the Brotherhood may not be involved, there is likely someone who has these two Haders."

"Then there are a couple others spread out across the Fiefs Kingdom," Kitoh said. "One deep in the Endim Mountains, and another at the port city Limbo. There may be others, but we haven't been able to locate them."

"So there's at least five of these stones," Lanek said, "and Rilv already has one of them. How did you get a hold of it?"

"The same way we will get a hold of all the others," Rilv said. "By any means necessary."

Lanek didn't like the way Rilv answered this. Not only did she avoid a direct answer, but it implied she really was willing to go to any length for these stones. This wasn't entirely surprising, but he was hesitant to have any part in it. He gathered it was Rilv's intention to have him fly the team around in his airship, which would go along well with what Rilv said when he arrived—how he had "passed the test." Rilv wanted to obtain all the Haders as quickly as possible, before rumor of the operation spread across the continent. If hundreds of people started searching for the Haders, reliable information would be harder to come by—and the less the Brotherhood knew, the less they would be able to interfere. And the less they would be able to prepare for Rilv's strike against Augurc. Thanks to Kitoh's device, they now knew where Augurc was in the world—it was likely that he kept his Elpis fragments with him at all times.

"What if other people already have these Haders?" Lanek asked. "I doubt they'll give the stones up freely."

"We will be willing to negotiate," Rilv said, "but as you say, it is unlikely they will exchange such power for anything. Chances are we will have to take every Hader by force."

Lanek lowered his head a little and stared down at the table. He didn't want to get caught up in dangerous missions like this—not after what happened the last time he worked for Rilv. He and Suran nearly died on several occasions, and in the end Suran *was* killed.

Rilv continued. "Because of the danger involved, I will lead a small but capable team. Lanek will pilot an airship—the fastest one in the kingdom."

Lanek frowned. "You're not even going to ask me to help?"

"Feel free to say *no* if you are not up to the task," Rilv said.

Lanek stared at her a few seconds. On one hand this was a chance for him to help bring down the Brotherhood... The organization that brought his sister's death was still alive and at large. Shouldn't he do everything he could to bring it down? But on the other hand... he had doubts in trusting Rilv. She was clearly for the Fiefs Kingdom, and likely willing to give up her very life for the royal line. But how far was she truly willing to go for all this? Lanek didn't like the idea of relying on ancient magical stones again, or the idea of making an enemy of every single person or organization that possessed a Hader.

How much of this world am I going to have to fight before this is through? Lanek thought.

"Right," he said. "I'll help how I can." It wasn't like he really could deny the request... especially right in front of the king.

"Good," Rilv said. "You will pilot the airship, and Kitoh will accompany us."

"Me?" Kitoh asked.

"Yes," Rilv said. "You will be able to continue your tests with the Elpis and Haders as we travel. I also know both you and Lanek are capable fighters. To round off the group, I will ask that Lynx assist us."

Lanek nearly stood up to yell an objection, but Lynx beat him to it.

"What? I can't be away from the Brotherhood that long. They will suspect treason."

"Sit down and calm yourself," Rilv said. "I know what your goals are, and I intend to help you fulfill them. In return, you will assist us in putting an end to the Brotherhood."

Lynx sat back down but didn't respond.

"This is a bad idea," Lanek said. "He could stab us all in the back. If he's a Brotherhood member, he might be an experiment himself. Just look at his mask! He can't be entirely sane."

Rilv raised a hand and glared at Lanek once more. "I understand *all* the risks, Lanek. Even those you are not aware of. I intend to keep an eye on Lynx, and I imagine you will as well."

"If it were up to me, he'd be dead," Lanek said. "This very instant."

"You will have to cooperate with him," Rilv said. "For the sake of obtaining all the Haders, we will need to enter the Shire Kingdom. Lynx has information we need, and will be an invaluable help in matters concerning the Brotherhood."

"He will turn against us," Lanek said.

"If he does, you can kill him," Rilv said. "But I imagine Lynx will have no reason to do so."

"I have no intention to," Lynx said, "but I don't appreciate being thrown into an operation like this without warning."

"We can't risk the Brotherhood learning of this plan," Rilv said. "If we manage to obtain enough Haders quickly, we may begin work to bring down Augurc once and for all. At that point you will be free to live however you wish."

"I expect so," Lynx said.

Just looking at him as he said this filled Lanek with rage. The very idea that Rilv wanted to cooperate with this man... and then expect Lanek to cooperate with him! It was incredulous. Unthinkable.

"This sounds dangerous," Kitoh said. "There is no telling what the other Haders are capable of. It may be best if we just continue our studies of the

Elpis, search for a way to counter Augurc's power through the fragments in our possession."

"Augurc's power is spread amongst a number of experiments capable of easily killing a hundred people in minutes," Rilv said. "He hasn't quite reached the point where he could launch a full invasion on the Fiefs Kingdom, and I would like to keep him from getting there. The hit-and-run procedures of the Brotherhood are bad enough as it is. It is my duty to serve the royal line in every way possible, and I don't intend to just let the kingdom suffer increasing casualties like this."

Kitoh nodded, but looked away from Rilv while doing so.

"Sounds like you have your team," the king said. "If there's no further points to share with me, I suggest you head to your first destination. I will discuss further items of business with the rest of the council."

"Very well," Rilv said. She stood up, then looked to Kitoh, Lanek, Lynx, and the colonel. "Lynx will walk with me. Lanek will walk with the colonel, behind us. Kitoh will walk between us."

Everyone got up and left the room as Rilv instructed. Lanek tried to think of a way out of this crazy mission—and a way to kill Lynx—and a way to bring down the Brotherhood.

He didn't know what to think at all, it seemed. He couldn't believe he was being asked again to search for ancient Nexi stones of unspeakable power.

Was this path going to bring him even more sadness? Or could it bring him the peace and contentment deep down he was searching for?

•

Augurc walked through the town, listening in on every passing conversation. There were only about a thousand people who lived there, but many travelers passed down the wide road that ran down its center. Nobody paid him attention, and thanks to the light rain, he was able to conceal his scarred face and Nexi-covered arms with a hooded cloak.

Nobody had mentioned her yet. Nobody spoke of a disaster. Nobody even had bad news to talk about.

This was precisely what Augurc wanted to hear.

He walked the entire length of the village, and then walked back. The preset meeting spot was in a small grove a hundred or so meters past a turnip and pumpkin farm just outside of the town.

He was pleased to find Project VI standing atop of a tree stump, waiting for him. There were only a couple bloodstains on her silver and black uniform— her work was getting cleaner.

"I didn't hear anyone speak of you," Augurc said. "Or of a murder."

"They're all dead," Project VI said. "There were no witnesses."

"And the bodies?" Augurc asked.

"Buried in the ditch," Project VI said. She stared straight through Augurc's eyes—it was as if she didn't even recognize he was there... As if she spoke to a wall.

From what Augurc could tell, there was no sound of alarm in the entire town. No commotion whatsoever.

All while twenty select people were murdered.

How long would it take before people realized what had happened? Augurc wondered. Surely by tonight, people would wonder where their husband went, where their wife went, where their child went, where their friend went, where their neighbor went. What would the authorities think when they suddenly realize twenty completely unrelated people went missing?

Would they ever find the bodies?

Augurc kept his eyes on Project VI's. "Follow me."

He walked on down the trail away from the town. Though he couldn't hear her footsteps, Augurc knew Project VI was following him. It had taken some time to make her obedient, but through the power of the Elpis, the vampire's emotions were guided just as Augurc wished.

"Your next test will be in Istal," Augurc said.

He said nothing more. He did not need to feel proud of his experiment. There was no need to thank her. Her performance met his expectations, and that was all he needed.

If only everyone in the world was this beautifully predictable.

•

Hidden amidst the shadows of the dim mangroves, Borely shut his eyes and listened for the approaching monster. Somewhere out there, Nivakil was watching, and Borely intended to show the old vampire his own tried and true method of taking down an enemy.
All the woods around him were silent, motionless. All Borely could hear was the slow beat of his own heart, the hallow air sifting through his lungs. After a couple minutes of sheer concentration, he realized his breathing had slowed down far more than he was used to. He was breathing at the unnaturally slow and quiet rate of a vampire in the middle of a hunt.

Breathe normally, Borely ordered himself. The last thing he wanted was to start acting like a vampire, even if he technically was one now.

It had been a rough five years, ever since the culmination of the grand battle between Terico Fiefs and Delkol Shire. To keep Borely from dying at Augurc Shire's hand, Areo injected her vampiric venom into Borely's bloodstream, effectively turning him into a vampire. On one hand Borely was thankful, given that he would have died otherwise. But on the other hand, Areo had condemned him to a long, miserable life as a vampire.

The beings who killed his parents. Who turned his brother mad. Who forced him to kill his own brother. Who took away everything that was good in his life.

Just make the best of it, Borely thought. *Show everyone that I don't have to succumb to their methods. I can still keep being myself. I don't have to stoop to their level.*

Nivakil—the mentor who had taught Areo to fight—and his other pupil Jenba, were quick to take Borely out of the scene of the battle while Borely underwent the painful transformation of becoming a vampire. Then before Borely knew it, he was being carried on Jenba's back, taking a dark forest road toward the vampiric city of Istal. Nivakil was determined to help Borely transition to the life of a vampire, if only because it would have been what his pupil Areo would have wanted him to do. Admittedly, Borely recognized later on that he probably would have died had the old man not force-fed vials of blood down Borely's throat each day. Still, at the time, the very thought of drinking blood was a living nightmare.

There was no helping it, though. Borely couldn't help but acknowledge he had become the very thing he hated, but he was determined now to not let his transformation bring him down. He wasn't going to let the vampires win.

He heard something. The sound was barely audible, but he could tell there was something out there. It was something he felt more than heard. Was this monster approaching him, or slipping away deeper into the darkness of the thick, leafy mangroves?

Borely leaned out and slowly searched through the dense branches and undergrowth of the forest. His eyes could see well in the dark, and could spot minute details from great distances away. He noticed the slightest of movements, far to his right. Or rather, he felt there was a movement. Looking at the remote trees, he couldn't see anything out of the ordinary. Perhaps it was just a faint breeze. It could also have been Nivakil, though Borely doubted he'd be able to spot the old man—Nivakil could probably hide in an empty room if he wanted to.

Maintaining focus on the spot he sensed movement in, Borely's vision grew a little clearer, a little stronger. It wasn't something he liked to admit, but a vampire's senses were incredible, especially in tense situations such as this. Somehow Borely's body was able to heighten its abilities when it sensed danger... It only reassured him that he was on the right track. There was definitely a monster out there.

Borely glanced a bit to the left, guided by an intuition that kicked in during situations like these. A tree moved, camouflaged amongst the other trees. Branches moved in trees ahead. Borely sprinted silently toward the shuffling in the distance, convinced this was the prey Nivakil assigned to him. The old man hadn't told him what he'd be facing, but Borely was determined to take it down his own way, rather than through methods a vampire would rely on.

Careful to make as little noise as possible, Borely took long, quiet steps. He glanced up and down, keeping an eye on the faraway movement and on the ground ahead of him, cautious to keep from stepping on twigs and piles of leaves that would give away his location to the monster.

There wasn't much Borely could do to hide his scent, but if he was quick enough he'd be able to surprise the creature and land a finishing blow before it could fight back.

He spotted movement amidst the mangroves just ahead of him. A tree moved a few meters to his left. Borely slipped behind a tree and peered to the side. His heart pounded madly—he still hadn't quite seen what the creature entailed, but it was suddenly a lot closer to him than he expected.

He caught sight of a massive earthworm sliding silently across the forest floor, slipping between trees at a remarkable speed. It was long—at least twenty meters long, though it was hard to tell with it slipping away so quickly. In seconds it vanished amidst the trees, its dark segmented flesh blending perfectly with the dirt and leaves. The creature had to be at least a few meters wide and tall, and though it took Borely a few seconds to realize it, the beast apparently had thin trees growing out of its back. The mangroves Borely thought he had seen move were just the thick leafy branches sprouting out of the giant earthworm.

Not wanting to lose it completely, Borely ran in the direction the earthworm took off toward. The monster hadn't noticed him hiding just a few meters away—Borely felt certain he'd be able to land a good hit on it from behind. But would the thick, fleshy creature die that easily? He had no idea where the vitals of such a creature would be. His best bet was to pound the beast's brains in, though Borely didn't know what means of defense the monster had. He was up against something much larger than he expected to face. It was probably Nivakil's hope that Borely would feel it necessary to rely on his claws and fangs. Borely didn't intend to fight the vampire way, however.

He ran as hard as he could, searching through the trees for any more shuffling branches, moving trees, or even any wide impressions in the dirt. Strangely, this earthworm didn't seem to leave any tracks—almost as if it were hovering a few centimeters above the ground.

Borely pushed himself faster, shifting his focus to distant sounds of rustling leaves to guide him in the right direction. He finally caught sight of movement amongst the trees, then forced himself down a path straight to the creature.

Just as he arrived within a few meters of the beast, the giant earthworm turned its lumbering body toward Borely. It had somehow sensed him, despite all of Borely's efforts to approach as quietly as he could manage. Suddenly the beast's faceless head was upon Borely, far faster than he expected. A bloody mouth ripped open, as if cut into and torn apart by force. The creature did not scream, but dozens of long red teeth emerged from all sides of the opening simultaneously.

Borely leaped forward as high as he could muster, crashing straight into the earthworm's head, just above the gaping maw. With his metal-gloved fists charged with orange Nexi energy, Borely slammed a full-powered punch against the beast's head. The creature folded back slightly as Borely rebounded off of the earthworm's thick, hard flesh. The beast immediately sprung back forward, and Borely timed his second punch into the side of the earthworm's head, keeping it from chomping Borely in half.

Borely landed back on the ground as the earthworm reeled back a few meters. It still didn't scream—it seemed incapable of making noise, strangely. How much it was damaged, Borely couldn't tell. For all he could see, the earthworm might not have even been bruised.

The trees on the creature's back—at least a dozen of them, perhaps, though it was hard to tell—each grew a little taller. The earthworm bent its middle upward, forcing the trees to stand higher, like the arched fur of a stretching cat. With a deafening series of explosive cracks, each of the trees bent in half, folding down like the arms of a praying mantis.

The giant beast slid toward Borely, silent once more. With only a second to act, Borely leaped up the branches of a nearby mangrove and turned back toward the earthworm. The beast snaked up to Borely, running its teeth through impending branches. Borely jumped past the worm's head. At the same time, the beast jabbed the folded half of a tree from its back toward him. Focusing on the Nexi energy within his fist, Borely punched through the tree, snapping it in half in a burst of sharp wood chips. Borely landed on the earthworm's back, careful to keep his footing gripped on the creature's segmented body. Immediately another folded tree on the worm's back swung down for him. Borely dodged, powered an orange Nexi, then punched into the base of the tree, knocking the whole thing off the earthworm's back.

The creature turned sharply, forcing Borely to leap away before being thrown off. A tree from the earthworm's back leered toward him. Borely jumped back, and the tree slammed against the ground. Just as Borely landed, the front of the earthworm turned and lunged toward him. Borely swiveled in place and readied another punch. He slammed a Nexi-powered fist against what he would have called the worm's chin, but the exhausting attack did little to slow the beast down. The front of the worm flopped up a bit, but in mere moments it was lunging toward Borely again.

He turned to run, but was stopped by a folded tree swinging in front of him, reaching down from the worm's back. Too tired to power his fists again, Borely activated the dark blue Nexi on the metal band across his forehead. A sharp stream of water pushed aside the thin tree, giving Borely a path to escape the worm's fang-filled maw.

This is precisely what Nivakil wants, Borely thought. *He wants me to get frustrated with this beast—one that's seemingly impossible to kill with my Nexi stones. He wants me to tear it apart with my claws, or to sink my fangs and disable it by injected venom into its bloodstream. But I'm not going to do it. I'm going to kill this beast my own way.*

The train of thought gave Borely an idea. He leaped against a mangrove and back onto the earthworm's back. A folded tree swung for Borely, which he dodged and quickly ran past. He couldn't afford to wear himself out from overusing his Nexi, so he barreled past the next tree, his innate senses helping him know when to pause and when to run.

The front of the worm turned again and arced toward Borely. He jumped backwards off the rampaging creature, facing the giant crimson mouth of the beast's looming head.

Borely landed on the ground and powered all the energy he could into the orange Nexi of his right metal fist.

"Come on!" Borely said, staring straight into the jaws of the monster.

Like the crack of a whip, the huge creature swung down and snapped its teeth for Borely's head. Borely stepped to the side and leaned back at the same moment, then swept a punch against one of the beast's thickest protruding fangs. The bloody ivory burst from the creature's mouth, but it did not roar in pain. Instead it turned to Borely and lunged again. Borely dived forward and rolled on the ground. The earthworm passed over him, and Borely snatched up the freed tooth in the process.

Borely leaped to his feet, dodged the swing of a folded tree, then slammed the sharpened end of the earthworm's fang into the fleshy side of the creature. Borely had to use the power of both his orange Nexi to exert the necessary strength to penetrate the beast's tough, dense skin. The earthworm slid several meters in the process, and Borely managed to slice down a great length of the creature before another tree jabbed down for him. Blood poured from the creature, but as far as Borely could tell he hadn't managed to inflict any serious damage on the beast. He needed to jab the fang into a vital region somehow.

The earthworm swung around again. Borely ran straight to the beast's head, clenching the worm's large, bloody fang tight. Faster than he expected, the creature flew forward, and in an instant the beast's gaping mouth was upon him. Borely leaped straight into the dark opening, avoiding all the creature's jagged teeth.

Once landing inside the worm's throat, Borely immediately slammed the fang into the top of the roof of the creature's insides. He powered the orange Nexi stones in his fists in order to push into the skin and through to the other side, then slide the fang forward to cut further down the creature. Still the beast was silent, but Borely forced himself to keep slicing down the length of the worm from the inside, tearing through the top of the beast and the roots of the trees within it.

The giant earthworm ripped apart, spewing all manner of liquids and organs in the process. Borely kept pushing himself until he reached the end of the worm, leaving its dissected remains a strewn, ghastly mess amidst fallen, bloodstained trees and branches.

Borely dropped the large fang and walked away from the grisly scene. He almost stumbled and fell to the ground, exhausted from his repeated use of the orange Nexi stones, but managed to keep standing when Nivakil arrived.

The vampire looked to be in his late fifties or so, but was likely hundreds of years old, as far as Borely knew. The old man was short, dressed in black, and had thick, dark rings beneath his yellow eyes. He wore a strange black hat with golden letters—a flat-topped, triangular hat that held some cultural significance to Nivakil, Borely imagined.

"So that's how you're going to be," Nivakil said. "Stubborn to the bitter end."

"I do things my way," Borely said. "You should know that by now."

Nivakil turned his head and stared blankly out toward the monster's torn-up corpse. Though the vampire was blind, he could still tell where anything was with his other senses. It was this devotion to hearing, smell, and touch that gave Areo and Jenba a unique style of fighting. Borely had gleaned some of this style from Nivakil as well, though he did everything he could to keep from using methods that were specifically vampiric in nature.

"Far too stubborn," Nivakil said. "Even more stubborn than Areo."

"Hey, I killed the monster like you wanted," Borely said.

"You killed it, but not like I wanted," Nivakil muttered.

Borely continued, "And there's no comparing me to Areo when stubbornness is concerned."

"I suppose you're right," Nivakil said, suddenly turning to face Borely. The old vampire's eyes stared straight through him. "Areo's stubbornness at least had some sense to it. Your stubbornness is only a hindrance."

Borely didn't care to respond. He didn't even wish to think about Areo right now. Not unless they were finally going to do something about her.

"You look like you're about to pass out," Nivakil said. Before Borely could retort that Nivakil couldn't see anything, the old vampire continued, "Go drink some of that monster's blood."

"No thanks," Borely said. "I'm fine."

"You're not fine," Nivakil said. "Any vampire with a lick of sense would know to drink some of the prey's blood at the end of an exhausting monster hunt."

"I don't need to," Borely said. "I'll recover with my own strength, like a normal person would."

"You're a vampire, Borely," Nivakil said. "You have to drink blood."

"I will when I need to." Borely could never stand it when conversations with Nivakil went this direction, as they so often did. Of course Borely knew he had to drink blood—he would die otherwise. But he wasn't going to seek out opportunities to drink blood. He was never going to let himself enjoy it. It was his intent to only drink blood out of necessity, and never out of any vampiric desire.

"Do you know why I've been training you all this time?" Nivakil asked.

"For Areo's sake," Borely said.

"And why have you been training?"

"For Areo's sake. Which is why—"

"Why you should follow my instructions to the letter!" Nivakil yelled.

"It's not getting me any closer to saving Areo though, if you haven't noticed." Borely threw his arms out. "We should be out there, looking for her. We should always be out there."

"You and Jenba don't have Rite Nexi yet, and wandering aimlessly won't help anyone," Nivakil said. "Your last dozen excursions certainly didn't turn anything up, and left you near-dead every time. Lucky thing I was able to track you down and drag you back here to Istal."

"At least I've been trying!" Borely said. "She's out there somewhere, in the Brotherhood's clutches."

"We don't even know if she's alive still," Nivakil said. "There's no reason to assume she is still alive. And if she is still alive, we have no idea where to find her. Augurc is not nearly as showy as his older brother."

Borely couldn't stand the fact nobody could figure out where Augurc's whereabouts were. There was nothing Borely wanted more than to beat Augurc to a bloody pulp and rescue Areo from whatever experiments he had performed on her. And then perhaps beat Areo up too, for turning Borely into a vampire. And then thank her for saving his life. And then...

Borely wasn't sure. He couldn't really decide how to feel about her, especially when so much time had passed since he last saw her. The days were passing by quickly, and though five years didn't mean much to a vampire, it still felt miserable. Just thinking of what the Brotherhood could have done to Areo was infuriating. Was she locked up in some cage somewhere? Borely wanted to find it right now. Just break it open and get Areo out of whatever prison or facility she was being held up in. He was ready to take down every Brotherhood member that stood in his way.

"If she is still alive, we will find her," Nivakil said. "We must go about things intelligently, however. The Brotherhood is not a menace to be trifled with. They may be fewer in numbers, but Augurc has made up for the lack of quantity with quality. These super-soldiers only grow more powerful with each passing year, thanks to his experiments."

Borely could remember fighting some of Augurc's men five years ago, and during some of his nighttime searches for Areo in subsequent years. For whatever reason, many of them never responded to his questions, even when they were maimed and severely injured. Instead, they would just keep on fighting. The others—those who didn't undergo experiments to their minds—were too difficult for Borely to defeat, their fighting skills heightened in other ways.

It was a strange, unpredictable world now, and everything about it had become foreign to Borely. Even himself.

"I won't give up on Areo," Borely said. "I don't care if it's unlikely she's still alive. I'll find her, and find a way to bring her back here safely."

"She may be an entirely different person from what you remember," Nivakil said. "She may not even remember you anymore."

Borely thought this over for a bit. What if Areo was turned into a soldier for the Brotherhood as well? Would he be able to fight her?

"I'm going to save her," Borely said. "And I'll save her my own way."

"You may not get the choice," Nivakil said. "Are you willing to do anything for her?"

Borely didn't respond, and Nivakil didn't push him to answer right away.

•

Once the monster's blood was gathered in a set of vials Nivakil had brought, Borely staggered through the forest, pushing himself to get back to the city before Jenba's fight began. Jenba was probably Borely's only friend in Istal, and the only one who seemed to understand Borely's desire to rescue Areo. The vampire trained hard each day to prepare for the Rite this year, his one chance to obtain the transformative Nexi stone that would allow him to freely travel the world in the daytime.

Borely hoped Jenba would win, of course, but it was difficult to say how great Jenba's chances were. Jenba was a hard worker, the kind of fighter who never gave up, but he didn't have the sort of talent Nivakil or Areo had. Borely even thought he could take on Jenba, despite the advantage Jenba held in his many extra years of training. Though Jenba looked to be in his forties, he had lived at least twice that length in time—though that still kept him younger than Areo. Borely wasn't sure if Jenba had ever gone into hibernation though, like Areo had.

The light of the small white Nexi stones hanging from the mangroves' branches started to grow a little brighter. Not bright enough to hurt his eyes, but it was now quite a bit easier to see. The path widened, flattened, and became more stable beneath Borely's feet. The main road to the city didn't get much traffic, given that Istal was a city of vampires, but it was in much better condition than the surrounding thin forest trails.

Borely dropped off the vials of thick monster blood at his home—a small wooden one-room building he shared with Jenba. It was little more than a couple cots, a desk, and some shelves, but Borely was used to small living quarters back when he was a sailor. This house in Istal was the only place that gave him any feeling of nostalgia, though at times it left him longing for the sea. It had been so long since he had stood on a ship, feeling the sway of the ocean beneath his feet. He missed the salty air, the crisp winds, and the cry of passing gulls. There had never been much glamorous about his life as a sailor, but it was what he was meant to be. It was right for him to be traveling the seas.

Not living in a city of vampires. The beings who ruined his life. Now he couldn't even feel the warmth of the sun, or view the beauty of a sunrise or sunset. He was trapped in a cold, dark hell, where not even the light of day was real. Just the dim, artificial glow of ghostly Nexi stones.

He placed the set of vials on a shelf, alongside a few other sets he and Jenba had filled over the last week. Borely had to admit to himself he was very thirsty, but he wasn't going to let himself start drinking blood every time he felt like it. He could hold out a little longer. Perhaps after Jenba's fight, he would have a vial.

Borely pushed himself away from the shelf and walked briskly out the door. The longer he looked at the blood, the more he knew he'd desire it. It was a part of his nature now, and he hated every bit of it.

I've got to get out of this place, Borely thought, walking down the city street. Though even if he did escape Istal again, that wouldn't free him from being a vampire. He would still need blood to live. What if one day he went insane, like his brother had? Would he start latching onto the necks of passers-by in the woods, killing innocents, destroying families?

He wished Areo was still around. Nivakil and Jenba did their best to help Borely out, but they only did so because that's what Areo would have wanted them to do. If Areo was still with Borely, he would have felt a little more at ease about all this. Perhaps because he had known her for a while before he was turned into a vampire? Perhaps because they had been through a crazy adventure together? Perhaps because she was the one who made the difficult decision of making him a vampire?

Perhaps because he still liked her. It was hard to say. It was hard to know.

There were a few other vampires in the area heading toward the outdoor arena where the Rite took place each year. Istal wasn't a huge city—it was more of a large town, if anything, especially when compared to the likes of Vursa or Setar. The arena only held about a thousand vampires, and it was one of the biggest events the city held each year.

Borely passed a series of wooden shops and a mansion made of stone, though obscured by the tall, tangling roots of a couple large mangroves. Ahead were the central government buildings—dark structures with golden trimming and red towers reaching toward the dizzying heights of the city's biggest mangroves. Borely had to wonder if even the trees of this forest were real, or if they were the result of some kind of Nexi experimentation. The setup worked a little too perfectly for vampires, he felt.

Down the trail a ways, Borely caught sight of a young vampire girl in a purple dress with white frills and lacing. She was running around, getting a hoop to roll down the road with a stick she beat it with. By her long violet hair and large yellow eyes, Borely recognized her as Analicia, one of the children Jenba visited each day at the orphanage. Borely sometimes went along with him, and usually regretted it.

These child vampires were an anomaly in the city, generally humans and elves who were turned into vampires by accident, or as the result of some series of unusual events. Analicia was bitten when she was eight, and though she had lived fourteen years now, she still acted like an eight-year-old. A very feisty one, to say the least.

She grabbed her hoop and turned to grin wickedly at Borely. "Hey, take me to the arena, Borely. I want to see the Rite."

"Okay," Borely said.

"What?" Analicia yelled. "You weren't supposed to agree so easily! You weren't supposed to agree at all..."

"Don't you want to go?"

"Of course I do! But everyone always tells me *no*. I wasn't expecting you to say *yes*."

"You're old enough to watch a couple adults brutally try to kill one another, and witness a grisly murder for the sake of being able to walk outside like any normal person," Borely said, folding his arms. "And you're a vampire yourself. You should be used to bloodshed."

"I'm not allowed to kill anything," Analicia said, a hint of sadness in her voice. "I'm too little..."

Borely remembered that though she was fourteen technically, she was still eight at heart, so perhaps she would never be allowed to go on a hunt. It made sense, of course. Who would send an eight-year-old out to kill monsters? She'd just get herself killed.

Not that Borely cared, of course.

"If you say so," he said. "Probably best you stay here then." Borely walked on down the road, but didn't get far before Analicia jumped onto his back and clenched his shoulders tight. He screamed and tried to shake her off, but she dug her claws into Borely's skin to keep a firm grip on him.

"Take me to the arena!" she cried. "I'm so bored! Let me watch the fight! It's Jenba today, and I want to watch!"

"What if he dies, you little brat?" Borely yelled through clenched teeth. "Do you really want to watch him get killed?"

Analicia only cried out louder. "There's no way Jenba will lose! He's the best there ever was! Now take me to the arena! It's almost time for it to start! Hurry up, Borely!"

All Borely wanted was for her to get her claws out of his skin. "Fine! Just get off of me!"

The small girl immediately plopped back to the ground and started to walk nonchalantly down the road. "Glad to know there's at least a few brain cells in your head."

Borely gripped one of his shoulders and scowled. "Is that what you say to someone doing you a favor? I'll pound you if you attack me again."

Analicia turned around and placed her hands on her hips. "If you're hurt so badly, just drink some blood, you idiot! If you're going to cry about it you can have some of mine." She tilted her pale neck to the side and strummed her tiny fingers across it.

Borely covered his eyes and groaned. "As if I'd do something that disgusting... I'd die before I suck *your* blood."

The child lowered her eyelids and smirked, as if trying to look seductive. "Don't lie to yourself, Borely... You know you want some of this."

Borely stomped past Analicia and walked at a brisk pace down the road. "This conversation is over! Come on, we're going to be late if we don't get going."

There wasn't much Borely was looking forward to in this Rite. There was a chance his one friend in the city was going to die, for one thing. But even if Jenba did win, would Borely get any closer to finding Areo? If Borely found out anything about Areo's whereabouts, perhaps he could nab Nivakil's Rite Nexi, and then go with Jenba to save Areo.

Borely tried to take his mind off the pain of the deep incisions in his shoulders, off his growing thirst for blood, and off of Analicia's incessant chatter.

•

Jenba's Rite match was going very poorly.

Borely sat between Nivakil and Analicia—a rather uncomfortable situation in and of itself—and watched as Jenba struggled to keep up with the vampire he was pitted against. Jenba's opponent was a large man who looked to be in his thirties, dressed in a white collared suit—which remarkably hadn't been stained in any blood yet. Perhaps this was to show just how confident he was.

Jenba repeatedly attempted to attack the man with bursts of flame from his red Nexi stone, but the opponent was quick to utilize his yellow Nexi each time he was hit. The glowing energy of the yellow barrier protected him from the fire, and the man was able to fight through Jenba's defenses quite easily. The opponent's efficient use of Nexi energy was remarkable in and of itself, but the fact he was a strong, burly man and a well-trained fighter made it difficult for Jenba to combat him.

And though Jenba was well-trained also, he looked almost frail in comparison to his opponent. Jenba's brown robes and yellow sash were splattered with blood, and even his red bandana had been clawed up to keep him from covering his eyes like Areo apparently had in her Rite duel.

It was painful to watch Jenba get repeatedly clawed, punched, and kicked by this opponent. Jenba was giving his all, and pulling off some really clever moves to keep from dying—but it didn't look like it was going to be enough.

At least, that's probably what Nivakil is thinking, Borely thought. There was nobody more pragmatic than Nivakil, and the old man had repeatedly insisted that Jenba not go through with the Rite this soon. Jenba was too anxious to save Areo to let Nivakil stop him, however. And Borely didn't want to give up hope on Jenba—or Areo.

"Come on, Jenba!" Borely yelled. "Finish this guy off already!"

Jenba gritted his teeth and fired off a giant burst of fire. The opponent activated his yellow Nexi, continuing his charge toward Jenba straight through the ball of flames. Jenba ran forward at the same time, claws ready to tear into his enemy.

He was fast. Faster than Borely had ever seen Jenba run before. *He was running into the massive burst of fire he had just created.*

A blood-curdling scream erupted from within the smoke flames.

The opponent's body flew through the air backwards, a bleeding hole in his chest. The airborne fires dissipated, and Borely turned to find Jenba lying on the ground, a burnt, bloody heap.

The enemy clenched his gaping wound and screamed, but managed to keep standing. He staggered toward Jenba, who struggled to push himself up.

Nivakil stood up, and Analicia gasped as the enemy stomped toward Jenba, claws outstretched.

"What is happening?" Nivakil asked. It was the first time Borely had ever heard the old man ask such a thing. Nivakil prided himself on always knowing what was going on, despite his blindness.

"Jenba's trying to get up, but—"

"He got hit again? How?"

"He jumped in the flames," Borely said. "That's how he jabbed his claws into the guy's chest. It was very unexpected."

"That... that *is* unexpected," Nivakil said. "Jenba wouldn't... That much fire will kill him unless he gets blood quickly."

"It was a last-ditch effort," Borely said, "but it still might not be enough. His opponent is—"

The man reached Jenba, who was still trying to stand up. The man swung back, ready to sever Jenba's head off with his elongated claws.

"Jenba!" Analicia screamed.

Suddenly Jenba was standing to the side of his opponent, shoving his claws straight into the man's stomach. Jenba had pretended to be nearly dead, just to get the enemy close to him.

The man stumbled backward, and Borely expected to see a second gaping hole in his body. Instead, Borely realized there was a faint yellow glow about the opponent's body. The man had activated his yellow Nexi as a precaution, just in time.

Jenba fell to his knees, screaming in agony—his claws had shattered upon impact with the man's barrier of energy. The sudden transition of feelings rushing through Borely was nauseating. One second it looked like Jenba was going to die, the next second it looked like he was going to win—and now it looked like he was going to die again. It was clear the man had been hurt by the quick and powerful blow, but Jenba's claws hadn't managed to pierce his body.

"You just... try that again!" the man yelled as his barrier faded, and he fought to catch his breath. He approached Jenba again, who now looked even worse off than he had before. It was obvious the same trick wasn't going to work again, and once the man finished Jenba off he'd be able to drink Jenba's blood and heal the gaping injury in his chest.

But before the man could get closer, screaming began to fill the far end of the arena. Borely looked across to find a large man walking past the table of startled judges. The man had a black vest, pants, and bandana, a scar across his nose, and at least a dozen green Nexi stones grotesquely implanted in his muscular arms. Vines coming from the green Nexi held several city guards tight, and held them up high enough for everyone to see. Jenba and his opponent both turned, the fight suddenly a secondary concern.

This was Augurc Shire, walking into the arena right in the middle of a Rite.

Borely and tens of others stood up.

It's him, Borely thought. *I'm going to get him to tell me where Areo is. And I'm going to kill him!*

Before anyone could make a move toward him, Augurc caused all his vines to squeeze the eight vampires he had captured even tighter. Drastically tighter. In a single moment, all eight of the guards were squeezed so tight they were each chopped up into a half-dozen bloody, screaming chunks.

Tens of screaming vampires leaped from the stands, rushing with claws outstretched, or Nexi stones raised. Augurc raised a hand, and Borely stood up, shocked at what he found. In Augurc's hand were two pieces of a stone, glowing bright, changing color with each passing moment.

Half of the Elpis.

"It's Augurc!" Borely said. "He has the Elpis!"

Just as Borely was about to leap down to the dirt field below, the arena filled with an overwhelming blinding white light. All the white Nexi stones of the mangroves above glowed brighter and brighter—a flash of white Nexi light that remained constant. All the vampires in the stadium were effectively blinded.

Borely shut his eyes tight, his ears ringing with the screams and groaning of a thousand vampires. He and Nivakil and Jenba would be able to get out without relying on their sight, but was this entire arena about to become a complete massacre? Augurc had just managed to overpower all of the white Nexi in the area without even batting an eye.

The sounds of dying screams filled the stands. Scraping metal accompanied bursts of fire, water, and earth. Borely could make out the sound of claws scraping against flesh. The gurgling cries of murdered innocents.

"I'll get Jenba," Nivakil said. "You watch over Analicia and find a way out of here. There's probably at least a hundred enemies here."

Borely tied a handkerchief around his eyes to help keep the increasingly blinding light from piercing through his eyelids. He heard Nivakil dash off down a stairway, then turned his focus to Analicia. The girl was screaming in pain—it had been years since she was exposed to even a fraction of this much light.

"Get on my back," Borely said, grabbing the girls arms and forcing them to drape around his neck. "Hold tight. I'm going to have to fight my way through this."

He was still exhausted from his fight with the giant earthworm. It was going to be strenuous to use more Nexi energy this soon, and any injury he'd sustain was going to hurt like crazy. He swore. If only he had taken some of the monster's blood to drink. He would have been ready for this ambush.

I've got to at least capture a Brotherhood member, he thought. *I've got to get answers... I've got to find out where Areo is!*

He leaped down the benches, pushing his way through frantic, fleeing vampires and huddled, shrieking children. Most of the people in the stands weren't going to be expert fighters—they were going to be slaughtered by the Brotherhood if something wasn't done. But what was Borely going to be able to do?

He reached the stairs, focusing on nearby sounds for any approaching Brotherhood members. If this was all part of Augurc's plan, then it was likely the ambush team had a way to see in the blinding light—or at least could fire large-scale attacks blindly into the stands.

Just as the thought came to Borely's mind, he sensed a series of large projectiles approaching—boulders perhaps. He sprinted down the stairs, careful to keep a hold of Analicia, who nearly flew off his back at the sudden burst of speed. Rocks exploded into the stairway behind Borely, and he struggled to listen for any other attacks. He heard footsteps everywhere— people fleeing, screaming.

The whoosh of a weapon. Borely turned and punched at what he expected to be the flat end of a blade. Instead, he bashed straight through claws. The vampire screamed and fell back—Borely continued to run, hearing the spread of flames across nearby wooden benches.

He wondered momentarily why a vampire had attacked him. He certainly had plenty of people in Istal who didn't think highly of him, but was this the opportune moment for any of them to attack him? Or were there vampires working with the Brotherhood? He remembered hearing of elites who broke away from Istal's government in past years, and how some vampires had been trained to fight in blinding conditions such as this. The vampire who fought Areo in her Rite duel was one, and his trainer one of the forerunners of a potential insurrectionist movement. Perhaps these vampires had helped Augurc and his soldiers reach Istal and bypass the city's defenses. A full-blown coup d'etat.

Borely reached the stage of the arena, where there was a bit more room to maneuver around. Was Augurc still down there? And what about Jenba and Nivakil? There was screaming everywhere. Bursts of flame, shattering of ice, whooshing of arrows. The field had turned to sheer chaos, and Borely couldn't see any of it.

Several sets of footsteps approached Borely. He was in no condition to fight multiple vampires or Brotherhood fighters at the same time, especially with a child in tow. He blasted a jet of water from his headband's Nexi and dashed ahead, coughing up smoke from a nearby explosion of fire. He nearly stumbled, but managed to keep running. The air around him suddenly turned cold—a light blue Nexi effect. He heard icicles sprout from the ground in front of him. He leaped over them, listening for other attacks, other enemies.

Something flew through the air, spinning toward him. Toward his head.

"Lean right!" Borely yelled. Upon landing he turned to his right as hard as he could, and Analicia leaned with him. What Borely took to be a knife flew just past his left ear. Footsteps ahead marked the assailant. Borely accessed the orange Nexi energy of his fist and punched the face of the enemy. A Brotherhood mask shattered upon impact, and Borely continued to run, hearing he was being followed.

He wanted more than anything to take down everyone in this arena, and to start questioning all the Brotherhood members he could about Areo. But there just wasn't time, and he didn't have the strength to keep this up much longer. If he could stop for just a few seconds to suck blood out of an enemy, he'd stand a better chance...

Borely heard the zipping of vines, the muffled groans of struggling victims. He kept running, careful to avoid a couple nearby figures, who may or may not have been enemies. There was a scraping of claws—two vampires fighting one another.

Though utterly spent, Borely kept pushing himself toward a stadium exit. There had to be Brotherhood members or vampires keeping people from getting out. The continued exposure to this blinding light was giving Borely an infuriating headache, and carrying Analicia like this was keeping him from fighting freely.

This might be my one chance to find out where Areo is, Borely thought. *I've got to find Nivakil and drop this kid off.*

A wave of dirt burst out of the ground a few meters away. Borely heard the cries of several vampires, but listened for the movement of the dirt. It was approaching him. He turned toward it to face it head on. Just as the wall of earth was about to encircle him, he shot off another blast of water, weakening the hardening dirt just in front of him. He headbutted through the earth and kept running. The person who made the attack stood just ahead. Borely raised an arm and clotheslined the attacker. He heard claws lengthening out just as he did so, marking this as another vampire.

He turned toward the exit—or at least what he believed was the direction of the exit. It was difficult to be certain, when he had moved in so many directions upon reaching the fighting pit of the arena.

Three sets of footsteps ran for him from straight ahead. Borely heard the unsheathing of a sword, then a subsequent charge of energy—perhaps orange Nexi energy for the sword. At the same time, Borely made out the taut pull of a bow's string. He struggled to make out the exact location of the archer. And a moment later, the third figure rushed toward Borely in an extra burst of speed—inhuman speed a well-trained vampire was capable of.

Borely gritted his teeth and leaped to the right the moment he heard the snap of the archer's bowstring. An arrow flew to Borely's left an instant later. A moment after that, the vampire reached Borely, swinging his claws for his head. Instantly Borely forced his own claws to elongate, and sliced the enemy's hand clean off in one quick swoop. As the man screamed, Borely kicked the man in the chest and ran straight over him. Borely listened for the swordsman. Three footsteps. Borely rushed to the enemy's right. The fighter swung his blade, charged with energy. Borely turned in place and leaned forward. The blade passed beneath Analicia. Borely kept turning, then jabbed his elongated claws into the enemy. It didn't matter where he hit—Borely shoved his claws through the assailant's body and pushed past him. At the same time, the archer had readied another arrow. Borely listened for the string.

Pull. Snap. With the enemy's location certain now, Borely side-stepped the arrow and rushed head-first toward the archer. The enemy ran for it at the last moment, but Borely managed to swipe his claws through the assailant's bow and on through his chest.

Struggling to breathe, Borely ran out of the arena, noting the change in the hardness of the dirt beneath him. He kept to the road, not confident enough to make his way through the thick forest without the assistance of his eyes. Minutes passed before he reached an area in the city that wasn't lit up like a dozen suns. The power of the Elpis was a terrible thing to behold—it seemed Augurc's studies of the stone had served him well. Perhaps he had found effective ways of using the stone in a way that would not poison him or fill him with agony, as had been the case for Terico and Delkol. Where Delkol's brashness and vigor had failed him, Augurc's patience and shrewdness was paying off.

It took time for Borely's eyes to adjust back to the dim light of the city's mangroves that weren't affected by Augurc's Elpis. He kept his eyes closed and his blindfold down, relying on his other senses to guide him further through the city. There was no sound of anyone chasing him, but he had the feeling he was being hunted. Something was stalking him—he could sense it. It gave him a strange sense of deja vu, only now he was in the place of the monster. Would he suffer the same fate as that giant earthworm? He was in much worse shape than that creature had been when it fought him.

"Borely."

The sound of a voice so close to him made Borely jump, the wind knocked out of him by the sheer suddenness of the beckoning. It was only Nivakil though. Borely slowed to a stop and struggled to regain his breath. How long had he been running for?

"Good, you still have her," Nivakil said, referring to Analicia. "Let her go. You're about to collapse."

The child got off Borely's back, and the lifted weight almost sent him floating up a few centimeters—or so he felt. It took some time to breathe normally again, but he was strong enough to keep standing.

"Jenba safe?" Borely asked.

"I'm fine," Jenba said. Apparently he was right there with Nivakil.

Borely lifted his bandana and squinted at the two figures standing before him. Once his eyes adjusted enough, he saw Jenba was alive and well. Presumably Nivakil supplied Jenba with some blood so he could regenerate from the near-fatal wounds his opponent had inflicted on him.

"We're going to have to flee the city," Nivakil said. "A Brotherhood scout spotted you running down the middle of the road, and is now gathering a team to take us down."

"We can't just run," Borely said. "We have to find out where they're keeping Areo. We have to help all those people in the arena." Though they were vampires, Borely still couldn't just stand by while the Brotherhood murdered helpless civilians.

"It's too late for them," Nivakil said. "This city is being overtaken by the banished elites. There's no stopping that." He handed Borely a vial of blood. "Drink this, quickly."

Borely didn't argue, knowing he'd need the energy if another fight did break out. And he fully intended to find a way to bring down some more Brotherhood members and accompanying vampires. This was finally his chance to get some answers, and he wasn't about to let Nivakil stop him.

Borely downed the blood in a couple gulps. He hated drinking blood, hated the overwhelming satisfaction it naturally gave him. There was nothing good about the taste, but his entire body felt thoroughly rejuvenated by the dark, undead power held within the substance.

"Can you run?" Nivakil asked. Borely turned to see he was talking to Analicia. The small girl looked like what little color was left in her face had been sapped out of her. She nodded blankly, her face pained and weary. Perhaps she was still adjusting to the more normal light. At least, more normal for her.

"You can all go if you wish," Borely said. "I'm staying to get some answers from the Brotherhood."

"Fine, go get yourself killed," Nivakil said, to Borely's astonishment. Was Nivakil seriously going to jet let him go? The fact Nivakil wasn't arguing and intended to just run for it placed the whole situation in a much darker light. Did he really see no hope at all in this situation?

"Are you serious?" Jenba asked, before Borely could. "There's way too many enemies for Borely to deal with here. Augurc is there somewhere, too. Even if all of us stayed, we wouldn't—"

"Now's not the time for us to run away," Borely said. "Jenba, don't you want to find Areo? This is our chance!"

"I do, but..." Jenba began. He glanced to Nivakil and frowned a little. He turned back to Borely. "But we should really follow Nivakil. If he feels the risk is too great, it's too great."

Borely was expecting more support than this. "Don't you care about Areo? I thought she was like a sister to you!"

Jenba grabbed Borely's shoulders, and for a moment it looked like he was going to scream something.

Footsteps approached.

Jenba turned away from Borely, just as a vampire lunged out of a nearby tree, claws outstretched. Analicia screamed. Two more vampires followed, and just as Borely began to turn, he heard the footsteps of two others from the other side of the road. Nivakil rushed to the nearest vampire. Borely forced his claws to elongate, knowing he was near his limit for Nexi stone usage. In an instant, dozens of claws scratched against one another—a frantic cacophony of scrapes and shoves.

Nivakil lobbed off the head of one, but then found himself pushed back by a woman with long, light blue hair. Her claws tangled with Nivakil's, and she grinned into his face.

"Hidif," Nivakil said. "I see you think you're in control of this situation."

"I always find my way to the top, Nivakil," the woman responded.

Borely managed to drive back the vampire that targeted him—a boy who was caught off guard by Borely's strength. Borely took the moment to assist Jenba, who had two enemies to deal with. Jenba lashed out at a man with blood red hair and a goatee, then dodged an attack by a vampire in a top hat. The moment he had an opening, Borely tore his claws into the second man's arm, forcing him away from Jenba.

The young vampire Borely fended off earlier raised a red Nexi and released a giant ball of fire into the fray. The fighters dispersed, and Borely used the moment of confusion to rush toward the vampire he had stabbed. The man was fumbling with a vial of blood, struggling to keep from screaming from his injury. Borely sliced off the man's arm and shoved him into the ground, claws pushed against the screaming enemy's neck.

"Tell me where Areo is," Borely ordered. "Tell me now!"

A figure leaped from a tree, landing a couple meters in front of the man Borely pinned down. It was a woman in a silver and black uniform.

Areo.

She is here? Now?

Borely was stunned speechless. He sensed he had to get away. But how was he going to? And why? What was going on?

Areo raised an arm toward Borely and caused her fingernails to lengthen into claws. Their jagged tips rushed straight toward Borely's face.

•

Claws flew to Borely, and though he couldn't believe anything that was happening, his body somehow managed to react by instinct. He dropped to the ground, forcing himself to fall backwards. The claws passed over him. Borely blinked, entirely dismayed by the fact Areo had attacked him. The claws shot down toward him, too fast to even see.

He rolled away, but still got a few claws jabbed through his left arm. Pinned down and screaming, he struggled to force his way out of Areo's grasp. The vampire Borely had beaten down scampered away, hurrying back to join the other vampires fighting Jenba and Nivakil. Borely looked up to Areo's face, finding it thoroughly void of emotion. Areo was never the most emotional person in the world, but this face was different. It looked like Areo, but there was nothing *Areo* about it. Almost as if her very soul was torn out from her body.

Areo retracted some of her claws, then forced them back out to stab Borely in the face and chest. Nivakil and Jenba couldn't save him—they had other vampires to deal with already. Borely forced himself to his feet and pushed his body further through the claws that impaled his arm. Areo's other claws still managed to hit him, but Borely managed to keep from getting his vitals punctured. His neck was badly scraped, and there were now several claws poking out his back. He coughed up blood, his entire body in agony.

He was alive, at least for a few more seconds. There was no way he'd be able to keep this up for long.

With his free arm, he powered the orange Nexi in his fist guard and punched at some of the claws impaled in his bloody torso. To his surprise, Areo didn't attempt to bring her claws back into her fingers. Instead, she held strong, and even with Borely exerting all his strength into the punch, he didn't manage to even dent the claws that pierced him. How had her claws become so freakishly strong? A punch like that could have shattered a block of steel.

Areo didn't register any pain in her face. Her claws kept Borely in place—the slightest of movements brought him excruciating pain. And Areo still had some claws free to jab straight into Borely's face.

"Areo! It's me!" Borely yelled. "I've been... trying to find you!"

Claws shot off toward Borely's face.

With what little energy he had left, he activated the dark blue Nexi on his forehead, releasing a burst of water at the approaching claws. They deflected slightly enough to zip by either side of Borely's head.

As soon as the thin stream of water subsided, Borely stared into Areo's eyes, which still registered no emotion. She didn't look upset or surprised. It was as if she didn't care either way if Borely lived or died—she was simply doing her job. A boring, everyday job she was just expected to do. She wasn't exerting herself. She was barely even trying.

All at once, Areo forced her claws to tear out of Borely, ripping out the sides of his body. He fell to the ground, a screaming, bloody heap.

He was dying, and there was no saving him if he didn't get any blood right away. Not that he could do anything to escape Areo at this point anyways. He couldn't even call out to her anymore, though he now realized there probably was no simple way to bring her back to her senses. Augurc had experimented on her to the point where she couldn't even realize she was killing the very person whose life she had saved—whom she was willing to give herself up for.

Areo retracted her claws back into fingernails, but left a few centimeters of claw on her right index finger. Her arm rigid and straight, she pointed down to Borely's lifted, trembling head.

Her claw lengthened out a bit more. Borely clenched his teeth.

Nothing more happened. She didn't finish him off. Areo's claw didn't grow any nearer to Borely. She simply stared down at him.

She was hesitating.

There was no hint of sadness in her eyes, or even confusion. And yet, she wasn't killing him.

A figure flew past Borely and Areo, but neither of them moved. Borely caught a flash of light blue—was it the woman fighting Nivakil, thrown through the air? The next moment Nivakil appeared in front of Borely. The old man swung his elongated claws toward Areo, who didn't seem to notice Nivakil's arrival.

Borely leaped against Nivakil's back, bleeding and screaming, feeling as if he'd fall apart if he moved any further. Nivakil's claws barely missed Areo's neck, and Borely realized she hadn't moved a muscle. But surely she had noticed Nivakil's attack?

"You fool! What are you doing?" Nivakil screamed.

"That's my line!" Borely yelled back.

Areo turned and ran, disappearing into the dim mangroves.

"Where are you going?" came a woman's voice. The elegantly-dressed woman with light blue hair stood up and rushed wearily toward the scene. She glanced from Areo's direction and back to Borely and Nivakil, her expression changing from confused to flustered to vengeful.

Nivakil shoved Borely off him and turned to the woman. *Hidif*, Borely recalled Nivakil calling her. She had a black eye and a deep gash near her collarbone, but she looked enthusiastic to continue her brawl with Nivakil.

Borely lay on the ground, his mind in a daze, his body at the breaking point, his soul tearing at the seams. Areo had tried to kill him. But then she stopped. And then Nivakil tried to kill her. And Areo ran away.

Why did Areo try to kill him? Why did she stop? Why did Nivakil try to kill her? Why did Areo run away?

Nivakil and Hidif charged toward each other, claws raised. They were fast. Much faster than Borely had seen two vampires fight one another before. Perhaps it was partly because he was dizzy and nauseous, but Borely could hardly tell how either of them were fighting. They moved too fast for him to keep up with, their every movement either scraping against claws or nicking the opponent's skin just a scratch.

"You can't hope to win, Nivakil!" Hidif yelled between breaths. "This city is mine now!"

"Congratulations," Nivakil said. "Your first act as ruler is genocide. By the end of the week you'll probably be the only one left. Just as Augurc planned. I may be blind, but I can see plain as day just how easily manipulated you still are. I better finish you off now, and save this world from your sheer stupidity."

"You were always one to talk big," Hidif said. A couple quick claw swipes forced Nivakil to step back, but his counter attacks didn't leave any openings for her. It was like watching two fighters swinging around ten long knives, and directing each one to a specific line of attack against the opponent. How either of them kept up with one another at this speed, Borely could hardly imagine. It was literally a blur of scrapes and sparks at this point.

Borely noticed Jenba was getting overpowered by the remaining two vampires—the young boy and the red-haired man. Jenba couldn't land a good attack on either of them, preoccupied with protecting Analicia.

Hidif's claws tangled with Nivakil's, and for a split-second Hidif lunged herself forward, attempting to latch her fangs into her opponent's neck. Nivakil slipped back, practically gliding across the dirt floor.

"Now, Analicia!" Hidif yelled, her eyes still focused on Nivakil.

Borely looked back to Jenba and Analicia, unable to get up and stop what he suddenly realized was about to happen. Analicia already had her claws out. She was already swinging them straight for Jenba's back.

Astoundingly, Jenba managed to leap over Analicia's attack without even seeing it—he apparently had heard the swing of her claws and reacted accordingly, all in the space of a single second. At the same time he dodged the jabbing of claws from the red-haired vampire.

Jenba landed just as the boy vampire raised an ice Nexi toward him. Immediately Jenba slipped out his own ice Nexi, and the two vampires each flung a jagged ice formation toward each other. The giant icicles collided with one another, and Jenba moved to attack the boy. He stopped quickly, however, realizing the red-haired vampire and Analicia were both about to attack him.

Nivakil was struggling to defend a series of Hidif's attacks, and for a couple seconds the woman managed to leave several deep cuts into him. Just when it looked like Hidif had an opening for Nivakil's face, the old man lunged a hand forward, his claws snapping back against the force of Hidif's guarding claws. She started to laugh, but suddenly found Nivakil's bloody fingers clutching her arm. Nivakil flung Hidif backwards, swinging her over his back, straight into a tree. The moment she was airborne and her claws free from his, he rushed straight at the red-haired vampire.

The man was about to swing his claws straight through Jenba's neck. In the blink of an eye, Nivakil rushed the claws of his good hand straight through the man's stomach, tearing him in half. Nivakil kept running, avoiding the shattering ice shards from Jenba's and the boy's Nexi attacks. A moment later, Nivakil had forced his claws through the boy, leaving Jenba free to turn toward Analicia.

Jenba dropped to the ground and rolled forward just as Analicia made another swing with her claws. The girl tripped over Jenba, landing flat on her face, arms stretched forward. Jenba and Nivakil both turned to where Hidif had been thrown, but she was nowhere to be found. Borely assumed she ran off to find Areo, but she might have simply decided it wasn't worth continuing to try to defeat Nivakil now that he had Jenba as back-up.

Meanwhile blood continued to flow from Borely's body, and he felt what little life was left in him begin to fade away. He couldn't speak. He could hardly breathe.

His vision was blurry, but he could tell Nivakil was kneeling beside him. The old man forced a vial of blood into Borely's mouth, and Borely begrudgingly drank the crimson liquid. Even at the brink of death, he still hated the fact he had to rely on blood like this. Would he be dead now if he weren't a vampire? How had Areo managed to slice him apart so effortlessly like that? She had always been a talented fighter, but this was on an entirely different level. And the fact it was Areo attacking him certainly didn't help matters. How could he bring himself to fight to the death with her?

The pain of flesh and muscle regenerating flowed through Borely's entire body. He struggled to keep from yelling, but it was such a sharp, all-encompassing pain. It was fortunately over in seconds, the wounds of his body healing away and replacing the pain with a dull ache and weariness.

"What were you thinking?" Nivakil yelled. "Because of your foolishness, you nearly got both of us killed." The old man took a drink from his own vial, stopping the flow of blood leaking from his fingertips.

"You were about to kill Areo," Borely said.

"She's not Areo anymore," Nivakil replied. "She's lost to us, Borely. Or do you think that was actually her wanting to kill you? Would Areo want to kill you, after all she did to save your life?"

"No," Borely said, forcing himself to his knees. "But she's still Areo, at least a little bit. She could have finished me off, but she hesitated. She's not completely under Augurc's control."

"We have no way of saving her," Nivakil said. "I imagine Augurc will keep experimenting on her, making her more and more powerful with that Elpis energy. We won't even be able to fight a monster like that."

"Now you're calling her a monster?" Borely yelled. "She's one of your precious students. Why don't you care about saving her?"

Nivakil turned away, gritting his teeth. "Of course I've wanted to save her! But now she's a killing machine. Don't you understand this, Borely? I don't want my precious student murdering hundreds of innocent civilians against her will anymore. This was probably my one chance to save her, and you ruined it!"

Borely shook his head and sighed. He shakily brought himself to his feet, his mind still in a daze. What was wrong with this old man? Nivakil was just thinking like a vampire, Borely decided. The old man naturally turned to bloodshed for an answer.

Wanting Jenba to support him at least, Borely turned to him. Before Borely could say anything though, he realized Analicia was still there, now standing beside Jenba.

"What is she still doing here?" Borely asked. "She nearly killed you, Jenba."

"I'd never kill Jenba!" Analicia said. "Get it in that thick skull of—"

Jenba placed a hand on Analicia's head to stop her. "Don't worry, Borely. Analicia was just trying to keep Hidif thinking she was on her side. Hidif was the one who made Analicia a vampire, and asked Analicia to fight for her at an opportune moment—a way to return the favor, I guess."

"I had to pretend to help her," Analicia said. "I whispered to Jenba that I would attack from behind, and he went along with it."

Borely thought it all sounded a little far-fetched, but he didn't care to argue about it. Analicia wasn't making any move to attack anyone right now—he'd just be sure to keep an eye on her a little more than he had before. She had always been a bit of a trouble-maker, but the possibility of her working for the vampire elite that helped spearhead this whole operation was more than a little alarming.

"Fine," Borely said. "But at any rate, we've got to go find Areo before that Hidif woman does. We can't let the Brotherhood keep manipulating Areo more than they already have."

"Let her go, Borely," Nivakil said. "What do you plan to do for her, exactly? Shake her back to her senses? Recount her life story to her to bring her memories back? Return her mind back to normal with a kiss?"

"I know you don't care," Borely muttered. "But Jenba, don't you want to come help me find Areo? She's *here*. Right now. In this city. This is our chance to save her."

Jenba looked to the ground and frowned. "I don't know. Saving her now... It sounds impossible."

"It might not be though," Borely said. "You have to at least try. She's your sister, Jenba!"

"I... I know," Jenba said. "I want to..."

"Now's not the time," Nivakil said. "Capturing Areo in our current state is impossible. If you still wish to retrieve Areo, I suppose I'm willing to help, but right now our priority is getting out of this forest alive. The Brotherhood and banished elite have effectively taken control of the city by this point. There's no going back there now."

"But—" Borely began.

"Areo will surely go with the Brotherhood—likely with Augurc himself— and be deployed to other locations. We will retrieve Areo at a more opportune time. Right now we're all exhausted, and we'd be severely outnumbered if we just marched back into the city."

It seemed Nivakil was trying to cooperate to some degree, and perhaps deep down he did have a little desire to try saving Areo somehow. And it was true that they had no plan for how to actually capture Areo, let alone bring her mind back to normal. Borely also knew he was in no state to fight anymore at this point. Blood could heal his wounds, but he could only keep fighting for so long.

"Okay, let's go somewhere safe for now," Borely said.

Nivakil bent down to one of the vampires he killed and rummaged through the corpse's pockets. He pulled out a pink Nexi stone.

"Check the others for Rite Nexi," Nivakil said. "You'll each want one if we're going to be on the move for a long time."

They did so, and were fortunate enough to find a Rite Nexi for Jenba, Borely, and even Analicia.

"Was hoping to actually earn this today," Jenba said.

"In your case, it was a good thing the insurrection happened when it did," Nivakil said. "Considering how you were about to be killed off by your opponent."

It was a cruel thing to say, even if it was true. Jenba looked like he was stabbed in the heart, but didn't respond to his mentor's jab.

The four headed away from the city, taking the trail further and further into the forest, where the lights of the mangroves progressively grew dimmer. The trail wound up a hill, but it was impossible to look back to the city through the mangroves. How many vampires were slaughtered at the arena that day? How many more were killed in the rest of the city? And how many was Areo forced to kill by her own hand?

Borely had never felt so powerless before. So much death, so much destruction—and he couldn't even help the woman who had saved his life.

And now he was leaving her.

I'm sorry, Areo, he thought. *I swear I'll find you again. I'll figure out a way to free you from Augurc's grasp. You can live your life again. And we'll do whatever we want.*

"Hold on," Nivakil said, stopping to pull a Nexi stone from his pocket. It was a teal one—one that allowed people to speak with others who had teal Nexis, even when a great distance apart from each other. Borely didn't realize Nivakil still had one, though he knew the old man had communicated with Rilv in time for him and a group of vampires to come assist Setar in fighting back Delkol's army.

"This is Nivakil."

Rilv's voice came from the stone, as if she were standing right there speaking with them.

"We have received word that Istal may be attacked by the Brotherhood in the imminent future. We ask that your city prepares accordingly."

•

Hour after hour, Lanek stared out at the sky ahead. A light blue. Some clouds here and there, every now and then. The sun above them a ways, to their left. Lanek stayed at the controls, but there really wasn't much for him to deal with at this moment. He just wanted something to focus on. To busy himself with something. To keep his mind off Lynx, sitting against the wall just a few meters behind him. The man who murdered Lanek's sister.

Meanwhile Rilv sat in the seat beside Lanek, asleep for now. She rested silently, barely breathing. She apparently had been up the entire night making preparations for this excursion. This strange mission, which Lanek felt only vaguely connected to. Yes, he wanted to bring down the Brotherhood. But he didn't want to go searching the continent for random magical stones again. And he certainly didn't want to be working with Lynx.

Of course, Rilv had warned both Lanek and Lynx to not create any trouble on this trip. Lynx was necessary for such and such reasons, none of which Lanek really bought. But perhaps Lanek could learn everything that happened to Suran. The events leading to her death. All the details Lanek had never gotten to find out from Terico. And perhaps Rilv was right to some degree—rather than simply trusting Lynx, perhaps they could actually use Lynx in some way to deal a fatal blow to the Brotherhood. It was an organization that truly needed to be destroyed, and the world would certainly be better off without Augurc Shire in the picture.

So Lanek decided he would wait. If Lynx chose to betray them, Lanek would be sure to drive his rapier straight through the madman's heart. In the meantime though, he would have to wait for a more opportune moment. Particularly one in which Rilv wouldn't be able to fling him around with her telekinesis stone.

Lanek glanced back to Kitoh, who sat on the floor with a stack of old books and a few scrolls. Apparently he was researching some of the materials lent to him by the linguist elf woman back at the council meeting.

"Anything interesting?" Lanek asked. He didn't want to interrupt Kitoh's reading, but he was tired of hearing nothing but the hum of machinery. Over the years he had made improvements on this ship, giving it a more aerodynamic design made of lighter materials, and providing it an engine that made the ship stronger and quieter than ever before.

"I'm just trying to understand how the Haders were created," Kitoh said. "It seems a council of elves came up with the concept, and some of the most powerful eigni at that time supplied much of the energy needed to craft the stones. There are accounts of people all around the world using the Haders though, vampires and humans included. The Haders brought about new power struggles much more often than they helped defeat kings who used the Elpis cruelly."

"Makes you wonder if this search will be worth it," Lanek said. "Perhaps we'll stop Augurc from using the Elpis any more, but now there will be a bunch of Haders in our hands."

"But in the end, precisely whose hands will be holding all these Nexi?" Kitoh asked quietly. "Rilv is leading this operation. There will likely be several Haders and a full Elpis involved before this is all over. What do you think she will do with that much power?"

"She can't use the Elpis, at least," Lanek said. "And she made it clear that she wouldn't be the only one in charge of the Haders."

"Who knows, though," Kitoh said. "My team has found some use for the Elpis. Perhaps there are other teams I don't know about. Perhaps Rilv has a plan in mind for when the four pieces of the Elpis are all gathered together. Or perhaps she just wants to use Augurc and the Elpis as an excuse to obtain a bunch of the Haders."

Lanek was worried Rilv was hearing any of this, but he watched her carefully, noting her slow breathing and the movement of her eyes—she was deep in a dream.

"Do you not trust her then?" Lanek asked.

"She has always been thoroughly loyal to the royal court, as far as I can tell," Kitoh said. "She may or may not have any ulterior motives, but either way it's dangerous for anyone to get a hold of so much power."

"It's fatal to use any of these things too much," Lanek said. "I don't think she wants to die. And neither do any of us. We'll just have to find a way to destroy the stones when we're through."

Throughout the conversation Lanek wondered if Lynx was going to comment on anything, but the masked man kept perfectly silent. Was he asleep? He sat perfectly straight, so it didn't seem likely. Lanek didn't like the fact he couldn't see Lynx's face, or know where his eyes were looking. There was no way Lanek was ever going to be able to trust him for anything on this mission.

"I guess we'll figure out what to do once it's time for us to," Lanek said. "Let's just focus on getting this first Hader for now."

•

•Part VIII•
TRANQUIL HAVEN

Lanek could make out the faint, ghostly mountains in the distance. The airship continued to travel at a brisk, smooth pace, hundreds of meters above the ground. Fortunately Kitoh was handling the flight much more easily than he had when he was on *The Finest Hour*. Perhaps that was partly because the boy had some books to read through. Or perhaps the situation simply called for him to be brave. Lynx's presence certainly wasn't comforting. Rilv wasn't very cheery company, either. And admittedly, Lanek had been feeling tense the entire trip.

But how was he supposed to feel? He couldn't take this calmly. He couldn't just pretend this would all go well. A Brotherhood member was on his ship, and there was nothing Lanek could do to take his mind off the fact this masked man had killed Suran.

He tried to focus on the distant mountains. But he couldn't let himself focus too much. He had to listen. Just in case Lynx tried to attack him from behind.

No, there's no reason for him to fight me now, Lanek reminded himself. *I'm the only one who can fly this thing, after all.* As far as he knew, at least.

Rilv paced back and forth on the bridge, her hands behind her back, rigid and proper. It was clear she was deep in thought, planning her every move for the upcoming days. Perhaps the upcoming years, for all Lanek could tell. The woman was always calculating details in her head. Admittedly it was something she was good at—it was largely thanks to her planning that Delkol Shire was defeated, though in the end it came at a great cost. The government of Fiefs was in shambles, but Rilv somehow managed to keep things together while the dukes of the kingdom were at each others' throats over the ensuing months.

Stability. That was what she wanted for the kingdom, more than anything else. It was probably the word that best described herself, as well. A sharp, jagged rock sticking out of the ocean shore, immovable amidst the constant torrent of crashing waves.

Perhaps more dangerous than the waves themselves.

And to continue the analogy even further, Lanek could picture himself as a peaceful, passing boat, with no desire to get swept up in the dangerous current, and no desire to collide with the rocks.

You can handle this, Lanek thought to himself. *You've handled worse than this before. And we know precisely where we're going, thanks to Kitoh's device.*

The boy was setting it up again right now, placing a map on the floor and the appropriate metal objects around it. The map was connected to a soft, thin wooden base, which allowed Kitoh to place needles into specific locations on the map. Lanek noted the silver triangular pedestal sitting in front of the map, where the two pieces of the Elpis stone were intended to rest.

"It's set," Kitoh said.

Rilv walked over and placed the two Elpis fragments into the pedestal. Apparently she had the Elpis with her all this time.

Lanek glanced back at Lynx, who continued to sit against the far wall. The masked man had one leg lying forward, the other propped up with his arm leisurely atop his knee. Was Lynx eyeing the Elpis pieces? Perhaps it was Lynx's goal to obtain the full Elpis for Augurc. Lanek didn't like the idea of Lynx being this close to the Elpis. It was quite possible that Lynx had been helping Rilv out all this time just for the chance to obtain the missing Elpis pieces for the Brotherhood.

Was this his chance? Rilv had the telekinetic Hader, and Lanek was here too. Not to mention Kitoh, who Lanek recalled could turn into a dragon when the circumstances called for it. Lynx would probably wait for a moment when he was alone with Rilv, or when everyone else was asleep. And probably when he wasn't in an airship in the middle of the sky.

Lanek had to keep an eye on him. If Augurc Shire obtained the full Elpis, there was no telling what disasters would befall the Fiefs Kingdom.

Lynx stood up and walked toward Kitoh and Rilv. And the Elpis.

Lanek stood up, his hand on the hilt of his rapier.

"Whoa, calm down now," Lynx said, holding his hands forward a bit, making gentle wave motions. "I'm just standing up. People do it all the time."

"Don't go any closer," Lanek said. "Sit back down where you were."

"Thank you for your caution," Rilv said, "but it does not matter if Lynx stands up and walks around from time to time. He can even watch our work here if he wishes. I will simply kill him if he tries anything foolish."

"There, see?" Lynx said. "Quit worrying so much, Lanek. I'm here to help you folks out, and besides—I know better than to mess with Rilv."

Lanek's frown only deepened. He hated the way Lynx was trying to act like everyone on this ship was on friendly terms.

"You will not speak to me more than is necessary," Lanek said. "This is not some vacation amongst good pals. This is my airship, and if I tell you to stay far away from the Elpis, I suggest you follow my command."

For a moment nobody moved. The bridge turned silent, save for the hum on the engine and muffled clanking of machinery. Lanek stared at Lynx's mask, gazing straight through the thin slits the killer had to be staring through.

"No need for another fight so soon," Rilv said. "Or would you like me to fling you both to the ground again?"

"It's fine, I'll just sit back down," Lynx said. He did so, slumping back with his arm again lying atop his propped leg. "I'll just rest here until our captain has cooled down a bit."

"Don't hold your breath," Lanek said, keeping a stern gaze down at the Brotherhood fighter. "As long as you're on my ship, I don't intend to be lax about anything. One wrong move, and I finish you off once and for all."

"You've tried killing me twice now," Lynx said. "Emphasis on *tried*. Quite frankly, your threat doesn't worry me much, though I am concerned about you pestering me for the entirety of this mission."

"You will have to put up with it, Lynx," Rilv said. "I have asked Lanek to not fight you unless you force his hand. Everyone needs to place the mission above all else. We have enough worry about as it is."

"What about when the mission is over?" Lynx asked. "Let's say we find the Haders and destroy the Brotherhood. Am I going to have to put up with Captain Elf trying to kill me the rest of my life?"

Rilv turned away from Lynx, but she didn't look toward Lanek either. "If you are cooperative for the entirety of the mission, and everything ends in success, I will guarantee your safety."

"What?" Lanek asked, forcing himself to keep from yelling. "This man murdered my sister. I will not just let him go free once this is all over."

"We will deal with this when the time comes," Rilv said.

Neither Lanek nor Lynx spoke up. With every fiber of his being, Lanek wanted to bring Lynx down. Deliver justice. Stab him through the heart. Fulfill revenge. Throw him off the ship. Anything. Anything to get rid of him. Anything to avenge Suran's death.

What did Suran do to deserve this? What did I do to deserve this?

Lanek was shaking, desperate—yet unable to pull the rapier from his hilt. He could kill Lynx. And if Rilv got in his way, he could kill her too.

No, I can't go down that road, Lanek thought. *She just wants to find these Haders. Bring down the Brotherhood. Help the Fiefs Kingdom. I just... have to go along with all this. Just for a while.*

"Sit back down," Rilv told Lanek. "Kitoh and I are merely going to check on the location of the Haders again, to see if anyone with them is on the move."

Lanek sat down slowly and reluctantly. It was difficult to keep from shaking, but he forced himself to take long, quiet breaths. He had to stare down toward Kitoh and his map, and do all he could to keep from thinking of Lynx.

Kitoh held a needle over the map, and somehow the Elpis fragments worked in conjunction with the strange metal blocks set up around the map. The needle moved slightly in Kitoh's grip, pointing toward the location the Elpis energy designated as a location of extensive Nexi energy. With slow, careful movement, Kitoh moved the needle toward the spot unseen forces were guiding it to. Once the needle drooped back down, Kitoh pushed it into the map—this one in a spot in Fiefs Kingdom.

He repeated the process several more times, then unrolled a second map marked with Hader locations from an earlier time. Kitoh and Rilv began comparing the pinned map to the marked one.

"This can't be a coincidence," Rilv said. "We've been compromised."

"What do you mean?" Lanek asked.

Kitoh pointed to a spot with three needles in the Fiefs Kingdom. "This is where we're at right now. Two needles for the Elpis fragments, and one for Rilv's Hader." He moved his finger to a spot with one needle in the mountains. "We're heading to this location, where there is likely another Hader." He then pointed at a spot with two needles, a ways northeast of the airship's location. "And here is someone who has what we're presuming to be two Haders."

"Could it be Augurc with two Elpis fragments?" Lanek asked.

"No, he is down in Istal," Kitoh said, pointing to two needles far to the south. "The force of the blocks is much stronger for Elpis pieces, so it's easy to tell them apart from the Haders."

"What is troubling is the fact the person with two Haders is on the move," Rilv said. "The subject is heading straight to where we're heading."

"He's definitely going in that direction," Kitoh said, "but there's no way to be sure of his final destination."

"How quickly has he been traveling?" Lanek asked.

"A speed similar to our own," Kitoh said. "He's traveled from the Shire Kingdom though, and has a bit further to go than us. We should have some time to find the exact location of the Hader before he does."

"How much time?" Rilv asked.

"Half a day. Possibly less," Kitoh said.

So even with all of Rilv's precautions, someone already knew of her mission to obtain all the Haders. But was this the Brotherhood working to find the stones, or some other enemy?

Or someone who wasn't an enemy at all, perhaps?

"Is there any chance this person with two Haders will cooperate with us?" Lanek asked.

"Unlikely," Rilv said. "There is a low chance that anyone with a Hader we encounter will cooperate with us."

Kitoh bit his bottom lip, and glanced around a bit. "But, we are planning to negotiate with the people we come in contact with, right? You said you've brought goods from the treasury to exchange with."

"Of course, we will try to reason with those who possess the Haders," Rilv said. "However, I am not confident anyone will be willing to give up such power, even for all the riches of the kingdom."

"You... you expect us to fight everyone, then," Kitoh said.

Lanek recalled Kitoh being nervous to fight the Brotherhood five years ago. He was just a child then, called to assist in a war effort at such an early age. The eigni was a strong, powerful boy, with an unparalleled link to Nexi energy. And yet he was still nervous about having to fight.

This was a good thing though, Lanek thought. It was wise to avoid a fight whenever they could. But Rilv seemed right—most people with Haders would probably react in a hostile way to any attempt to barter for the stones.

"Yes, I expect conflict in this operation," Rilv said.

"And that's where I come in," Lynx said. "You don't need to worry yourself, Kitoh. I can bring down an opponent in more ways than one, even if he's got *two* Haders."

Lanek held his tongue.

"But... what if someone has a Hader, and doesn't want to fight? And doesn't want to give it up?" Kitoh asked.

Rilv folded her arms and tilted her head a bit, considering the possibility of such an event.

"Our goal remains the same," Rilv said. "We take the Haders by any means necessary. If we have to fight, we will. Even if our opponents do not."

•

It took more time than expected to navigate through the mountains, but the next day the airship came in sight of a number of small villages. Kitoh used a map of the mountain range to try to discern more specifically where they needed to go, and they ended up flying by a couple secluded elf villages in their search for the Hader in question.

Eventually Kitoh and Rilv decided the most likely location for the Hader was higher up in the mountains, and Lanek guided the airship to what turned out to be an especially small village. To Lanek's surprise, there were many farms surrounding the area, the steep hills carved into steps for the crops to grow on. The homes were small hovels, most of them made of wood. There were a couple nicer buildings made of stone, apparently carved straight into the mountainside. It was a very quiet-looking village, a place cut off from the rest of the world. The slow, wispy drifts of fog gave the fragile village a mysterious atmosphere. It was a strange, precarious place for anyone to live.

Lanek understood that the elves here had to be living a very traditional lifestyle, with a strong emphasis on the elvish culture of centuries past—long before it became commonplace for elves and humans to live together in the various cities and towns of the Fiefs Kingdom. He wasn't sure what elves of a small traditional village would be doing with a Hader. Perhaps the stone was hidden in the mountains nearby, and nobody knew it was even there. Lanek hoped this would be the case—it would make matters so much simpler. He wasn't eager to lead an attack on these people.

It was difficult to find a good place to land. There were elves working on the farms, pointing up at his airship. Lanek imagined Rilv was hoping for a less dramatic entrance, or at least one that didn't take fifteen minutes to finish. By the time Lanek found a safe spot a ways down the mountain to land at, there was quite the gathering of people at the village, watching intently. It may have been the first time any of these villagers had seen an airship. It may have been a long time since they had had visitors at all, for that matter. This was going to be a big deal, whether Rilv liked it or not.

Once the ship was landed and anchored safely, Rilv led Lynx and Kitoh outside. Lanek followed them out once he had gone through a final check to ensure everything was secured. He ran to catch up with everyone, a bit upset they didn't care to wait five minutes for him. He was concerned about leaving just Rilv and Kitoh with Lynx, even though he knew both Rilv and Kitoh could probably defend themselves... Rilv had a Hader, and Kitoh surely had some Nexi stones. But what if Lynx caught them off-guard? They seemed to trust him more than Lanek did. And Lynx was far too unpredictable to take lightly. There was no way Lanek was going to go along with the idea Lynx was truly on their side in all this.

The terrain was rocky, and the air was cold. There was little wind, and it wasn't a biting cold—but it was a solid cold, one that lingered and seeped slowly through Lanek's body. Perhaps it was the lingering fog, giving the mountaintop an extra layer of chilliness.

He caught up with the group and followed them up the thin dirt trail leading toward the village. It was a steep climb, and it was difficult to see any of the buildings from this vantage point. Lanek kept an eye on Lynx, wondering what the masked man would attempt at the small village. Perhaps the Brotherhood member would use the opportunity to take the Hader for himself, and sneak off down the mountainside. Lanek had taken precautions to make it so only he could run the airship, but he had to anticipate the possibility Lynx could still break in by force, and it was technically conceivable Lynx knew enough about airships to be able to pilot it as well.

They soon came in sight of some of the terraced fields the villagers used to farm their crops. Corn and potatoes were the main vegetables Lanek noted, but caught sight of what looked to be a vineyard further ahead. There seemed to be plenty of crops to support the small village—a level of self-reliance that wouldn't be found in much of the rest of the world, with its interconnected cities, trade routes, and shifting supplies and demands.

As the path began to level off a bit, the group came in contact with a number of farmers, taking a break from pulling weeds, it looked like.

Rilv led the team a little closer, stopping just a couple meters from where the farmers had gathered. It was just a few seconds before anyone spoke, but Lanek found the pause a bit disconcerting. Perhaps he was expecting one of the farmers to say something, but they simply looked to him, as if he should introduce everyone to them.

Before Lanek could decide how to present themselves, Rilv spoke first. "Hello. My name is Rilv, and I am the head servant of the Fiefs royal court. These are my assistants, and we come on official business."

None of the farmers responded. They looked wary, suspicious. And for good reason, Lanek thought. It wasn't likely a government airship would come to a random little village in the mountains like this without it meaning there was some kind of trouble. Some of the villagers glanced from Rilv to Lanek, their eyes shifting back and forth a couple times. Perhaps they would have preferred to speak with him, considering he was an elf like them.

"Do not be alarmed," Rilv said. "We are simply stopping here temporarily. We have been on a long journey." It seemed she was downplaying what she had just said about official business. It was important to try to get the villagers relaxed so they'd be willing to share information and cooperate, though Lanek kind of doubted Rilv would be able to actually do so...

He decided to speak up. "My name is Lanek. I've never been up these mountains before, but I've got to say, you folks have a really nice view up here. I'm surprised there are villages up this high, and so far away from any kind of big town."

"We manage well enough," a man in a patched-up coat and pants said. "You work for the government too then?"

"No, I'm just an airship pilot and mechanic," Lanek said. "I spotted this picturesque little village though, and pointed it out to Rilv here. She was so impressed, she insisted we stop by and take a look for a bit. I was kind of hoping to walk around on some stable ground for a bit anyways. It's good to get fresh air when you can, and this seems as fresh as it gets."

Most of the villagers were smiling a little by this point.

"You flew that airship?" a woman asked. "I never imagined I'd see one here."

"Scared me half to death," a younger woman said, "though it is kind of amazing..."

"Feel free to come up to the village proper," an old man with a cane said. "There's not much to see, though. This is no tourist destination, to say the least."

"We hardly ever get visitors at all," a small girl said. "Where are you from?"

"A small town far from here," Lanek said. "At least, when I'm building airships. When I'm traveling, I suppose the airship you saw just now is my home."

"Well, feel free to make yourself at home here," an old woman said. "If you need a place to spend the night, I'm sure we can accommodate."

"That's very kind of you," Lanek said. He decided to neither accept or reject the offer right away, and wait to see how things would play out. Glancing up the mountain trail, he noticed some more villagers approaching, though these ones looked more at ease. Perhaps they felt calmer, seeing their fellow villagers engaging in friendly conversation with these strangers. Or at least Lanek.

He decided to finish introductions. "This here is Kitoh. He is an eigni, and though he's just a boy, he's an accomplished scientist."

"Well, not really," Kitoh said. "I'm just a researcher, just studying..."

A farmer boy looked visibly impressed. "You're a scientist? Do you not have to farm or go to school then?"

"An eigni?" a girl said to an older boy with a straw hat. "Is he..."

"Don't worry," the boy in the hat said. "Eigni are nice. And look, he's just a bit older than us. He's nice."

Lanek pointed to Lynx and added, "And this is a bodyguard. He's not allowed to speak, so don't try talking to him."

"I can speak all I want," Lynx muttered.

A few conversations continued all at once, and Lanek took the moment to turn back to Rilv and give her a slight smirk. He would have liked to see her flustered by Lanek's ability to manage the situation, but as always she refused to express any kind of interesting reaction.

Lanek shrugged and looked back to the small crowd of villagers. A young woman with light brown hair and a green and black dress approached Lanek, so he turned to speak with her.

"By the way, I was wondering what the name of this village was, Miss...?" Lanek said.

"Fenley," the woman finished. "Er, that's my name, that is. The village is Velm."

Lanek maintained the smirk he had given Rilv. "Oh? That's a lovely name."

Fenley blushed and glanced to the side. "Um... my name? Or the... village?"

"Ah, the village's name is nice too," Lanek said. "I'd like to see some more of it."

"It's... it's right this way," Fenley said, motioning toward the dirt trail. "I can show you around. You should at least see the shrine to the ancients. Well... at least if you're interested."

"That would be nice," Lanek said. "Let's go, Rilv."

Rilv stared at him with a straight face. Lanek wondered if she was upset with him to some degree, though she didn't show any displeasure in the situation. She was probably just analyzing things in her head—perhaps wondering if this shrine Fenley mentioned would hold any clue to where the Hader was. It was at least the most important building in this village, it seemed.

The villagers took the group of four up the rest of the way to the village, where small wooden structures rested a good distance from one another, with thin trails of smoke coming from small brick chimneys. Which buildings were homes and which were shops, Lanek couldn't tell. He decided he was thinking about the village structure the wrong way—what goods were sold were likely just bartered at homes, if everyone knew each other. Though the people were nervous to see visitors, they seemed like a friendly bunch. This village was probably a tight-knit group, perhaps out of necessity.

"That's my home over there." Fenley pointed at a nondescript hovel. Like all the other little buildings, this home was covered with dark wooden planks, unpainted, and lacking any kind of ornamentation. It looked sturdy and watertight, so the focus for this village was likely on practicality and resilience.

Even the shrine, as it turned out, looked very plain. It was about the size of nine village homes, three long and three wide, and made of stones mortared together. Instead of a door, it looked like there were some heavy black curtains inside the arched opening. There was a guard to either side of the doorway—elves dressed in leather armor, wielding a lance. Neither of them said anything when Fenley guided Lanek to the entrance, though she stopped before pulling the curtain back.

"Oh, I should mention only elves can come inside," she said.

A farming man with a thin mustache turned to Rilv and the others. "We can take you all to the administration building in the meantime. We have some food and drink for guests, and a fire can help you warm up."

Rilv glanced from the farmer to Lanek and back again, presumably trying to decide the best course of action. "Very well. Is this where the leader of the village lives?"

"No, but we can probably find him if you want," the man said. "Oh, you had business of some kind to deal with, right?"

"Nothing too big," Lanek said, before Rilv could make the situation sound grave to the villagers. "But we'd love to meet and chat with your leader, if it's not too much trouble for him."

"I doubt it'd be a problem," the farmer said. "Nullen hardly ever has anything official to deal with, as you might imagine. This'll be good for him."

Some of the villagers had dispersed at this point, perhaps to inform relatives of the arrival of visitors, while other villagers spoke quietly amongst themselves. Lanek only caught a few words here and there, but everyone seemed curious to find out what business the royal government had in mind for their little village. Perhaps it would have been good to make up a non-threatening story, but Lanek couldn't think of a good one. Hopefully Rilv would just converse with the villagers to break the ice some more before jumping straight to asking where the Hader could be.

"Sounds great," Lanek said. "Go ahead, Rilv. You and Kitoh and Lynx can go relax at the administration building a bit. I'll join you soon enough."

Rilv and the others went along with some of the villagers to the building in question—a stone building not much bigger than any of the homes in the vicinity. There was a large wooden sign nailed above the doorway though, with ancient elvish lettering intricately inscribed on it. Lanek could read elvish—not that he ever needed to use it much—but the swirling lettering on the sign seemed hundreds of years old. Despite this, the sign looked to be in pretty good condition.

"Sorry I couldn't let your friends come into the shrine with you," Fenley said, "but that's the rule. It's nothing against humans or eigni or anything..."

"It's fine," Lanek said. "I'm familiar with this sort of protocol." He was a little worried about leaving the others alone, especially with Lynx in their midst. But it seemed this was the best course of action to take—there was a chance Lanek would find something out about the Hader from this young woman, so it was important he not relinquish the opportunity to go inside the shrine.

Fenley opened the curtain to let Lanek in, as well as about a dozen villagers, most of them not much older or younger than Lanek. The inside of the shrine was surprisingly bright and spacious, the dark stone walls lit up by torches spaced just a meter or so apart. Between each torch was a work of art crafted from a thin sheet of light copper, cut into perfect circles. Lanek walked up to one and saw a depiction of a couple goddesses, surrounded by ancient elvish writing and a number of more intricate symbols. Lanek was familiar with most of the old tales of elvish religion, but he wasn't quite sure who these deities were. The other metal plates had other gods and goddesses inscribed on them, many of them holding objects that surely held significant meaning to those more pious than Lanek.

He looked back to the center of the shrine, where a large circular pool of water rested. At the very center of the pool was a stone platform with a statue of a kneeling goddess, her arms held forward dramatically, as if she were beholding some kind of miraculous sight a ways above her.

A boy pointed at the still, clear waters of the pool. "This is divine water. It will help you feel calm and happy."

"Really?" Lanek said. "That sounds... great?"

"It *is* great," a man with light brown hair said. "A weekly rest ritual does wonders. Puts your soul at ease. Helps you see things as they are. A sort of reminder to keep things simple in life."

"Simple..." Lanek said. "I could use a little simplicity in my own life." And he genuinely meant it. Perhaps he should forget Rilv and this crazy quest, and just set up shop in this little village. It was a silly thought though, considering he'd never have access to all the necessary parts for building airships at a secluded place like this.

"You should take part in a rest ritual then!" Fenley said. "I haven't had one yet this week, and was thinking of doing it tonight. You can do it with me, if you'd like."

Lanek felt his heart beat a little faster. He didn't know what this ritual entailed, for one thing. And in a strange way he felt like he was being asked out on a date, which seemed strange, considering he had just met this girl. Not that that would be a bad thing, Lanek realized. Fenley was actually very pretty, in a homely, unassuming way. Her light brown eyes matched her hair, and she had a cute, petite frame not so different from Suran's, back in Edellerston. He wasn't quite sure how old this girl was, though.

"That sounds like a good idea," the man said, now standing beside Fenley. "Have you ever gone through a rest ritual before?"

"No," Lanek said. "Can't say I have."

"There's only a few divine pools left in the world," the man said, "so that's not so surprising. Fenley can help you out, though. She knows everything about all the rituals."

"This is my brother, by the way," Fenley said. "His name's Yalmin and he just got married a couple weeks ago! Tria, his wife—she makes the most delicious soups in the world."

"She's probably going to cook some up soon," Yalmin said. "Perhaps I can head over and see if she can make some extra? You and your friends can come over tonight if you want."

Lanek didn't want to turn down such hospitality, even if he wasn't hoping to glean information off of these people. "That sounds nice. And so does the ritual. I'll go ahead and give it a try, if it's really as nice as you say it is."

"You'll love it," Fenley said. She turned to the other villagers and looked them over for a few seconds. "You've all had a rest ritual already this week, haven't you?"

There were several nods and a couple *yes*'s, so Fenley turned back to Lanek and folded her arms. "Looks like it'll just be us then." She smiled, and Lanek couldn't help but smile a bit too. This girl—and these villagers in general— just had a sweetness that Lanek didn't find in others much anymore.

He wondered if the village's seclusion simply made the people naïve, or if the people here were as genuine as they appeared to be. Perhaps he was just over-thinking things. Perhaps he needed to not let himself get so caught up in this mission, and take the time to get to know these people just for the sake of being nice. It had been a long time since he had been able to meet new people like this.

Once everyone else left, Fenley led Lanek to the back of the room, where there were a couple of shelving units filled with stacks of folded-up clothes—all of them a light gray, it looked like. There were also a couple free-standing folding walls, apparently intended for people to change clothes behind.

"The rest ritual is a simple one, Fenley said. "You lie in the divine water, and allow the gods and goddesses to clear your mind, calm your body, and purify your soul. If you focus on one thing long enough, you'll find clarity in what it is you should do, regarding what you're thinking about."

Lanek walked to one of the shelves and picked up one of the articles of clothing. It felt very soft and silky, but was a bit stretchy. "So we change into some of these clothes?" He unfolded the clothes he held and found it to be a one-piece bathing suit for women.

"You'll want to use the other shelf," Fenley said, "but yes, you probably don't want to get your own clothes dirty. The clothes provided by the shrine represent life in this world, which is neither wholly light or dark."

Lanek returned the clothes he held and picked up a pair of shorts from the other shelf. The ritual seemed strange, and a little pointless. Not quite like going for a swim—it was really just a bath, if anything.

Though it was with some nice company, Lanek remembered.

He pulled out one of the folding walls and changed into a pair of gray swimming trunks that fit him, while Fenley changed behind the other makeshift dressing room. Lanek waited for her to come out before walking to the shrine pool, not wanting to do anything to ruin the ritual.

"Are you ready?" Fenley asked.

Lanek stepped out and nodded. Fenley was dressed in one of the plain gray bathing suits, and though her figure was shown more clearly—and was quite a bit more womanly than Lanek expected—there was still a pure look about her. She held her hands together behind her back, and looked over Lanek a few seconds. For a moment Lanek thought she was going to blush, but instead she closed her eyes and smiled.

"Ah, this might be kind of awkward for you," she said. "If you've always lived in a city, you might have never done any rituals before."

"No, I'm fine," Lanek said. "And most of my life I lived in a village called Edellerston. There weren't any shrines for ancient elf rituals there, though."

"I'm glad you're fine with this," Fenley said. "Our village hardly ever gets any visitors."

Lanek thought it was more surprising that Fenley was fine with this, but she probably felt safe since there were a couple guards just outside the entrance. Not that Lanek was planning anything—he was simply curious to see what was so special about this ritual.

Fenley led him to the waters, and pointed to the statue of the goddess with outstretched hands. "Reali will help enlighten you, though it may take a little while since it's your first time."

Though Lanek had never been very religious, he was willing to place a little faith in this ritual for Fenley's sake. Perhaps he wouldn't find anything special about it at all, but it wouldn't be hard for him to act relaxed and edified. Lying in the water a bit would probably be nice at least, especially since there was a red Nexi at each side of the circular pool, keeping it warm.

Lanek let Fenley get into the water first so he could see if there was any specific way he needed to lie in the pool.

"Just have your hands and feet pointing toward the goddess," Fenley said. She lay down with her head propped back against the wall of the pool. Her eyes shut and her breathing slowed. Her face exuded a calmness and tranquility Lanek didn't expect to find so quickly. The pool was just deep enough to keep the rest of her body underwater, though her chest rose out a bit when she inhaled deeply. And as she had instructed, she kept her arms and legs pointed straight toward the statue kneeling on the pedestal in the pool's center. Though there was a rigidness to her position, she looked perfectly relaxed.

Lanek stepped in the pool as quietly as he could, not wanting to interrupt Fenley's concentration. The water was lukewarm—neither hot nor cold in the slightest. He assumed this was symbolic the same sort of way the plain gray clothes were.

"Feel free to speak up if you have any questions," Fenley said. "I've done this many times before, so I can regain my focus easily."

"Okay," Lanek said. He eased himself into the water and lay down beside Fenley.

She opened an eye and glanced at him, a smile spreading on her face. "You don't have to lie right next to me."

"Oh, do we need to spread out?" Lanek asked.

"No, it makes no difference," Fenley said. "I just wasn't expecting it." Some of Fenley's hair brushed against Lanek's shoulder, the water moving strands of her hair in slow, wispy motions.

"Our minds will conduct more power when we're close together," Lanek said. "And I'm a personal fellow by nature, anyways. Personable, too."

"That's good," Fenley said, to Lanek's surprise. "I sometimes wonder if people in the world are becoming more and more impersonal."

"Even in a village like this?" Lanek asked.

Fenley nodded. "Some people think it's best for everyone to mind their own business. Which... I guess is good to a degree, but..."

"People need to help each other," Lanek said. "You can't just focus on yourself all the time."

"Yes, people ought to be less selfish," Fenley said. She sighed and closed her eyes again, letting her body sink back into the water.

"Though it's good to keep your dreams in mind, too," Lanek said. "You have any big goals in life, Fenley?"

She smirked a little. "Nothing very big. I kind of just want to have a family and manage a house really well. You know... be a good wife and mother."

"Sounds like a big goal to me," Lanek said. "Those are things I'd never be able to do, at least."

Fenley opened her eyes. "What? Why's that?"

"Well, I'd make a poor wife and mother," Lanek said.

Fenley laughed a little. "I thought you were saying you'd never have a family."

"Ah, well..." Lanek paused a few seconds. "I guess I haven't given it much thought."

He also hadn't stuck with a girl long enough to begin considering anything even close to marriage, but he didn't want to bring up this aspect of his social life with Fenley. The last five years had been good for Lanek in terms of winning the hearts of lots of women, but he never tried to form a lasting relationship with any of them. None of the women who fell for him seemed to mind when Lanek moved on—most of them were just as lustful and vain as he was.

"That's right," Fenley said. "You fly an airship. I guess you wouldn't really want to be tied down to one place."

"Well, I'm usually just building airships," Lanek said. "And to be honest, I'm not anxious to be flying around for this excursion I'm on."

"It must be hectic, working for the government," Fenley said.

Lanek couldn't hold back a weak laugh. "Oh yes... In fact, a part of me would rather I just sit in this pool for the next few weeks, than continue on this... endeavor."

"I guess you can't give me details," Fenley said. "And I guess a part of you knows you have to continue it."

"Yes... a part of me knows I have to see this through to the end."

"Do you... have plans for afterward?"

It was a question Lanek wasn't expecting, and certainly wasn't one he had been thinking about ever since learning of Rilv's plan to collect the Haders. When was this mission going to be finished? Would Lanek really be able to put up with Lynx for weeks on end? Or even months? For that matter, would he even be able to put up with Rilv for that long? As Fenley said, Lanek didn't enjoy working for the government—but the fact was he inherited his parents' legacy of creating very fast airships, and this was something the Fiefs Kingdom would not be able to ignore. Especially when the Shire Kingdom was making its own advances in the field of aviation.

"I'm not the kind of person to think very far ahead," Lanek finally said.

"Maybe this is a good opportunity to try?" Fenley said. "As the god Pilekshim said, the only person who can make you do something is yourself."

"There's always consequences to deal with afterward though."

"Yes, Pilekshim said that as well."

The girl's reliance on the ancient religion was a little peculiar to Lanek—at the very least unfamiliar—but it somehow came off as a cute quality for Fenley. Perhaps she was just that good-natured. Perhaps she was just that much like Suran.

"Fenley, if you don't mind my asking... How old are you?"

"Oh, it's kind of embarrassing... But, um, I'm seventeen."

"How is that embarrassing? That's a lovely age."

"I'm already seventeen, and still not married," Fenley said. "I guess it's been on my mind a lot lately, since my older brother just got married. But it's fine for boys to marry when they're a bit older. My relatives are worried about me, but I don't really like the boys they've tried to pair me off with."

Lanek saw this conversation going a number of ways, none of which he felt he ought to entertain right now, given that he was supposed to be focused on figuring out where the Hader was.

"I'm sorry," Fenley said. "I've ended up chatting with you, instead of letting you take part in the ritual. I'll be quiet now." She shut her eyes and repositioned her body to lie perfectly still beneath the water. Only her head remained above water, and her hair continued to slowly sway to either side of her. Lanek was surprised when she opened her mouth again. "Oh, but feel free to ask any questions if you have any, and maybe I'll be able to help you out. With what to focus your mind on, and such."

She had certainly left Lanek with plenty of things to think about. What was he supposed to focus on? He looked over to Fenley's soft, tender face, as reposed as a sleeping princess's. He watched the slight rise and fall of her breathing, and the subtle motions of her legs. Lanek imagined she was already gaining the tranquility and enlightenment this ritual offered.

He lay his head back and shut his eyes, still trying to decide what he ought to think about. Perhaps the ritual could help him figure out where the Hader was? This seemed the wisest choice, but Lanek had a feeling nothing would come of simply thinking about the Hader. Did he actually care about finding it? It wasn't his idea to go looking for the stones. And though he did have an interest in bringing down the Brotherhood, he didn't care for this method of doing so. There was no guarantee the Haders would enable them to defeat Augurc's experiments. And there was the possibility of ill side effects. Lanek wasn't about to forget what happened to Terico, who died from overuse of the Elpis fragments.

What is it Fenley is thinking about? Lanek wondered. Marriage was certainly on her mind, so it made sense for her to focus on that subject. What would she end up realizing? That she ought to marry Lanek? It was clear she had an interest in him.

This rest ritual was probably just wish fulfillment. People just think what they want to think. There was no reason to believe the ritual would solve anyone's problems, just by lying in the water and meditating for a little while.

It was silly, how this random girl felt Lanek could suddenly be a part of her life like this. He hardly knew her. And as soon as he found the Hader, he'd be on his way, and never see her again. Why would she care about him? He should have just been seen as a random passer-by, like any other visitor. She didn't know anything about him, save that he made and piloted airships. There was no way for her—or anyone—to know that she'd be compatible with him.

Just thinking about this was a little ridiculous, though Lanek wondered if he had been focusing on it too much. Or enough for the ritual to start to affect him. If it could affect him.

I'll just focus on the Hader and see what happens, Lanek decided. He forced himself to think only of the Hader hidden somewhere in or near this village. If he was going to be a part of this mission, he might as well give his all. The sooner he found the Hader, the sooner the mission would end, and the sooner the Brotherhood would come to an end. And the sooner Suran would be avenged.

It was right to do this, wasn't it? The world would be better without the Brotherhood. Safer. Augurc would be gone, and so would his devastating experiments. And his terrible followers. Lynx included. There was no way Lanek was just going to let Lynx go.

The Hader. He had to get the Hader. Lanek had to be the one to find it. He needed leverage against Lynx. The more power Lanek had, the more capable he'd be to kill Lynx.

Where is it?

Where is the Hader?

Where is it hidden?

How can I obtain it?

How can I wield it?

Lanek lost track of time, and even forgot he was lying in water, its gentle pushes and pulls against his body dissolving into background noise—

impossible to notice as all his thoughts turned to the Hader.

He didn't know why, but he decided to open his eyes. It made no sense to do so. Wouldn't that break his concentration? And yet it came to him effortlessly, naturally, seamlessly. He stared straight above himself.

Something was hanging in the air. The goddess statue was staring up straight at it, just as Lanek was, though from a different angle. It was a glowing stone, shifting from a dull red to a bright yellow. The two colors swirled within the Nexi, radiating a light very similar to that of Rilv's telekinesis stone.

It was a Hader. Right there in the shrine, hanging from a fancy-looking white rope and some netting. How had Lanek not seen it right when he walked into the building? Perhaps it wasn't actually there, but was some kind of vision? He had focused for a good while on the Hader, but he had never felt certain he'd actually find it. It was more of a foolish hope, if anything. And yet... here it was. Just a few meters above where he lay. With the help of one of the shelving units, Lanek would be able to easily cut the rope with his rapier and take the Hader.

If it was actually there. It seemed kind of impossible for it to be there, when it had clearly not been there until now.

"I see something," he said. "There is something hanging above us. A Nexi stone of some kind."

Fenley opened her eyes and smiled. "It's the Stone of Truth. If you can see it, that means your focus has reached a conclusion. If you had a deep question in your heart, there is now an answer—a key resting in the lock, waiting for you to turn it. Just as the water calms the body and the silence calms the mind, the Stone of Truth calms the soul."

So this Stone of Truth—or rather, this Hader—had appeared once Lanek had focused on something hard enough. It was ironic that it was the Hader itself Lanek had been concentrating on. The revealing of the stone was the sign and the answer all in one.

"How do you feel?" Fenley asked.

Lanek chuckled. "Enlightened."

•

The Hader and the string it was tied to disappeared before Lanek got out of the pool. He made a point of remembering precisely where it was, though it wasn't hard—he only had to look to where the goddess statue was looking. Perhaps there was a story about her finding the Hader floating in the sky—or rather a Stone of Truth, as the texts would likely put it.

Once they changed back to their old clothes, Lanek followed Fenley to the shrine doorway, his thoughts lingering on the Hader. How was he going to get it? Perhaps the guards wouldn't be around in the middle of the night, and he could just sneak in?

It felt wrong to do, of course. Everyone in this village had been nothing but kind to him so far. It wasn't right to return the favor by stealing their most precious treasure. The Hader clearly held special meaning to the villagers, and likely had many years of religious history stored up in it. It certainly held great significance to Fenley, at the very least.

Lanek doubted he'd be able to keep the Hader a secret from Rilv for long. She would find a way somehow to pin down the exact location of the stone, and would probably not be willing to leave before obtaining it.

Plus there was the possibility Lynx would get the stone. Lanek couldn't let the murderous Brotherhood member lay hands on the Hader. The consequences would be horrendous, and would put a great risk on the mission. Not to mention on Lanek himself—plus Rilv and Kitoh. Lynx was dangerous enough as it was, and there was a good chance the masked man had spearheaded this mission for the sake of getting the Haders for himself in the first place.

And Lanek remembered there was someone else approaching the village. Someone with two Haders was coming, and could very well be willing to go to any length to take the Hader in this village. It was very unlikely this enemy was on the side of the Fiefs Kingdom, at the very least.

Fenley guided Lanek from the shrine to the administration building, where presumably Rilv and the others were going to speak with the leader of the village. Lanek had noticed a bit of a spring in Fenley's step. She looked quite pleased with herself. Perhaps she was happy with the insight she gained from the rest ritual.

It worried Lanek a little. That girl likely had two things on her mind: him and marriage—and regardless of what the Stone of Truth put in that head of hers, it just wasn't going to work out.

A part of Lanek legitimately entertained the idea of a quiet village life. But it simply didn't feel right for him. How could he just hide away atop an empty mountain, leaving everything behind him? Ever since Edellerston was destroyed, ever since his parents were killed, ever since he became entangled in quests for the Fiefs Kingdom, ever since Suran was killed... there was nothing that could ever be the same. He could never really be himself again, though he had long pretended he could.

What am I now? Lanek wondered.

Perhaps that's what he should have thought about in the rest ritual. Maybe next week.

But there wasn't going to be a next week for him. Or for anyone. He was going to steal the Hader and be off in his airship, likely tens of kilometers away from the village before anyone caught wind of what happened.

Or maybe he wasn't. How could he live with himself after doing something like that?

It is for the greater good, he could imagine Rilv saying. *The Fiefs Kingdom needs the Hader more than this village does. And we can always return it once our mission is complete.*

Imagining Rilv saying this didn't make Lanek feel any better about the prospect of stealing the Hader. In fact, it just upset him more.

Fenley knocked on the door of the administration building, which was promptly opened by a man in a white jacket and black pants. He smiled at Fenley, but raised an eyebrow at Lanek.

"Hi, Chei," Fenley said. "This is Lanek, another visitor. He just went through the rest ritual with me."

"Ah, was it your first time?" Chei asked.

"Yes," Lanek said. "I think it went well."

"Really?" Chei grinned, the tip of his tongue poking between his teeth. "It took me several months before I felt I was getting any kind of inspiration."

"Wow..." Lanek said, pretending to look shocked. "That's a long time to be sitting in the pool. Your whole body must've been covered in wrinkles."

Chei laughed so hard, Lanek and Fenley jumped back a little. "It's not like I was in there several months straight. I still just went once a week, and never longer than an hour. Can't just sit around all day, after all. Far too much work to be done."

The man led Lanek and Fenley from the entryway to a decent-sized room with several plain wooden chairs. Rilv, Kitoh, Lynx, and a couple elves sat in a circle, leaving five other chairs sitting against the far wall. There was a brick fireplace with a subdued fire going behind Kitoh and a middle-aged woman with short black hair. The only other point of notice was a rather plain green and yellow rug hanging limply behind a middle-aged man, who had a series of scars down his neck and a red scarf over the top of his head. Lanek assumed one of these elves was the village leader, since Chei didn't seem the type.

"Did you learn anything interesting?" Rilv asked, always going straight to the point. It wasn't like Lanek could just blurt out that he found the Hader though, so presumably Rilv was expecting Lanek to say something in code, or something.

"I wish I had the privilege of going through the rest ritual every week," Lanek said, deciding to not bother hinting whether or not he found out anything about the Hader. He could talk to Rilv later, when they weren't surrounded by villagers. For now, he needed to just pretend he was still trying to find out about the Hader, since he didn't want Lynx to catch on that he had found it in the shrine.

"It is a relaxing ritual," Chei said. He motioned a hand to the two elves sitting in the circle. "Allow me to introduce you to Ioliv and Neve, the village coordinator and village representative."

"Nice to meet you," Lanek said. "Does that make you the village leaders?"

"No, that responsibility falls to Nullen," Chei said. "He should be here shortly."

"Ah." Apparently Rilv and the others hadn't even gotten the chance to speak with the leader yet. "And what's your position then, Chei?"

"Village idiot," the scarred man said.

"I've been promoted?" Chei asked.

"Don't congratulate yourself too much," the raven-haired woman said. "It's not actually a step up from village fool."

"He's actually the village greeter," Kitoh said. "And he greeted us very well."

"Everyone in this village has a title, it seems," Rilv said. "Though it appears they all farm." She looked thoroughly disinterested in the situation. She had her arms folded, one leg crossed over the other, and her head slightly tilted forward.

"Whenever we don't have visitors, at least," Chei said.

"Which isn't very often," Lanek said. "At least, that's what Fenley tells me."

Chei looked shocked for a moment, then turned to Fenley with a stern look in his eyes. "Giving away all the village's secrets, eh?"

"Well, I am the village speaker," Fenley said. This elicited a laugh from the other two elves.

"Well, you are very good at it," the woman said.

"At speaking, that is," the man added. "Whether there are visitors or not."

Before Fenley could respond, the front door opened once more. Chei hurried to the entryway to greet who Lanek assumed to be the village leader.

Following Chei back into the sitting room was a man who looked to be in his sixties, at the very least. He had long white hair, with a series of multicolored beads strung in several of the strands hanging in front of his pointed ears. He wore robes that looked to be a strange amalgamation of different-colored robes—one sleeve was blue, the other was red, the top third was white, the middle third was gray, and the bottom third was black. And though he was an elderly man, he was also quite tall, and held a commanding presence upon entering the room.

The elves who were sitting down immediately stood up, and Lanek noticed Rilv managed to stand to attention the exact same time. Kitoh stood up a second later, upon realizing what was happening. A few seconds later, it took Rilv tapping Lynx on the shoulder to get him to stand up. Lanek wondered if he had fallen asleep—Lynx probably didn't converse with the elves the whole time Lanek was away, and it wasn't like anyone would be able to tell right away that the masked man snoozed off for a bit.

The old man chuckled as he glanced over to Lanek, Rilv, and the others. "I assure you, we're hardly ever this formal." Everyone relaxed a bit, then sat back down one or two at a time.

"Worth a try once in a while," Chei said.

Lanek sat down in a chair beside Fenley, while Chei pulled out a chair for the village leader, who Lanek remembered was named Nullen. Everyone rearranged their chairs a bit, so Nullen sat in front, facing the village's guests.

"I hope you've enjoyed your stay so far," Nullen said. "I'm sorry I was a ways down the mountain when you arrived. I go on walks from time to time, and sometimes find myself a lot further from the village than I intend."

"He goes where the wind pushes him," the scarred elf said.

"So best hope he never stands too close to a cliff," Chei added.

Nullen frowned deeply at Chei, who simply smiled back in return.

"At any rate," Nullen said, "I hope our guests have been well received." He looked down to Kitoh for a couple seconds.

"Ah," Kitoh said, a little surprised. He probably expected Rilv to do all the talking. "I really... The elves, er, everyone here's been nice. The food was really good."

"What did you have?" Nullen asked.

"Bread and tea," Kitoh said. "The bread was really warm."

"That's how we like to eat it," Nullen said, patting his stomach. "Helps keep the fire going, though mine will probably be diminishing soon, regardless."

"Can't keep a fire going forever," the woman a few chairs from Lanek said.

"And can't keep a guest waiting forever," Nullen said. He turned to Lanek and asked, "Now, I'm kind of curious. How exactly are you all related?"

"You don't see the family resemblance?" Chei asked.

Of course, there was none, given that the group consisted of an elf, an eigni, and two humans, one of whom was masked.

"We're just all working together, you could say," Lanek said. "Rilv here is the one leading the group. She can best introduce us." He didn't want to say something wrong, given the delicacy of this operation.

Rilv gave her name, as well as Lanek's, Kitoh's, and Lynx's. "I am the head servant of the Fiefs Kingdom, and the four of us are traveling together to conduct an extensive search."

"Amazing," Nullen said. "I never expected royalty to step foot in our humble village."

"We are not royalty," Rilv said. "But our business does concern the royal court."

Nullen pointed at Lynx. "And why's he masked, exactly?"

Lynx tilted his head to the side, and held it there silently for several seconds. Lanek wondered if he was going to respond at all, but Lynx eventually cleared his throat and answered. "Well, let's just say that after I was born, my mother decided any future children in the family would need to be adopted."

Nullen and the other elves laughed, and even Kitoh laughed a little. Lanek admittedly found the joke a little amusing as well, but he was never going to let himself laugh at one of Lynx's jokes, even if the masked man was poking fun at himself.

"Well, feel free to keep it on," Nullen said. It seemed that the old man—and everyone else in the village, for that matter—didn't recognize Lynx's mask marked him as a member of the Brotherhood. Did the people in the village even know what the Brotherhood was? It was quite possible, Lanek realized, that the elves here were so cut off from the rest of the world, that they didn't know any specifics about the Brotherhood.

He couldn't let Lynx become good friends with the people here. He would manipulate them, trick them, betray them. He didn't want anything bad to happen to these people.

And yet he was planning to steal their Stone of Truth.

Nullen and the elves got sidetracked into a discussion on masks used in some of their yearly festivals, but Lanek's thoughts were elsewhere.

Lanek couldn't stand himself. What was it he was trying to do, exactly?

I just have to accept it, he thought. *I just have to accept the fact these people are going to be hurt. Someone is going to be leaving the village with that Hader. I won't let it be the person who already has two of them. And I definitely won't let it be Lynx. I have to be the one that takes it. I'll do it in the middle of the night. These people will probably have us spend the night. I'll get up and steal it, then get Rilv and the others to come back with me to the airship without waking anyone up. And then... I'll just have to forget this village.*

He wasn't sure he'd be able to. He had never been to a place quite like it before.

His eyes met Fenley's for a moment, and he realized she had been looking at him. Not wanting to look as troubled as he felt, he leaned back in his chair and folded his arms, and gave her a look to show that he had caught her staring. She glanced away, but not without a smile creeping across her face.

Though he kept it to himself, Lanek regretted his continued interaction with Fenley. After tonight, there wasn't going to be any further developing of their relationship together. She was just going to be another girl who fell for his dashing good looks. Just another girl Lanek would need to leave behind and forget.

But again... he wasn't sure he'd be able to. He had never met a girl quite like her before.

Nullen and the other three elves realized they were rambling, and the village leader laughingly steered the conversation back to the matter at hand.

"Sorry, sorry," he said. He turned to Rilv, a large smile still on his face. "I should get to the point, I suppose. What is it you're looking for, that our village would have?"

"A Hader," Rilv said.

Lanek nearly slipped out of his chair. *So to the point! What is she thinking?*

"What is a Hader?" Nullen asked. The questioning look on his face looked genuine enough, but Lanek assumed that nobody in the village had connected their Stone of Truth with any of the abnormally powerful Nexi stones used in centuries past.

"Haders look something like this," Rilv said. She took the telekinesis Hader from her pocket to show to Nullen. Just as it had at Setar Castle, the stone continually gave off a swirling purple and blue glow.

"Oh!" said Fenley, accompanied by some quiet recognition from the other elves.

Except for Nullen. He stared at it curiously a few seconds before responding. "Is this a Nexi stone of some kind?"

"Yes," Rilv said. "And I take it there is another stone like it in this village, given the reactions by your fellow citizens."

"I've never seen a stone like this before," Nullen said. "And I don't recall anyone ever saying anything about a stone like this before." Nullen looked to the other elves and asked, "Have any of you ever seen one of these in the village?"

"Don't think so," the woman said.

"No," the scarred man added.

"It certainly looks nice, whatever it is," Chei said.

There was a long pause, perhaps ten seconds long. Rilv was calculating the responses, likely thinking the same thing Lanek was thinking: Nullen was lying, and the villagers were just following his lead.

But Rilv surely thought they were trying to keep secret a powerful weapon. Lanek knew the villagers saw their Hader in a completely different light—it was nothing more than an object of religious import. It somehow made a connection with their minds in some way while they rested in the shrine's pool, but they didn't seem to use it in any other way. As far as Lanek could tell, they couldn't even see it when they weren't achieving enlightenment in the pool.

Rilv looked to Fenley. "Have you ever seen a stone like this before?"

Fenley shook her head. "It's very pretty. What does it do?" She understood not to reveal anything now, but was hesitant to say an outright lie. The villagers likely felt they were justified to lie in a situation like this, to preserve their religious practices, though Fenley appeared to find it a bit more difficult. She seemed like the type of girl who probably hoped to go her whole life without lying, or doing anyone harm. And yet she managed to look calm, her face now only showing curiosity in the Hader that Rilv held.

Rilv, on the other hand, looked profoundly dissatisfied—but then again, she always did, to varying degrees.

She looked to the village leader again, and sat up even straighter than usual. For a moment Lanek thought she was going to stand up, but she retained her position. "If there is a stone like this in the village, it is of the utmost importance that I locate it. It could very well be a deciding key in the preservation of our kingdom."

"I will let you know if I see one," Nullen said.

"If you know where it may be, the kingdom will gladly assist this village in any of its needs," Rilv went on. "And, of course, you will all be substantially compensated for your assistance. I am capable of awarding the village goods with a combined value exceeding nine hundred thousand in monetary value."

"A generous offer," Nullen said, "but our village has no need for riches. We are a content, self-reliant people. I doubt any of us would feel at home in a palace of jade and gold and silk. It's best we keep things as simple as possible."

"I understand," Rilv said. "The offer to assist your village in any other way still stands, however. I work directly for the king, and am willing to procure anything you or your people desire. This could include the manpower to construct buildings and roadways, the means to produce better crops, or even a collection of ancient elvish texts that could prove invaluable to better understanding your religious beliefs."

"There is nothing we need from the government," Nullen said, surprisingly quick in his answer. "And I'm afraid nobody here knows anything about these Haders you speak of. Very few of us ever leave this village, so we tend to just know about the things we need to."

"Very well," Rilv said, pocketing her Hader. "If you don't mind, we would like to explore the surrounding area for a bit before we leave, just to make sure it isn't simply lying around somewhere."

"That's fine," Nullen said. "Just be sure to keep the peace, and don't go searching people's shops and homes without asking first."

"Of course," Rilv said.

There was another long pause. There was clearly a strange tension in the room, one that was likely difficult for everyone to pin down. Nobody had made any threats yet, but there was that clear possibility, from both Rilv and Nullen. What it was Nullen could ever do, Lanek wasn't sure. As far as he could tell, he, Rilv, Lynx, and Kitoh could probably defeat everyone in this village if a fight broke out.

The thought reminded Lanek of the couple guards at the shrine. It meant that at least some of the elves here were probably trained to fight, and surely the average citizen had access to the base Nexi stones, such as red, blue, and orange.

Also, Rilv surely saw there were guards at the shrine, and had probably already decided she would investigate the site as soon as possible. She would certainly see the possibility that the guards were protecting the Hader, rather than the sanctity of the shrine.

But she wouldn't see the Hader there—and neither would Lynx. As long as the villagers kept quiet, there was essentially zero chance of either of them locating the Hader. It was invisible, and there was no way for either of them to bump into it.

Would Rilv or Lynx force someone to tell them the precise location of the Hader? Certainly Lynx would be willing to beat the information out of someone, but Rilv would probably continue trying to keep things from escalating out of control. She was the type of woman who liked to keep everything *certain*. She likely had a plan forming in her head right now, if she didn't have one formulated already.

The elves helped Rilv and the others out of the administration building, some of them engaging in idle chatter to help deflate the tension a bit. Surely everyone was going to act as normal as they could, but chances were they were all going to be keeping a vigilant eye on the visitors—constantly. They weren't going to let anyone take the Stone of Truth.

Lanek wondered what everyone was thinking of him. They knew Fenley had taken him into the shrine and had gone through the rest ritual with him. There were only two options they could be thinking of. One: Lanek was not successful in the rest ritual, and therefore did not see the Stone of Truth. This wouldn't be so surprising, since it was his first time attempting the ritual. And two: Lanek *did* see the Stone of Truth, but had purposely chosen not to say anything. If this were the case, that would mean he was on their side. After all, he was an elf like them. That's what they'd believe.

Someone grabbed Lanek's shoulder. Before he could react, he was spun around violently, then was grabbed by the other shoulder. He found himself staring directly into Chei's eyes. They were no longer friendly eyes—they were callous, dark, morbid.

And yet his voice sounded friendly when he spoke. "By the way, how *did* your rest ritual go?" Because Lanek was turned toward Chei, Rilv and the others couldn't see Lanek's situation. In fact, it looked like everyone was leaving them behind.

"Oh..." Lanek uncharacteristically stumbled for a response. "It went well. The water was nice."

Before Chei could say more, Fenley walked over. "The ritual was thoroughly enlightening, for the both of us."

She said it calmly, without emphasizing anything—and yet the message was perfectly clear to Chei. Fenley was letting him know that Lanek had indeed seen the Stone of Truth, but had chosen not to reveal this to Rilv. The other elves likely heard this too, but Rilv, Lynx, and Kitoh wouldn't understand the hidden message. They didn't know that enlightenment in the shrine entailed seeing the Hader hanging from the ceiling.

Chei loosened his grip on Lanek slowly. He was a brave one, considering that Lanek's rapier was in plain sight all this time, and the others in Lanek's group were nearby and also armed.

"I'm glad you had a good experience," Chei said. His eyes now matched his voice again, and all was back to normal once more. It was worrisome just how quickly Chei was able to shift back and forth. Was he pretending to be a silly, jovial fellow all this time? For all Lanek knew, it was all an act.

For all he knew, everything was an act.

Was it possible that Fenley was also just pretending to be Lanek's friend? Or did she actually suspect Lanek? What was it that she really thought of him?

The village leader and his supporters guided their visitors through the town, showing each of the homes, and noting anything remotely of interest. What constituted a special site in such a small village included things like a tree that had been struck by lightning, and a small hillside with some artwork made of rocks grouped into simple patterns—apparently set by children.

Of course, there was no sign of the Hader in the short tour, which was maybe a half hour at most, even with everyone walking at a slow, careful pace, and several random villagers stopping to greet them.

Everyone was thoroughly friendly, kind, considerate. Several people offered to let the visitors spend the night at their place, but Fenley made sure to let them know Lanek had already agreed to stay at her brother's place, where they were all going to have dinner.

By the time the tour ended, Lanek could tell Rilv was growing impatient. She was surely concerned about the person with two Haders approaching. Would this person arrive tonight? Lanek felt certain it would take a while for this opponent—for this was surely an opponent—to locate this specific village, so well-hidden in the mountaintops.

The village leader and his associates split up and went about their separate ways, save for Fenley who stayed with Lanek. He noticed Nullen and the others talking with more villagers, some of them casting glances toward the visitors. Were all the villagers being told to keep an eye on them? It wouldn't take long for word to spread through the entire village that the visitors were suspicious, though Lanek recalled there was already some wariness amongst many of the people the moment they arrived.

"It's probably about time for supper," Fenley said. "I can take you and your friends over to meet my brother and his family, if you'd like."

Lanek thought it best to check with Rilv, to find out what course of action she was going to take. When he turned to her, he found she was already looking at him.

"Go ahead," Rilv said. "We will meet up with you shortly."

"Okay," Fenley said. "We live in that house, right over there." She pointed to a house in the distance, at the top of a small incline. "The one with flower boxes hanging from the window. I'm growing some red tulips in them."

Lanek kept his eyes focused on Rilv's. "Are you sure? I don't want any trouble to start with..."

"I will have Lynx's full cooperation," Rilv said, readily understanding

Lanek's concern. "We will come within a half hour—otherwise you can come find us. In the meantime, I request you... learn more about this village. And I suggest you go quickly."

She wanted Lanek to get useful information from some of the villagers before they were told to be watchful of the visitors. If the people Lanek spoke with suspected him and the others of foul deeds, they wouldn't say anything about the Hader. Of course, Lanek already knew precisely where it was, and he was pretty certain the others had no way of finding out themselves at this point.

"Got it," Lanek said.

Fenley took his hand and eagerly brought him down the path leading to her brother's home. From what Lanek could tell, nobody had gone to that house since the village officials separated, so Lanek felt safe talking with Fenley's relatives. And really, there was no reason for him to be worried. He could protect himself well enough, and Fenley would be there to keep any trouble from escalating. Lanek just had to count on Lynx not causing any strife. Or Rilv, for that matter, though for very different reasons.

"So you eat with your brother and his wife?" Lanek asked. "What about your parents?"

"They've passed away," Fenley said. "A couple years ago, they fell ill." She didn't elaborate, and though she didn't sound sad, Lanek felt bad for bringing it up.

"I'm sorry," he said. "My parents died a few years ago too. My sister as well. It's difficult to know how to go on sometimes... after something like that."

Fenley stopped a few meters from the front door of the home and looked up into Lanek's eyes. Her eyes were wet, but she wasn't quite crying. "I'm so sorry. I felt terrible... for days. And I still feel terrible at times. Even now. But I've still had my brother. And the whole village. We all support each other when anyone dies. In a way, losing a fellow villager is almost like losing a family member."

Lanek at least had Suran after his parents and friends all died in Delkol's attack, but after Suran was killed... Who did he have left? He had only himself. And there were many days where he wondered what the point of anything was. It often felt like there wasn't much reason to go on living at all.

It would have been nice if there had been someone left alive, who could have understood what he had gone through.

"I'm sorry," Fenley said. "I didn't mean to get like this all of a sudden."

"It's fine," Lanek said. "I think it's a good sign. It shows you're still attached to the ones you love."

It was just something to say. Lanek didn't really think about it until after he finished the sentence. How much had *he* grieved these past five years?

Not very much. He didn't let himself grieve. It wasn't that he didn't want to. After his parents died, he wanted to be brave for Suran. She needed someone to support her, and Lanek was glad to be there for her. On top of this, he was thrown headfirst into a mission to help retrieve a piece of the Elpis, and then assist the nation in defending the capital against the Shire Kingdom's armies.

Then after Suran died, he felt...

It was difficult to put to words. He kept wondering how he was supposed to feel. How he was supposed to act. What he was supposed to do. Even who he was supposed to be. He was no longer a villager or student in Edellerston. He was no longer the training mechanic under his parents' tutelage. And he was no longer Suran's brother.

What was there for him? Only revenge—it was the only thing he could think of. Suran's killer still loomed at large, and so did the Brotherhood as a whole. Terico had gotten rid of the immediate threat—arguably the greater threat—but it wasn't over yet. It wasn't finished.

Fenley wiped her eyes and thanked Lanek. He was relieved to see her smile again, then knock at the door to her brother's home.

It was her brother who answered, and he showed them in to the front room of the home, which served as both a kitchen and a dining area. As Lanek expected, the house was just as humble inside as it was out, with little in the way of convenience or ornamentation. There was a thin table with four chairs, all of which looked scratched and battered over the years. And hanging near the hearth was a circular woodcarving of a number of deities, some of which looked similar to those in the shrine. Lanek tried to spot the goddess whose statue was carved in the shrine, but wasn't certain which was her.

Checking a pot in the fireplace was a woman who Lanek assumed to be the wife of Fenley's brother. She had the top of her blonde hair covered in a bandana that was half-black and half-white, and wore a fairly basic green and brown dress. She turned to Lanek and smiled.

"You must be one of the visitors," she said. "Lannick, was it?"

"His name's Lan*ek*," Fenley said. "*Eh. Eh.*"

Lanek chuckled, then glanced back to Fenley's sister-in-law. "It's good to meet you. And this soup you're cooking smells wonderful."

"Better than soup," the woman said. "This is a stew."

"By the way," Fenley's brother said, "when do you think your friends will show up?"

"Don't worry," Lanek said. "They just ate, so they're fine. They might not show up for a while, so no need to keep you waiting." Of course, if Rilv and the others took too long, he intended to check outside to see what they were doing.

In the kitchen area, an elderly couple gathered bowls and cups, and prepared a sweet-smelling tea. Though their motions were slow and weary, they were always smiling, and whispering and laughing to each other. Lanek helped bring everything to the table, while Fenley's brother helped the elderly man sit at the end of the table, and then the elderly woman sit to his right.

As Fenley's sister-in-law added some more spices to the stew, Lanek learned and relearned names—her brother was Yalmin, and his wife was Tria. The elderly couple were Tria's parents, who were the happiest old people Lanek had ever seen. Perhaps they were still in a cheerful mood from their daughter's wedding. And now that Lanek thought about it, he noticed Yalmin and Tria smiling as well. And so was Fenley. They were all simply *joyful*, and Lanek didn't feel any of it was ingenuine. They weren't just pretending to be happy in front of guests. And it made sense, Lanek realized. They all had each other. They loved each other.

Since there weren't enough chairs, Lanek and Fenley knelt on folded blankets at the end of the table, which was low enough for them to eat from comfortably. Yalmin and Tria had offered to kneel, but Lanek was quick to kneel himself, knowing they were probably tired from preparing the meal.

The food turned out to be a spicy vegetable stew, and Lanek was glad to enjoy a hot, fresh meal he didn't have to prepare himself. He wasn't a bad cook, but he felt it was nice to eat food prepared by someone else. Somehow the act of sharing a home-cooked meal could build a relationship in a deeper way that other daily interactions couldn't.

Everyone was curious to learn about Lanek and his life as an airship mechanic and pilot. He didn't give many details about his life, not wanting to ruin the light mood at the table, but he was able to tell them all the basics about airships. Everything was new and fascinating to them, and Lanek felt glad to at least provide something interesting for them to discuss with their neighbors—perhaps for the next couple weeks.

"You seem like an elf with a head on his shoulders," Tria's father said. "The village could use a few more young men like you."

"Oh yes," Tria's mother agreed. "A kind, strong man who would protect these humble hills."

Lanek held his spoon in his stew, studying it a few moments. "Well, I may have grown up in a small town, but I'm not really the type to live in a place so off-the-beaten-path. A place like this doesn't lend itself well to an airship mechanic."

"Think so?" Yalmin asked. "You're practically in the air to begin with up here. And you could always fly down the mountain to Riul to pick up whatever parts you'd need, I imagine."

"I suppose things could be worked out," Lanek admitted. "I'm just not sure what I'm doing with my life right now."

"My parents just like to voice their opinion to people," Tria said. "Only you can decide how you want to live."

"Of course," Fenley spoke up, "we *would* love to have you here."

Lanek looked over to Fenley, and her pure, bashful smile. He didn't want to look too long—he wasn't quite sure what he wanted to say about all this. He didn't like how indecisive he had become since getting to know the people of this village. Was he going to be on the village's side or on the government's side?

When he put it that way, the answer suddenly seemed rather obvious. The choices may as well have been Fenley's side and Rilv's side.

The dinner conversations turned to more trivial things, and Lanek tried to clear his mind a bit and focus on the delicious stew. But just when he was getting worried about what his teammates were up to, a knock came at the door. Yalmin got up to answer it, and Lanek looked back to see Kitoh at the entryway.

"Ah, welcome," Yalmin said. "Come in and have some stew, if you have the time."

"Hello," Kitoh said. "I just came to give Lanek a message really quick."

"What is it?" Lanek asked.

"I... I didn't think she'd act right away," Kitoh said. "But she's going. Right now."

Lanek felt the blood drain from his face as his mind registered just what Kitoh was telling him. Rilv was already on the move. She was going to get the Hader. Right now.

He got to his feet and hurried to the door. "Sorry, I have to go." He grabbed Kitoh's hand and pulled him forward down the trail. There were voices coming from inside the house, and Lanek was pretty sure Fenley was getting up to follow him. But Lanek couldn't stop to explain anything. If Rilv had somehow figured out where the Hader was so quickly... Or perhaps was just taking drastic measures to get information out of the villagers...

"Where is she?" Lanek asked.

"Heading to the shrine," Kitoh said. "She had me make a map of the village, and we used the Elpis... She wanted me to just check that you were still at that house, but I decided to let you know the current situation while I was there."

Lanek quickened his pace, and Kitoh ran along beside him, managing to keep up. Soon enough Lanek came in sight of the shrine, its two guards still positioned to either side of the curtain entryway. Hastily scanning the area, Lanek caught sight of Rilv and Lynx approaching the shrine from the other direction, walking at a resolute, determined pace.

What is she doing? Lanek thought. He slowed his pace a little in order to catch his breath, and to keep it from looking like he was running in a hostile way. Instead he jogged as if he was simply hoping to catch up and join Rilv, not wanting it to look like he was trying to stop her. It was still possible that Rilv wasn't certain the Hader was in the shrine, and at the very least there was a good chance she didn't know it was invisible.

Rilv and Lynx continued past a couple villagers who tried to greet them, made their way past a small girl playing with a jump rope, and marched straight toward the shrine entrance—and two disconcerted guards.

"I'm afraid only elves are allowed inside," one guard said, while the other lowered his lance a bit. "If you'd like, you can—"

"Set them aside," Rilv said.

Lynx leaped forward and plunged knives into each guard's neck.

"No!" Lanek screamed. He immediately sprinted forward, while Kitoh stumbled to the ground in shock at the turn of events.

Rilv scowled at Lynx, perhaps not intending for him to outright kill the two guards—but she continued to the black curtain, unperturbed by the screams and cries of villagers in the vicinity. The entire village was going to be in a panic now. Or worse—in a vengeful frenzy. Lanek had to stop this now. *Somehow.*

Rilv and Lynx were inside the shrine by the time Lanek reached the entry, and as he hoped, they didn't appear to know precisely where the Hader was. They were looking around in the large, empty room, finding nothing that stood out save for the pool and its goddess statue centerpiece.

"I can blow this place apart," Lynx suggested.

Lanek drew his rapier before Rilv could respond. She glanced back to Lanek, the way one would express displeasure at a friend's bad joke.

"We have no time for this, Lanek," Rilv said. "I apologize for Lynx's rash behavior, but we have no time left. Someone with two Haders is nearly upon us, and this operation will be severely undermined if we do not find this village's Hader before him. I suggest you tell us everything you've learned from the villagers regarding the stone's location."

"I don't know," Lanek said. "Nobody knows anything about the Hader. Now let's just get out of here and leave before you let that deranged psychopath kill any more people!"

"Tch," Lynx muttered.

"We can not leave without the Hader," Rilv said, glancing back to the entryway. There was clearly a commotion outside—villagers were gathering fast.

Kitoh ran inside, out of breath and panic-stricken.

"The Hader's not here," Lanek said to Rilv. "Everyone's going to be up in arms over this, and I'm not going to let a needless fight break out!"

"Let's hurry," Kitoh said between breaths. He pointed up in the direction of the statue, staring straight toward the Stone of Truth. "Just take the Hader and go."

Could he see it?

"I don't see it anywhere," Lynx said, rummaging through the shelves of gray clothing. He pushed aside the fold-out dressing walls, then started pulling off the decorative metal plates from the wall.

"It's right there, where I'm pointing," Kitoh said.

Rilv and Lynx stared right at the Hader, but they didn't show any sign of recognition. Lanek couldn't see it, and Rilv and Lynx couldn't seem to see it.

Of course, Lanek realized. *Kitoh is an eigni. And one with a particularly strong connection to the Nexi. He can see the stone without even going through the ritual.*

Several men rushed into the shrine, each of them wielding a weapon and a Nexi stone.

"Get out immediately!" a middle-aged man yelled. He and the rest stopped a couple meters in front of the curtain, which was now pulled aside so other villagers could look in—many of them also armed with Nexi stones, as well as farming scythes, cleavers, and pitchforks.

"Give us the Hader, and we will leave," Rilv said.

"You will leave, or suffer the consequences!" the man replied.

A red Nexi skipped across the floor, flying straight toward the seven men.

"Get back!" Lanek yelled.

The Nexi stone exploded in a massive ball of fire, blowing up straight into two of them, and sending the rest flying backward. The curtain burned away and a good portion of the wall to the left of the entryway blasted apart in the process, eliciting cries from the elves gathered outside of the shrine.

Lanek turned to find Lynx sprinting toward the men who weren't incinerated in the powerful fire attack. Lynx had a sword raised forward in one hand, and a second red Nexi in the other. Lanek ran in front of Lynx and slipped a yellow Nexi out from his pocket.

This was his chance. This was his legitimate chance to kill Lynx. The masked man hadn't betrayed the team, but Lanek wasn't going to put up with this village slaughtering a moment longer.

"Out of my way!" Lynx yelled. He swung his sword.

Lanek leaped straight to the blade, activating the yellow Nexi just before it hit his side. The protective energy forced the blade to deflect off his clothes. Lanek slammed his shoulder against Lynx's chest, knocking them both back. Lanek recovered quickly and jabbed his rapier forward. Lynx activated his red Nexi to force Lanek's blade back. With the yellow Nexi still activated, the flames passed to either side of Lanek harmlessly.

He couldn't keep it up for long—not without tiring himself just as the fight had begun. He pushed through the flames and smoke to attack in Lynx's general direction. Lanek struck metal. Lynx let up on the red Nexi and countered, forcing Lanek to block and hold Lynx back.

"You can see the Hader, Kitoh?" Rilv asked.

"It's hanging from a string," Kitoh said. "Some kind of spell is keeping everyone from seeing it, though it's not strong enough to stay hidden from me."

"Get it and we will be on our way," Rilv said.

The men who were injured by Lynx's fire attack were on their feet again, and joined by a number of other armed villagers. There were several bystanders approaching the entryway as well, Lanek realized—civilians who would be killed quickly and easily by Lynx if Lanek didn't end this fight right away, or at least hold him back. But then there was still Rilv...

"You want to die, Lanek?" Lynx asked, blocking each of Lanek's attacks. Lynx returned a series of blows, but Lanek was quick enough to defend each swing of Lynx's blade. They were evenly matched—just as they were five years ago. Lanek had kept up his training all these years, just in hopes of being prepared for this very moment. He had to find a way to overwhelm Lynx. To take him by surprise. To get the upper hand.

Lanek managed to pull out a light blue Nexi while Lynx pushed him back with a strong swing of his sword—a heavier, thicker blade than Lanek's rapier. With a flick of his wrist, Lanek released a gust of cold air. Lynx was quick to jump to the side of the blast, but Lanek timed his motion to freeze the floor where Lynx landed. Immediately Lanek leaped forward and jabbed his blade toward Lynx's stomach, but the masked man kept from slipping on the ice, and twisted in such a way to avoid Lanek's attack.

Lynx turned his head suddenly, as if startled. Before Lanek could use the opportunity to attack, Lynx pulled out a yellow Nexi stone. A thin trail of fire exploded straight into Lynx. A burst of light, nearly too fast for Lanek to see. It enveloped Lynx in a blinding, roaring swath of flame. Past Lynx, a giant chunk of the shrine wall blew apart, but the flames remained around Lynx. It was hot—extremely hot—and Lanek had to quickly step back a ways to keep from getting burned.

He looked to where the fire attack had come from. Standing a few meters away was Chei, his eyes as fierce as they were when he had grabbed Lanek a little while ago. Chei held a red Nexi in his hand, glowing a bright, violent red. It was a fast, powerful attack, and Chei was keeping the flames going, knowing Lynx may have activated his shielding Nexi in time. If Chei could overpower Lynx's yellow barrier of energy, Lynx wouldn't last one second in such intense heat..

"Let me know when you're going to let up," Lanek said. "I'll run in and stab him the moment he deactivates his yellow Nexi." It was going to be like Lynx was underwater, holding his breath, and the moment he broke free would be the moment Lanek could attack. He simply had to time the attack for a moment when Lynx would be too weary to defend.

A giant mass of gray sludge exploded from within the fire, then flowed like a violent torrent straight for Lanek and Chei. It was swamp material from the brown Nexi, but altered in some way.

The gray Nexi, Lanek realized. The substance was poisoned, and likely lethal upon contact. The fact Lynx was able to combine the two Nexi abilities like this, and while maintaining a strong shield with a yellow Nexi... It was more than uncanny—it seemed utterly impossible.

Lanek ran out of the way of the sticky gray substance, but the material continued toward him—Lynx was somehow guiding it perfectly, even with senses obscured by flames, smoke, and screams.

There was no opening. Everywhere Lanek turned, there was more of the sludge rushing toward him. He used his ice Nexi to freeze the substance before it could reach him, then turned to check on Chei's situation. While running back from the rushing gray swamp, Chei let up on the fire pounding against Lynx. Immediately Chei released another sudden burst of fire, blasting straight through the poisoned swamp substance.

The fire around Lynx dissipated, but his yellow barrier was still barely activated when the second blast of fire slammed directly into him. This explosion sent Lynx flying straight out of the shrine, through the gaping hole that was created from the first massive fire blast.

Chei fell to his hands and knees about a meter from the settling swamp substance. He was shaking from head to toe, exhausted from Nexi use. Lanek couldn't stop to help him though, and he didn't have time to check on Lynx either. More than anything, Lanek wanted to find Lynx and skewer his heart, just to make his death definite—but the villagers were surrounding Rilv and Kitoh. The battle for the Stone of Truth was commencing, and Lanek didn't want it to last another second.

Several villagers rushed toward Rilv at once. She pulled out her Hader and activated its power, forcing the assailants to fly backwards violently. From a safe distance, one villager threw a knife, but Rilv was able to deflect this as well. At this unbelievable sight, many of the people ran away, unable to see any way to get near Rilv as long as she had the ability to effortlessly fling them back. But many of the villagers simply became riled up, and shouted for others to help them try overwhelming Rilv.

"Stop the fighting!" Lanek yelled to the stirring crowd. "We'll leave!"

"Kitoh, grab the Hader and go," Rilv said. "I will create a path for us."

The eigni boy nodded and raised a green Nexi stone, pointing it toward where Lanek knew the Stone of Truth was hanging.

A series of icicles, a couple arrows, and a spear flew toward Rilv and Kitoh. Rilv managed to deflect all of the weapons with her telekinesis Hader, but Kitoh stumbled back in surprise, the onslaught fended off mere centimeters away.

Vines flung toward where the Stone of Truth hung, which became visible the moment it was snapped off its string. The vines didn't come from Kitoh's Nexi, though. Lanek watched as the vines brought the Hader down to the village leader, standing just outside the blown-off entryway. He was accompanied by the two elves Lanek met in the administration building, each of them armed with a couple Nexi stones.

"Quickly, Lanek," Rilv called out. "Retrieve the Hader, and we will be on our way."

"No," Lanek replied. "I will not fight these people."

Rilv did not look any more upset than she usually did, and didn't seem to be surprised. More villagers were approaching her, rejuvenated by their leader's success in protecting the Stone of Truth. She turned to Kitoh, a concerned frown spread across her face. "I can not continue using my Hader so much. Fend these people off and I will retrieve the Hader myself."

"I don't want to fight these people either," Kitoh said. Lanek smiled, relieved that Kitoh at least wasn't about to turn against the village. But Lanek had hoped Nullen would call off the villagers' ambush by now. Nullen had the Hader, and there was no way Rilv was going to be able to fight off all these people by herself—right?

And yet the leader simply stood and watched, his companions ready to defend him in case Rilv did anything drastic.

"You want to die?" Rilv asked Kitoh.

A young man swung a scythe—Rilv leaped back while Kitoh ducked. At the same time, an older man released a jet of water, but missed them both entirely. Rilv punched the man with the scythe hard in the face, grabbed his scythe, and tossed it aside as he stumbled backward. Another villager threw a spear, while two others sent waves of dirt rushing toward Rilv and Kitoh.

Lanek didn't see how he was going to stop the fighting. The people were in a frenzy, dismayed to see their beloved shrine half in ruins. After all the hospitality they had shown their visitors, it had to be unbelievable that in return their most valuable treasure was nearly stolen. He tried standing in the way of some of the villagers and yelling for them to stop, but they pushed past him, desperate to keep Rilv from taking the Stone of Truth. Lanek had to somehow convince her to give up on taking the Hader.

Which seemed about as easy as convincing a river to start flowing the other direction.

The people continued to attack Rilv and Kitoh, and a few had started surrounding Lanek as well, recognizing him as one of the visitors, but not knowing anything more of his situation. He sheathed his rapier and raised his hands, making it clear he didn't intend to fight, but the people remained in his way, reluctant to let him join up with Rilv and Kitoh.

The eigni boy wielded a dark blue Nexi, creating a large spray of water to deflect the villagers' attacks. He wasn't fighting them, but was protecting himself and Rilv. The water compacted and began swirling around the two, creating a rapid whirlpool of water in the air surrounding them. The weapons and Nexi attacks thrown at them were pushed to the side by Kitoh's power—a utilization of the water Nexi that Lanek had never heard of before, let alone seen. Water was simple enough to release from a dark blue Nexi, but it took extreme skill to maneuver it the way Kitoh was managing.

Rilv charged forward, and Kitoh ran along beside her, keeping them protected from the villagers' attacks. The villagers tried to find openings, either by timing their weapon throws to reach Rilv and Kitoh in between spurts of the rushing water, or by using Nexi attacks that could reach Rilv and Kitoh from above. However, Kitoh spotted every attack in time, and controlled the water in such a way that he was able to defend every attack and still be able to see where he and Rilv were going through the anarchy of the shrine.

They passed where Lanek and some of the villagers stood, and Lanek watched Nullen and the people outside quickly back away—nobody was certain how to get past Kitoh's defense. Lanek could hear Kitoh and Rilv speaking to each other, but he couldn't make out what they were saying. He hoped Kitoh was trying to call this whole thing off, though it didn't seem likely the boy would be able to persuade Rilv to give up on this Hader.

"Let me try to stop them," Lanek told the villagers blocking him. Before he could try to push past them though, he spotted Chei on his feet again, pointing his fire Nexi at Kitoh's barrier.

"Wait!" Lanek yelled.

A third massive burst of fire erupted from Chei's Nexi stone, slamming directly into Kitoh's rapidly circling water. The wild collision flung Rilv and Kitoh away a couple meters, throwing them against the ground. The fire dissipated before it could continue toward Rilv and Kitoh. Chei fell back to his hands and knees, breathing heavily.

Amidst the explosion and panic, Lanek slipped past the villagers and hurried outside. Most of the people outside had fled a ways, though Nullen and his supporters were a good six or seven meters away from Rilv and Kitoh.

Rilv pushed herself to her feet and pointed her Hader directly at a small girl a few meters away from everyone else—it was the girl who had been jumping rope before all this madness had escalated in the shrine.

Effortlessly, Rilv forced the girl to float in the air, higher and higher. A couple villagers ran toward Rilv, their makeshift weapons raised.

"Stop!" Lanek yelled, as other villagers began to point at the floating child. Panic spread as everyone realized Rilv was holding the child hostage. The men who were about to attack Rilv stopped, their eyes turning up to the crying girl suspended in the air, now a good ten, fifteen meters high.

"What do you think you're doing?" Nullen yelled.

Rilv spoke loudly and clearly, but resolutely. "The moment anyone attacks us will be the moment this child plummets to her death." The panicking girl was now positioned high above the shrine building, where nobody would be able to catch her if she fell.

"Now tell everyone to back away and drop their weapons," Rilv continued, staring straight toward Nullen. "Then hand me the Hader. We will leave as soon as we have that stone. The girl will be safely returned to the earth, and nobody more will have to get hurt."

The village leader stared back at Rilv a long time, perhaps trying to come up with some way to stop Rilv without having the child die in the process. A vine Nexi could be used to grab the girl, but that would take time, and Rilv could very well fling the child away if she wished. The telekinesis Hader was no ordinary Nexi, and Rilv seemed to have a good grasp for how it operated, even in this wearied state she had to be in.

"Everyone back away," Nullen said. "Set your weapons down."

The villagers complied, dropping their swords, knives, scythes, pitchforks, bows and arrows, spears, and Nexi stones. Some of them backed into the shrine, while others backed away outside, giving Rilv and Kitoh plenty of space. Lanek stayed put, remaining about four or five meters away. He was not far from what used to be the shrine entryway.

He looked over all the villagers standing outside in the distance, most of them looking frightened, the rest looking furious. Lanek spotted Fenley a ways down the trail, standing with her brother and his wife. They all looked confused and worried. What they must have thought about him right now, standing in front of the smoking, broken-down shrine...

"Let's stop this," Lanek said to Rilv. "The Hader isn't worth all this."

"I am not leaving without the Hader," Rilv said. "Do you want our kingdom to fall to Augurc's experiments? They are powered by the Elpis—even a well-trained troop of our best soldiers are slaughtered when they encounter the Brotherhood these days. We need power in order to defend the Fiefs Kingdom. I have tried reasoning with these villagers in every way I could, but they do not care about the greater good. They only care about themselves. And now they must suffer the consequences, if they refuse to cooperate. Even now, I am offering to leave without anyone more coming to harm."

She stretched her hand out toward where Nullen stood. "Hand me the Hader. Now."

Nullen gripped the stone and held it against his chest. This was the last thing he ever wanted to give up, of course. It was probably his greatest responsibility as village leader. That stone was of the greatest importance to these people.

"Now, Nullen," Rilv said. She twitched her Hader a bit, causing the hostage girl to shake in the air a little. The child cried out, screaming for her mommy and daddy.

Villagers pointed and gasped, some of them in tears.

"Stop this, Rilv," Lanek said. "You've gone too far."

"You have ten seconds, Nullen," Rilv said, still staring at the trembling village leader.

"No," Kitoh whispered. "This is wrong."

"Stop this, Rilv!" Lanek yelled.

"I will not stop," Rilv said. "Five seconds, Nullen."

The village leader only clutched the Stone of Truth tighter. His eyes moved from the girl to Rilv, back and forth. Frantic. Desperate.

"Now, Nullen!" Rilv screamed.

"Hold it!" a man yelled, even louder.

A human leisurely walked out from behind a small hill in the other direction. He was tall, and perhaps a year or two younger than Lanek was. His hair was a violent red, short and spiky. He wore a light tan jacket, dark brown trousers, and an assortment of pouches tied to his belt, arms, and legs, all obscured by a cloak as red as his hair. There were several weapons on his person—a sword sheathed on his back, a dagger on his arm, a couple knives on his belt, and some kind of rod tied to his right leg.

"Stop," Rilv said. "I will let this child plummet if you continue."

The young man kept walking toward her, as if he hadn't heard a word she had said.

"Doubt it. I know a bluff when I see one."

He simply kept walking. Did he even know what was going on here? Who was this person?

"Don't worry, everyone," the man proclaimed to the onlookers he passed by. "I will most certainly save your village."

He grinned a long, sadistic smile at Rilv. Gripped in each of his hands was a Hader.

•

To Be Continued...